boomerang

Also by Noelle August

COMING SOON
Rebound

boomerang

Noelle August

wm

WILLIAM MORROW
An Imprint of HarperCollins*Publishers*

BOOMERANG. Copyright © 2014 by Wildcard Storymakers, LLC. All rights reserved. Printed in the United States of America. No part of this book may be used or reproduced in any manner whatsoever without written permission except in the case of brief quotations embodied in critical articles and reviews. For information address HarperCollins Publishers, 195 Broadway, New York, NY 10007.

HarperCollins books may be purchased for educational, business, or sales promotional use. For information please e-mail the Special Markets Department at SPsales@ harpercollins.com.

FIRST EDITION

Designed by Diahann Sturge

Library of Congress Cataloging-in-Publication Data has been applied for.

ISBN 978-0-06-233106-9

14 15 16 17 18 OV/RRD 10 9 8 7 6 5 4 3 2 1

*To Lisa, my first literary agent, my constant reader,
and my best friend. Love you, Blister.*

*And to Brenda, for all you do,
and for your big, gorgeous heart.*
—LO

*To Lolo, who wrote half of this, but still.
You are wonderful.*
—VR

Chapter 1

Mia

Q: Have you ever had a one-night stand?

*O*n the single most important day of my life, I wake with the thought: *Oh crap, where are my panties?*

I think this because I also happen to wake in the bed of a stranger, with a wicked shaft of lemon-hued LA light bisecting my bare thigh and not a shred of underwear or any other garment in sight.

This is *so* not me, and yet here I am, tangled in warm sheets that are most definitely not my own.

Vague snippets of the night before push through my hangover-muddled brain. I remember sitting at Duke's after my interview with Adam Blackwood, wired with anticipation and the feeling that, finally, I was set to *launch*. I'd be able to finish my film about Nana, turn it in, and say *sayonara* to college. And I'd turn this internship with one of the biggest media companies in the country into a real film career where I could find myself, find *my* style, not just the styles I'd been parroting during my years in school.

I *almost* remember the guy too. Broad shoulders, an easy manner, and that feeling of heat and possibility. But that's about it. No face. No name. No idea how this—this minor miracle of actual real-life *sex*—came to pass.

Sadly, this mystery may remain unsolved. I've got to get going.

I struggle up, gingerly tugging strands of my curly hair from beneath the shoulder—the toned and nicely tanned shoulder—of my new friend. My head feels like the inside of a blender set to frappé, and the taste in my mouth suggests something crawled in there and died.

Swinging my bare feet onto the cool concrete floor, I rise, willing away the queasiness that threatens to grab hold.

Thanks a bunch, Patron Silver.

I creep around the bed to see if I'll have better luck finding my underwear—or really, *any* item of clothing—on that side of the world. And, I'll confess, I'm dying to take a look.

My curiosity is most definitely rewarded. Even though the guy's face is mashed against his pillow, and his short caramel-brown hair lies matted against his head, he is about twelve kinds of hot. He has a strong, beautifully sculpted jaw with just a hint of a cleft, full lips, and the kind of dark sweeping eyelashes that girls need to gob on mascara to achieve.

Stretched out with just the barest corner of sheet covering him— my bad for hogging the blankets—his feet almost dangle off the bed. Which means he's tall. And even in sleep, his face holds an in- teresting furrow-browed intensity, like he's dreaming about saving the world. I know he has to have a stellar personality or there is *zero* chance I'd have woken up in his bed.

I don't see any condom wrappers, which makes me wonder what, exactly, did happen last night. It's definitely not like me to be reckless. So maybe nothing happened? But again: no panties.

While I puzzle over this, my glance drifts over to his bedside clock. The numbers 8:02 a.m. carve their way through the haze, and adrenaline floods my every molecule.

My internship at Boomerang—the answer to becoming more than the daughter of a famous photographer, to stepping into my *real* life and preserving the life of the dearest person in the world—kicks off in exactly fifty-eight minutes. And I have no idea where I am or where my frickin' underwear went.

"Crap, crap, crap." I push my hands through my hair, do a quick inventory of the room, and decide the clothes must have landed elsewhere.

This should be fun.

Hurrying down a narrow hall, I catch glimpses of sports photographs and motivational posters with soaring eagles and mountaintop sunrises. One says, "Life begins at the end of your comfort zone," which means my life is definitely beginning. Right. Now.

I find myself in a living room with the expected lumpy bachelor sofa, smudged glass coffee table, and giant-screen TV that blots out the sunlight attempting to pour in through two tall Pendleton-blanket-covered windows. It's also got the requisite single-guy funk: booze, sweat, and a kind of dead-possum tang for the kicker. Books and magazines lie scattered over most surfaces, along with a host of remote controls that suggest an underground lair somewhere; a laptop that looks old enough to belong to Fred Flintstone, and various articles of clothing—a sweatshirt, gym shorts, and— score!—my dress from last night.

I snatch it off the floor and inspect it. It's so wrinkled it looks like a dump truck backed over it, and it's stiff in spots, with a V-shaped stain spreading over the top.

Trying to shake out the creases, I wish I had chosen something a little less *slinky* for my meeting with Adam Blackwood. But I went with this, and he'll get to see it again today. Only this time it'll look like I wrestled it off a hobo.

I hear a creak of bedsprings and then a door opening and closing, followed by the rush of water from a shower. So, the guy's awake. Great. Maybe he can give me a hand with Mission Impossible: Underwear Edition. There's no way that will be awkward, right?

After searching around the entire living room, picking up clothing, pizza boxes, video game cases, and various pieces of sporting equipment, I manage to find my shoes, purse, and—draped over the kitchen pass-through—my bra. But no underwear.

Did they just disappear? Dissolve right off my body? In that case, kudos to the guy. *Evan?* No, that's not it. And all the more reason to wish I could remember, oh, even a couple of minutes of last night.

The microwave clock says 8:09. I gather up my shoes, bra, and dress and race back into the bedroom. Dumping everything onto the bed, I knock on the bathroom door and push it open at the same time. Niceties went out the window sometime between my meeting with Adam Blackwood and my clothing being fired around this apartment like t-shirts at a Lakers game.

"Uh, hey—(*What the hell is his name?*)—there," I say lamely. "Um—not to be weird or pushy, but I'm in a ridiculous hurry. New job. Do you mind if I come in and . . ."

He draws back the shower curtain and pokes his head out, giving me an eyeful of chiseled torso in the process. Add in his soulful blue eyes and the water pooling in the deep grooves of his collarbone, and, well, it's a lot to take in this early in the day.

Clearly, he feels some of that as well. His eyes make a quick circuit up and down, and then he stammers something.

"What?" I say and lift a hand to my lips. "Do I have something in my teeth?"

He laughs. "You're so *naked*."

I give him a smile. "Sorry, yeah. Is that okay?"

Between modeling for my mother, spending eight shows a week nude in a summer stock production of *Hair*, and being the go-to "drop trou" girl for my fellow film students, I feel like I spend half my life naked. Am I going to spend half my life blushing and apologizing for myself? No, I am not.

His gaze sweeps over me, and his lips quirk into a smile, though he makes an excellent effort to look into my eyes when he speaks. "Definitely. *Definitely* okay. Do whatever you need to do."

"Great." I turn away and leave him to his shower. Palming the condensation off the mirror, I get a look at myself, especially at my hair, which always constitutes a *situation*. It frizzes out in a million directions, but it has definitely been worse. Which means, I realize with a pang of regret, that we definitely didn't have sex after all.

Sex—good sex, anyway—makes my hair go insane. Like giant mushroom cloud insane. Right now, it's at about Defcon Three, which suggests some vigorous making out but not much more.

Looks like the dry spell continues.

I find a brush and tug it through my hair then dab a line of toothpaste onto my finger and apply it to my teeth. After that, I gargle about a half-gallon of his mouthwash and gulp down a few handfuls of water from the tap.

"Dumb question, but do you have any idea where my underwear went?"

He turns the water off and reaches an arm out for his towel, which I hand around the curtain to him. He pushes aside the striped fabric, the towel draped around his waist to accentuate an impressive contoured abdomen.

"Not sure," he says, grinning. "Let me just put on some clothes, and I'll help you find them."

Back in his bedroom after a quick shower of my own, I slip on my bra and dress, feeling weirdly asymmetrical without my underwear.

"Where's work for you?" he asks as he buttons a crisp white dress shirt.

I have a flash of him wearing a suit the night before and of snaking my arms beneath the jacket to run my hands over his strong back. He looks used to good clothes, so probably something professional. But he has a ton of sporting equipment. Maybe he's a basketball coach. They wear suits, right?

"Where did you say you need to be?" he asks again, and I realize I've totally zoned.

Flushing, I say, "Century City, and I'm going to be so late."

His hands still on the buttons. "Me too," he mutters, more to himself than to me. "But it's twenty minutes in good traffic. You can make it."

That means I have to leave *now*.

He helps me search around the apartment, turning over chair cushions, checking behind curtains. "Are you sure you had them on when we got here?"

"You think I came here *without* my panties?"

Did I come here without my panties?

He yanks a tie from the ceiling fan over a small kitchen table, smiling as he holds it up for me. "Seems possible. I'm a little fuzzy on the details myself, but the evidence suggests we had a hell of a time."

Maybe not quite as good as you think, I want to say, but why get into it? I find a rubber band on the kitchen counter and fashion my hair into a low bun.

I give my dress another inspection and realize there's just no way I can show up looking like this.

"Hey, would you mind loaning me a shirt?" I say. "Like a dress shirt. I'll . . . um, get it back to you." While I hope this doesn't make me sound like a weird stalker girl, my need to not look like I just pulled my clothes off a tavern floor overrules my concern with first—or second—impressions.

"Yeah, sure," he says, and heads off to his room. He returns with a blue button-down shirt and hands it to me. "Might be a little big."

"I'm sure it will be," I say, but I put it on and cinch it tight around my waist, covering the worst of the problem. Now I just look like a rumpled weirdo. Though if my new boss spends any time with film people, I definitely won't be the *only* rumpled weirdo in his life.

The guy picks up a pair of black-checked boxer briefs from a kitchen chair. "I was wearing these last night, so we're getting warm."

I grow more and more anxious as he locates items of his own clothing.

"Sorry, Mia," he says after he's opened every cabinet and looked in every nook and cranny of the modest apartment.

I feel a little flush of pleasure that *he* knows *my* name, quickly supplanted by embarrassment at the fact that I'm the jerk who doesn't remember his.

In the kitchen, he pours himself a glass of juice from the fridge, sliding one across the pass-through for me too. "I don't see them anywhere."

Where the hell can they be? And is it better to be late for work on my very first day or to flash all my new co-workers? Decisions, decisions.

I fish out my cell phone—8:29—and sigh. "All right," I decide. "I guess I'll do without."

"Commando." He grins. "I like that in a girl."

"Why, thanks. If you find them, feel free to keep them as a souvenir."

"I'll treasure them. Unless they're granny panties. But then those might have been easier to find."

"They are most certainly *not* granny panties. They're—"

He laughs, his back to me. "Hot pink? With white butterflies?"

"Yes! How did you—"

He steps to the side and pulls open the door of his glossy Breville toaster oven. There, draped across the toasting rack, lie my panties.

Chapter 2

Ethan

Q: On dates, do you prefer to go Dutch, or pick up the bill?

For a few seconds, I can't shake the picture of Mia's pink thong sitting in my toaster oven. It's like time stops, and then I'm picturing her wearing them, and then *not* wearing them, until Coach Williams's voice filters through the pounding in my head.

If you're on time, then you're late.

That gets me moving, as it has for the past four years. I can only imagine what Coach Williams would think of me now: late to the internship that's supposed to change everything for me, and so hungover I'm still buzzed.

I leave the kitchen and head into the living room. The girl I woke up with—Mia—leans on a hip as she sifts through her purse, so I take a second to appreciate the view.

Damn, she's hot. I give myself a mental slap on the back.

"Can I get your address?" she asks, pulling out a cell phone. "I need to call a cab."

An image of last night flashes through my mind. She and I jumped into a cab as soon as it pulled up outside the bar. We were in too much of a hurry to be alone together to wait for a ride with Jason and Isis. But why the hell did we come here instead of her place? My apartment's a biohazard.

"Forty-four Creston Drive," I say. Pushing aside socks and shin guards, I sit on the battered couch and pull on my oxfords. "In Westwood."

Mia makes the call, speaking in a rush to the dispatcher, but I get the feeling it's not just because she's late. The tone of her voice is smoky and colorful, like she talks often and laughs a lot. She's petite. No more than 5'3", but the heels she slips on give her a four-inch boost. My shirt pools forward as she bends down, giving me an excellent angle of her perfect rack.

"Five minutes?" Mia says. "Thanks." She hangs up and turns her attention back to me. Her eyes are green, but not the weak hazel color people try to pass off. Mia's are clear and bright.

"All set?" I stand.

"Yep, all set." Mia drops her phone back into her purse and pushes a coil of black hair behind her ear. Her eyes make a quick trip up and down my body, and then she glances at the front door. "So . . . thanks for the juice?"

I sidestep, blocking her path. One-night-stand protocol is to get in and get out, so to speak, but I can't let her go yet. She's not the only one who needs to get to Century City, and it's too late for me to bike there. "Can you hold on a sec? I have to talk to my roommate."

She looks around the apartment, her jaw dropping. Five seconds ago, our clothes were everywhere. "You have a *roommate*?"

"Yeah. Jason. And Isis. She's Jason's girlfriend, but she pretty much lives here. I think you met them last night at Duke's."

Mia gives me a shaky smile. "Okay, I feel awful admitting this, but I'm trying to remember whether your name is Evan or Ethan. So it's safe to say I'm sketchy on some details from last night."

Shit.

I wasn't after anything serious, obviously. After two years with Alison, non-serious is a requirement. But this girl doesn't even remember my name? That sucks, but I shrug and play it off.

"No problem. It's Ethan. Ethan Vance."

"I'm Mia Galliano."

"Nice to meet you, Mia Galliano." We stand there for an awkward second. Introductions seem beside the point, considering I'm pretty sure I slept with my hand on her ass. "Give me one minute," I say, breaking the silence. "Help yourself to more juice."

Nice one, Ethan. Because that's what the girl wants. More PowerAde at 8:33 in the morning. I head to Jason's room, knock on the door once and swing it open.

Jason and Isis are sitting up in bed, watching the door like they've been expecting me. Isis breaks into a smile and starts slow-clapping. Jason's less subtle. He lifts a vuvuzela to his lips and blows. The loud beehive hum of the horn cuts into my brain, sending my headache to Code Red.

"Yeah, Ethan!" Jason laughs. "How'd it go, man? Was it like riding a bike?"

"A little more fun than that," I say. But, damn. I wish I really knew.

"Did she leave?" Isis asks.

"Not yet, but she needs to."

"Ethan!"

"Easy, Isis. We *both* need to leave. She has a job, and my internship starts today."

Isis snorts. "That sucks. You look like crap."

"Then I look better than I feel. J, I need some cash." The words burn in my throat. I hate asking for money. "I have to chip in for a cab."

Jason shakes his head. "Sorry, bro. I'm out. You emptied my wallet last night."

"I did?"

Isis laughs. "Don't you remember? You and Mia were doing body shots."

Christ, *body shots*? Did I revert to being a freshman? "Never mind."

As I head back to the living room, I consider fishing through my sports bags for stray change, but I don't have time and I still wouldn't find enough to pay my way. There's only one option left. It's going to gut me, but screw it. It's the only way.

I find Mia standing by the front door, a sexy half-smile on her face, and my brain shorts out as I picture licking salt off her olive skin.

"Did I just hear a vuvuzela?" she asks.

"Yeah. My roommate thinks he's funny. So, about that cab . . . Mind if I catch a ride with you?"

Mia frowns, and I can tell she's surprised. I'm surprised too. This isn't how I expected this morning to play out. "Sure," she says. "No problem."

"Cool. And uh . . . One other thing?" *Fuck.* I'm about to blow my chance of ever seeing this girl again—and I want to. If nothing else, to figure out what the hell we did last night. But I'm up against a wall. "You mind paying for it?"

Chapter 3

Mia

Q: Are you a lone wolf, or do you run with a pack?

The poor guy—Ethan—looks like he's just requested a nail file to the eyeball. So he doesn't like asking for favors. Interesting.

"Yeah, no big deal," I tell him. It takes all of my self-control not to reach out and touch him, straighten his red color-blocked tie or smooth the slight cowlick that rises over his straight, serious brow. Air molecules thicken between us, scintillating with that delicious energy of attraction.

Or, okay, lust.

It's been *so* long since I've felt that, and I would love to just stay here, anchored in this moment. But I have *no* time.

A car horn honks, punctuating my thought.

"Guess our ride's here," I say.

He leans in front of me to open the door, and I become intensely aware of both his height—he has about six inches on me, and I'm in four-inch heels—and of his scent: smoky and tantalizing, like a beach bonfire.

Another flash comes to me: the inside of a cab, streetlights shading and then revealing his beautiful, serious face. He hauls me across the seat, pulling my leg over his, and bracing me with powerful hands against my back. Then the memory pinholes shut, leaving only the uptick of my pulse and the reminder that I really, *really* have places to go.

I precede him onto a narrow balcony, blinking in the crystalline light that turns everything to shimmering green and gold. On the street below, a cab idles, and I head toward a rickety-looking aluminum staircase to make my way down.

I'm aware of him behind me. The feeling of him—tangible and light at the same time, his quick certain footsteps shaking the entire staircase as we descend.

Head in the game, Galliano. This is about becoming who I want to become. Finishing my film. Finding a way into the business on my own. This is most certainly *not* about a dude whose big move consists of hiding my underwear in an appliance.

I slide into the cab first and give the address of the Boomerang offices.

Ethan climbs in on the other side. "Olympic and Avenue of the Stars," he tells the driver. "Probably close to where she's headed."

The red-haired driver turns and gives us a look. "Yeah, real close."

I barely know that part of town, but at least that makes things easy.

Ethan's shirt swims on me, and the jersey fabric climbs my thighs. This is not good. Maybe there's still time to gather my forces so I don't stroll in looking like "Little Ms. Hot Pants," as Nana would say.

I call Skyler, who seems to answer before the phone even rings.

"Oh, my God. Tell me everything. Right. Now."

I guess I must have given my roomies a heads-up that I wouldn't be home last night. Sighing, I say, "Good morning to you, too."

"Screw that. What happened? Where are you? Was it delicious? Did he—"

"Hey, Sky," I interject, certain Ethan can hear her every word. "I need a favor."

She picks up on my tone immediately. "Is he there?" she asks. "Like right there, now? Aren't you supposed to be at your new job?"

"I'm on my way," I take a deep breath to tamp down my exasperation. "I—um— overslept—"

"I'm disappointed you slept at all."

"Sky, come on!"

"Okay, okay. So, he's there now?"

"Yeah, we—uh—" I feel Ethan's gaze on me and turn to meet it. He smiles in a way that seems both impossibly sweet and impossibly sexy at the same time. I smile back, wishing I had a portable cone of silence I could activate for privacy.

But the privacy ship sailed sometime in the middle of the night. "We're sharing a cab now. Anyway, listen, I—"

"Facetime me," Sky says.

"What? No way. Can you please just focus? I need you to do something for me."

"Facetime me, and I will."

"You'll do it anyway because you're my best friend, remember?"

"Do it."

"I will kill you."

"Facetiiiiiiime."

"Fine!" I swipe the icon on my screen, and Skyler's face appears before me: all blond hair and smudged Cleopatra eyeliner. As usual, she's got her hand wrapped around the neck of her cello and fingers the strings as we talk.

"Show me!" she demands.

My entire body goes cold, then hot, then cold again. "Why do you hate me?"

"I love you with the fire of a thousand suns," Sky says. "Now show me."

Oh, what the hell. I'm wearing last night's clothes while sharing a cab with my one-night stand. Was I really going to *use* that last bit of self-respect?

I turn the phone toward Ethan, who grins easily at the screen. The tips of his ears glow pink, though, and I'm oddly reassured to know he's as embarrassed as I am.

"*Whoa,*" says Skyler. "Hello to *you.*"

I roll my eyes. "Ethan, this is my *former* roommate, Skyler Canby," I say. "Skyler, Ethan."

"Hey, Skyler." He tips a two-fingered salute, and another memory unfurls. Ethan giving that same salute to the bartender at Duke's, pushing the hem of his navy jacket out of the way as he sat in a high-backed stool next to me.

"Celebrating?" he'd asked, and his eyes held a lively interest that made me straighten and turn to fully face him.

"A little work and a little play," I said.

"Same here," Ethan said, and we clinked glasses. "To work and to play, in almost equal measure."

Now, though, I have to put the play behind me and get to work.

"Okay, listen," I tell Skyler, as we turn onto Santa Monica Boulevard. "Can either you or Beth get to Century City in the next . . ." I check the phone for time. "Shoot. Like eighteen minutes? Is that even possible?"

"Your lucky day. Beth's got an audition at Fox. She's probably been there since six, stalking the director."

"Call her for me, see if she's got anything with her that I can change into. Even just a jacket."

"Okay, but no jacket. You can't cover those boobs."

"Skyler!"

"I second that," Ethan murmurs.

I turn to him, surprised. That smile again—sexy, a little shy. And those blue, blue eyes, so deep they're almost black.

"They're, uh . . . a great asset," he says. I get caught in his expression, direct and teasing, and I don't know if it's a memory or a fantasy, but I can feel his hands on me, his fingers smoothing away the strap of my dress . . .

"The man speaks the truth," Sky says. "Jackets make you look boxy."

I get a mental grip on myself. "Whatever. Just please and thanks." Seriously, anything's bound to be an improvement over my current ensemble.

"Stop talking to me so I can take care of this. I'll text to confirm."

"Thanks, doll." I really do have the best friends on earth.

"No worries," says Skyler, who then treats me to a big, toothy grin. "Tell Ethan he's a hot piece of ass."

He laughs beside me, and I shake my head in mortification.

"I'm pretty sure he already knows."

Chapter 4

Ethan

Q: Do you plan dates, or do you like to be surprised?

The cab moves down Wilshire at a crawl. I can't stop my leg from jittering, even when it's clear Mia notices. I want to swing the door open, throw off my jacket, and sprint to Century City. I know I could get there faster. I smile, thinking of my dad's favorite comment when he comes to visit. *Why is everyone in such a damn hurry here?* But if you want to get somewhere, you accept it. Successful people live their lives in a damn hurry.

"Do you work for ESPN or something?"

Mia's question surprises me. Then I remember she must have seen my weights and soccer gear.

"No, I wish." Earning a living from sports would be great. I came close to making that happen. Set a few records at UCLA. But a knee injury junior year ruled out pro soccer for me. After ACL surgery, it was never quite the same.

"I'm starting a new job today," I tell Mia, focusing on the future. "Marketing for an online business." I can't bring myself to say "internship." I have a degree from a top university. You'd think I could find a way to get paid to work, but that'll change soon enough. "What about you? Swimsuit model?"

I don't know why I'm flirting with her. I won't ever see her again, and we've already hooked up. Not that I remember it. But she's hot, and there's something intriguing about her. She's a little mystery, wrapped in my favorite dress shirt.

"Well, of course." She smiles and pats her hip. "With all this to work with, what else would I be?"

She's so comfortable with her body. Amazing after two years with Alison, who still wanted the lights off when we slept together. I don't think Mia and I even started in bed. We ended up there though.

"What else?" I say. "I don't know. Vegas showgirl?"

"Wow, thanks. That's so progressive of you."

"Just my imagination speaking. So, what's it really? What do you do?"

Mia crosses her legs, and I manage to keep eye contact. "Well, actually, I'm still in school."

"School . . . great." Please be eighteen. She *has* to be. "What year and where?"

"I'm a sophomore at LA High."

I almost choke on my tongue. "You're *what*?"

She bursts into laughter. "Sorry. I couldn't resist. Actually, I'm a senior at Occidental. Studying filmmaking. But I took on this position for my last semester to get some real-world experience."

"You're a filmmaker? That's cool. I love this one art house film. *Star Wars*? Maybe you haven't heard of it. It's an obscure title."

That's all I can come up with to cover my lack of film knowledge. I don't watch movies; I play soccer. When I'm not playing soccer, I read books about history, or biographies—subjects a girl like Mia would probably hate.

She narrows her eyes like she's deep in thought. "*Star Wars*, you say? It doesn't ring a bell, but you know us film majors. If it's not some grainy black-and-white transfer, dubbed into Slovak and then back into English, it's *so* not worth the time."

She stretches her legs into my personal space. I can't tell if she's flirting or just at ease. Either way, I like it.

"What about you?" she asks. "What excites you, other than toaster panties?"

I laugh. "Hey. That wasn't my doing." Though, who knows? It actually might have been. I have a quick debate with myself about whether to tell her about my soccer career and decide against it. "I just graduated from UCLA in June. So, you know, marching bravely into my adult life and all that. First day on the job for me today."

"And we're both starting out with hangovers. Sweet."

"But at least we're both wearing underwear."

"At least there's that." Mia leans her head back against the seat and smiles. There's nothing flirty about it. Nothing forced or fake. It's just a really great smile.

Suddenly we're trapped in a staring contest. Her gaze is so direct and her green eyes are like prisms. They hold so much light inside them. There are questions and jokes and stories in her eyes. I know right then I want this again. To be looked at by her again.

"Look, Mia, I know this isn't how—"

The cab jerks to a stop.

"Eighteen dollars," the cabby says.

Mia reaches in her purse. "I'm paying for his fare, too. Can you add it?"

"Sure thing, lady. Still eighteen dollars."

Mia and I lock eyes. I can't believe this. We've come to the *same place*? There's no way.

Someone lays on the horn behind us.

The cabby curses and pulls closer to the curb. "Twenty-one hundred Avenue of the Stars. That's what you wanted, right?"

"Right," we blurt at the same time.

"Okay. Wow," Mia says. She shoves some bills at him, and we get out of the cab.

The office building rises up in front of us, a smooth wall of smoke-tinted glass that jets to the sky. It blew me away when I came here for my interview. I remember thinking this was the place that would start my future, but I'm not thinking that right now. I'm trying to figure out the present.

Mia and I walk through the doors and join a cluster of people waiting at the bank of elevators.

We haven't said a word to each other since we left the cab.

We haven't looked at each other.

I don't even know if we're standing together, or just in the same vicinity.

I shift my shoulders, telling myself that it's the suit that feels strange and constricting.

The elevator arrives and the doors part. I hold the door, letting a dozen people flood past me. Then I step inside and reach for the button for the seventeenth floor, but it's already lit.

Mia stands lost behind a wall of dark suits. The urge to shove toward her comes over me. That seems desperate, though it also feels awkward *not* to stand with her. But then it's too late. The doors slide closed and I'm trapped in the front, staring at the seam between the steel panels.

We hit the seventh floor, and four people step out.

It's not until the doors close again that I realize I've been holding my breath.

Mia's still on the elevator.

Twelfth floor. Two people leave.

Fourteenth. Three more.

I glance at the elevator controls. Only one floor is still lit.

"Well, this is a surprise." Mia is still a few feet behind me. I can't tell, but I think she's smiling. I want to ask her at least one of the questions charging through my brain, but doors slide open to the glass-walled Boomerang lobby, and we both step out.

Chapter 5

Mia

Q: Dress like a wreck, or dress for success?

*M*y brain decides it's an excellent time to go on strike, leaving me with zero resources to puzzle through the fact that I, a) woke up next to this lovely male-type person after engaging in activities I tragically can't recall; b) ended up in a cab with him, which; c) took us to the exact same destination; until d) we found ourselves stepping out on the same floor. A floor that houses one business and one business only: Boomerang.

My new place of employment.

And apparently his too.

"So, this job of yours?" I say. A corkscrew of hair drops into my line of vision as if to underscore my rattled state.

"Internship," he replies, and the word comes out heavy, like a confession.

"For Boomerang."

He nods, and his hands busy themselves with the knot of his tie, reminding me of my own less-than-professional attire. I'm itching to get to my cell phone, to find out if Beth's made it yet. "You too, huh?"

I'm too shell-shocked to frame a reply, so I just nod like a dummy and start what feels like one of those weird dream-walks through a space that seems to shrink and expand with each step.

I joked about never having seen *Star Wars*, but looking down a long expanse of gleaming bamboo floors, "The Imperial March" sounds in my head. The place is more Ridley Scott than George Lucas, though, with its curving white walls and recessed purple lighting. The cubicles have low smoked-glass walls and funky half-circle workstations. As Skyler would say, it looks like someone drank a feng shui cocktail and puked the decor.

We pass a few cubicles occupied by girls in thick black glasses with asymmetrical haircuts and guys in skinny jeans with various configurations of facial hair. Hipster Central, it seems, though Adam Blackwood, Boomerang's founder and president, looks like the love child of Ryan Gosling and . . . well, Ryan Gosling.

"I'm supposed to . . ." Quickly, Ethan amends, "I guess we're supposed to check in with HR, fill out some paperwork, surrender our firstborn. That sort of thing."

"Crap, I already surrendered my firstborn at the *last* job. Do you have a spare?"

He grins at me. "How would I have a spare *firstborn*?"

"Oh, fine, you're going to drag logic into the conversation?"

A towering blond woman in an emerald-green suit with lapels sharp enough to slice cheese stalks toward us, her expression set somewhere between rabid and murderous.

"You have got to be kidding me!" she shrieks as she comes alongside us and casts a tundra-cold glance in my direction.

Immediately, I think she's talking about my clothing, which, while not precisely appropriate, wouldn't seem to merit a Teutonic hissy fit. But her eyes bounce away from me again, and she presses her hand to her ear. "If this guy doesn't work out, I will have no problem jamming an ice pick up your skinny ass, Paolo," she says, and I finally notice the Bluetooth device tucked up next to a chignon tight enough to give her cat eyes.

She clips away, leaving flowers to shrivel and birds to drop from the sky in her wake.

"Jesus," Ethan mutters, and I realize I've actually grabbed onto his arm in terror. "Here's hoping she's not the HR rep."

I allow myself a moment's enjoyment before releasing him. "Here's hoping she doesn't even *work* here."

He smiles. "Here's hoping she's leaving on a ten-year cruise."

"To Antarctica."

"To reunite with her clan, the snow beasts."

I laugh. And my eyes find his again. Maybe I've lucked into more than just an internship here.

"Sorry to break up the party," says a voice behind us.

I turn to find Beth standing near a doorway marked with a pink heart made of two boomerangs. She wears a stick-straight black wig over her kinky hair and rocks a ridiculous blue gingham romper. Like some kind of vampire farm girl—from Harlem.

Rattling a plastic bag at me, she says, "Chop, chop, girl. Let's jump in here and get you fixed up. I have another go-see at noon, and it's way the hell up in Burbank."

"Thank God you made it." I rush to her side, calling out a quick intro as I push open the door to the ladies room.

Her shrewd black eyes take in every inch of Ethan, and she reaches out a perfect set of purple acrylics to shake his hand.

"I like your . . ." Ethan makes a sweeping gesture that manages to encompass pretty much all of Beth.

"Yeah, I like yours too." She slaps my butt, moving me through the door. "If you're a good boy, maybe Mia will share sometime."

"Beth!"

The door swings shut on his gape-mouthed expression, and she lets out a big, open-throated laugh. "That boy did not know what hit him."

Before I have a chance to respond that I know the feeling, she has my dress off over my head and has replaced it with a violet silk blouse. Beth comes from a long line of dressers and stage managers, so this is a feat I've witnessed several times before, though it's my first time on the receiving end.

"Where'd this come from?" I ask.

"It was on my body when I left the house this morning," she tells me. "Or did you think I walked around looking like some broke-down Dorothy from Oz?"

She drops to the floor and pulls a heather-gray skirt from the bag.

"Step in," she orders, holding the garment open for me, and I do.

She stands, spins me around, tugs down the bottom of the blouse, zips up the skirt, and then reaches her hands beneath my clothes to do some adjusting.

The outfit is, not surprisingly, absolute perfection.

I plant a hand on Beth's shoulder as I zip on her pair of soft leather boots, which she trades for my strappy sandals. "You really are so good to me."

"As good as *Ethan*?"

I straighten and look in the mirror. My skin looks sallow in the fluorescent lighting, and half my hair has escaped its bonds, making me look like the spawn of an anemone. But still, it's an improvement. "You're going to kill me, but I barely remember."

She tsks. "What a shame. And also why I don't drink." Then she grabs my hair like reins. In a flurry of purple nails and chunky silver rings, she wrestles it into order, smoothing it into a neater version of the low bun I'd attempted.

It seems a *pinch* ungrateful to remind her that she actually stopped drinking after accidentally making out with her cousin.

"I'm glad you had yourself a little fun, though, Mia. You deserve it after *that tool* Kyle."

"Thanks, gorgeous." I give her a quick hug, and then I turn last night's dress and shoes over to her. I think of returning Ethan's shirt to him, but some impulse makes me hand it to her too. "And thanks so much for this. You're a lifesaver."

She drops them into the shopping bags and then considers me for a moment. "Looking good, but you could use a little lipstick."

"What have you got with you?"

"You like this?" she asks, pointing to the bright poppy stain on her full lips.

"It's gorgeous. Can—"

Beth grabs my face and plants a firm kiss on my lips.

"Voilà!"

She thumbs away the excess, spins me toward the door, and then gives me another slap on the butt. "Now? Go show this place who's boss."

Chapter 6

Ethan

Q: Rule breaker, or rule maker?

*M*ia rushes off with her friend, leaving me alone in the lobby. Between starting the internship and everything this morning, I'm beginning to feel like I stepped into someone else's life—except this is the job I'm gunning for. The one that's going to launch my professional career. At least that feels right.

I've barely made it to the receptionist desk when I see Rhett Orland, the HR manager, striding down the hall.

During my interview for the internship, I learned that Rhett is in his early thirties, divorced with no kids, and has recently gotten *very* into biking, swimming, weightlifting, and running. The guy is always amped up—probably because he's an energy-powder distributor on the side. I'm almost positive I landed this gig because he wants me to give him some training tips, but hey, if it's what got me in the door, I'm fine with it.

"Ethan!" he booms as he pumps my hand. "I've been expecting you, man! Day one!" Rhett's face actually looks like he works out constantly, sort of skeletal and muscled, like a pit bull. "You're looking good. Been logging some extra time in the gym?"

"Nah. Just doing some cycling lately." Because I can't afford a car.

"Nice! I knew it. Come on, let's get you saddled up!" Rhett loops an arm over my neck and tugs me down the hall. It's awkward because I'm taller. And because it's really fucking awkward.

As we leave the lobby, I glance behind me, but I don't see her.

"Forget something?" Rhett says.

Yes, I'm tempted to say. *Maybe the greatest night of my life.* But I shake my head. "No, I'm good, man. So, how's the training going? You ready for the triathlon?"

For the next half hour, I sign some paperwork in his office as he updates me on his progress. By the time he walks me back out, I know his current weight, BMI, resting heart rate, daily caloric input and output. By my guess, we're about five minutes away from a full detail on his bowel movements.

It's not that I don't care or that I'm not interested in the guy. It's just that for me, being fit isn't about numbers. It's about the game. The beautiful game, as soccer's called in Brazil. Playing allowed me to push my physical limits—which was a big draw—but soccer is also about being part of a team. Belonging to something greater than yourself. Rhett's angle on sports couldn't be more different than mine. He's basically a one-man team.

I stop at his door. "Hey, Rhett. I don't mean to cut you off, but I thought there was only one internship position."

His eyes go wide. "Oh!" He leans in like we're sharing a secret. "You met Mia, huh? What'd you think? Sweet piece of—"

"Yeah, I met her," I interrupt. After one hazy night with her, I shouldn't care, but I feel like I might punch him if he finishes that thought. "So, what's the deal? Did they create another position?"

"No, no." Rhett's hand thumps down on my shoulder, and we're moving through the halls again. What kind of HR guy doesn't understand personal space? "Boss man wants to be the one to give you the details, or you know I'd tell you everything."

He gives me a look, like he and I are tight.

"Got it," I say. But I don't. I didn't expect this.

This being Mia.

I'm already wondering—no, I'm already *sure* she's going to be a distraction. Or a temptation.

Shit. She'll definitely be both.

Rhett takes me into a glass-walled office. The furniture is modern, but not fragile or stark. This space looks like it belongs to someone organized, stylish, and rich. Sleek chairs made of wood, accented with glossy black leather. A desk that's a single thick piece of glass, with nothing but a laptop, a cell phone, and a small bronze tiger resting on its gleaming surface.

Adam Blackwood looks up from his laptop when Rhett and I walk in. Behind him, Los Angeles stretches out, sun-bathed and bustling. It's an unusually clear day, and you can see all the way to Santa Monica.

He stands and comes around the desk, silver cuff links flashing as he offers his hand. "Ethan. Good to see you again. Welcome to Boomerang."

Adam is twenty-two, only a year older than me, and already president of a multimillion-dollar enterprise. Of course, it helps when you start your first company at fifteen. He went to Princeton, evidenced by the tiger on his desk, and Boomerang is the third company he's founded.

Last night at Duke's when we met for a drink, it felt like every woman in the place orbited our table. I get checked out here and there myself, but nothing compared to what I experienced being in his company.

The thing about Adam is that he's always ten steps ahead of everyone. That's why he's so successful. I know I'll learn a lot from him.

"Thanks, Adam. It's good to be here."

Adam dismisses Rhett, who leaves with a disappointed pit bull look on his face, then gestures to a chair in a seating area away from his desk. "Have a seat, Ethan."

"Thanks." I sink into a soft leather chair. A series of huge modern paintings of ocean waves line one of the walls. I make a mental note of that. Blackwood might be Ivy League, but he's also a surfer—or an art collector.

He pushes his suit tail back in a movement that's as unconscious as the way I juggle a soccer ball. "How'd it go last night after I left?"

I smile, because part of me wants to tell him the truth. *Well, Adam, I met the other intern, did some body shots with her, took her back to my place and probably spent the duration between her thighs. So, pretty good night, all in all.*

I go with the safer answer, though. "Great. I met up with my roommate. We did a little celebrating."

"Good. That's what I like to hear." Adam's eyes move past me, and we both stand again as Mia enters with the blond woman we saw in the hall earlier.

"Morning, Cookie," Adam says.

"Adam, intern. Intern, Adam." She gives Mia a little push and then swivels on a stiletto and leaves.

The glass door is on one of those slow-closing hinges, so we hear and see her retreat for what feels like forever. "I need that presentation, Paolo," she says, pressing a headset that appears to be implanted in her ear. "Get them to me in an hour or I'll have your Puerto Rican ass deported, and no, I don't care if that's impossible. I could find a way and don't you doubt it for one goddamn . . ."

The door closes, and we settle back into our seats, sharing a moment of tense silence. From the corner of my eye, I can tell that Mia's wearing new clothes. I want to see how she looks, but checking her out is not an option right now. Besides, I already know she'd look good in anything. She looks really good in *nothing*.

Adam smiles and crosses his legs. "I'm very fond of talented, hard-working people, and Cookie happens to be both, as do both of you. You'll notice that among my staff, I'll forgive eccentricities as long as the work that's produced is on time and of the highest quality—but I do have a few rules." He stiffens slightly and shakes his head. "I'm sorry. I'm forgetting my manners. You two haven't met yet."

He introduces Mia and me, and we shake hands, pretending to be strangers who did not, in any way, see each other naked one hour and ten minutes ago. I can't tell if we sell it well enough. Adam watches us with a curious expression, like he knows something that we don't know. Or like he knows the something that we *do* know and are trying to hide.

"Where was I?" he asks.

"Rules," I say.

"Work of the highest quality," Mia adds.

"Yes, thank you. I know you'll produce good work—you wouldn't be here otherwise—but the terms of the internship need to be clarified. You'll help in marketing. I understand you both have different areas of interest, but the Boomerang brand can always use an injection of fresh, creative thinkers. And it's the best place to learn about what we do. Only one of you—the one who contributes the most—will receive the offer of permanent employment in the fall. Prove your mettle, and you'll earn your place in one of the fastest-growing media businesses in the world, but I want to be clear: there's only one spot. Only one of you will stay on."

He pauses, letting that sink in. And it does. Like ice water. I took this internship because of the promise of a job at the end of the summer. I did *not* sign up to work my ass off for free, only to end up with nothing.

I can't afford that. I will starve if I don't get this job.

I'm too close to it as it is.

I feel Mia's eyes dart over to me. This girl showed up in my life less than twenty-four hours ago. I've slept with her. I've shared a cab with her and given her my dress shirt to wear. But this new situation is a game-changer.

Officially, Mia is now my competition.

"Is that understood?" Adam asks, his eyes narrowing on me and then shifting to Mia.

I nod.

Mia says, "Yes."

"Good." Adam folds his hands together. "Now for rules. There's really only one. This business sets up people who want no-strings-attached company. That's what I sell. Relationships for people on the rebound. People who want fun, without any emotional entanglement. But the office policy is no relationships, tangled or entangled, or in any form at all. Ever." Once again, he looks from me to Mia, his blue eyes glinting. "Have I made myself clear?"

This time Mia nods, and I'm the one who answers.

"That won't be a problem," I say.

I need this job. And I always play to win.

Chapter 7

Mia

Q: Do you forgive and forget, or hold a grudge?

That won't be a problem.

Ethan's words ricochet around in my already battered brain as we accompany Adam Blackwood down a long corridor.

I drop back, letting the two of them stride along in front of me. Beth's boots pinch my toes, and I have to take about six steps for every two of theirs. I feel deflated, bruised, and not really sure what bothers me more—that this great opportunity turned into a cage match or that I just took a sucker punch to the ego from someone I don't even know if I want.

That won't be a problem.

Probably, if I'd woken in my own bed and wasn't nursing the hangover of a million rock stars, I could shrug off those five words.

But they keep twinging inside me, like muscles you forget are sore until you stretch the wrong way.

I'm here for the job, I remind myself. Not the guy. I couldn't even remember his name an hour ago, and now I'm pouting because he wants to focus on his work? This is better. This makes it all that much easier to crush him.

Um, I mean *earn this fantastic opportunity on the basis of my merits.*

Bits of their conversation waft back to me as we move in and out of halos of LED lights: *market penetration, abandonment rate.* Ethan's already grabbed the baton, and here I am moping along in the background. Is that the Mia Galliano who's going to take on this mother-flippin' world? No, it is not.

So I need a plan. One that includes leaving Ethan in the dust.

I steel myself and take a few healthy strides to catch up to them. Wedging myself next to Adam, I force Ethan to shoulder-bump the wall.

"I've already got a hundred great ideas," I tell Adam Blackwood. "How about a more *cinematic* approach to your promotions? Like a visual narrative we can carry out along all kinds of transmedia platforms. What do you think?"

"I like the sound of that," he says and gives me a wink that would relax Medusa's hair.

I keep him chatting until we reach an alcove with a massive partner desk in Plexiglas and chrome. Tablet computers rest on each side, with additional wireless keyboards and fancy tri-fold monitors spread across the desktop. The geek girl in me salivates—classily, of course.

On a long concrete countertop nearby, a towering espresso machine alternately hisses and gurgles, its four nozzles caked with foam. Beneath it, cabinet doors gape open, and a profusion of cleaning supplies and paper cups spills out onto the floor.

Adam glances at the kitchen area, his expression darkening, and then gestures us to the sleek white leather captain's chairs flanking the desk. We both go for the same one, smacking inelegantly into one another. Ethan puts a hand on my shoulder to keep me from tottering, and that delicious beach-smoke scent of his hollows my insides.

Focus, Mia.

I ease away and flop into the oversized seat, the wheels of which promptly roll me about six feet across the space.

"What's first on the agenda?" asks Ethan. He settles into his chair like he was born to it, though his legs are so long that his burnished Oxfords end up under my side. I roll back up to the desk, feeling overly conscious of every bit of him—his feet right near my own. His toned legs and broad shoulders perfectly encased in his suit. His ink-blue eyes, inquisitive and friendly, focused on Adam. Not aggressive. Not overeager. Just deep and thoughtful, alive with his desire to dive into a challenge.

"Today, I want you to get signed up on Boomerang. You need to have the client experience to know how to sell it, right? And everything we do—this dating site, our film and TV properties—it's about tapping into a certain zeitgeist. Really understand how to speak to our audience, and you can write your own ticket. So, take a look around the site, fill out member profiles, get familiar with it all."

Brushing imaginary lint from his sleeve, he says, "In fact, I want you two to fill out bios for one another. Get to know your competition." His shrewd eyes move back and forth between us, and a knowing smirk makes a fleeting appearance. "All right?"

Ethan nods and fires up his tablet. "Great."

I sit back but hook a toe around my desk leg so I don't roll away again.

"Sure," I say, glancing at Ethan. "That won't be a problem."

Chapter 8

Ethan

Q: Tell us a little about yourself.

*A*dam walks away, leaving us at our new desks.

For a few seconds, Mia and I just stare at each other. I wonder if she's as tired as I am. Whatever we did together last night, sleep didn't figure into it much. I don't drink coffee, but I'm tempted to fire up the massive coffee machine on the counter and mainline some espresso.

"Should we get started?" she asks, her tone a little too bright. She's not happy about competing for something that was supposed to be a sure thing either.

I have a wild urge to bow out of the running and let her have the damn internship. Then I remember the box crate in my closet filled with utility bills, student loans, and law school applications. Bowing out would be really fucking dumb. I barely know this girl.

But apparently that's about to change.

Mia taps on the keyboard in front of her. "Do you want to take turns or go at the same time?"

"Let's go at the same time. That's usually more fun."

Her eyes snap up to me. Guess I'm not the only one with a dirty mind.

"I'll start." I open the laptop in front of me and find the Boomerang Profile icon, clicking it open. "Last name?"

"Galliano. Two L's. One N."

"You're Italian?" All morning I'd been thinking she's Greek or Brazilian.

"Half Italian, half Jewish," she says. "Guilt is my Kryptonite."

Her eyes are on the screen, but I can tell she's fighting a smile.

"Vance for me. Just how it sounds. Age?"

"Twenty-one," she answers. "I'm an early bloomer."

I get the feeling her sense of humor cannot be contained. That's trouble. This would be much easier if she were more like Alison, who'd go on emotional benders for weeks for reasons I never understood. Mia can't be this easygoing.

"Twenty-one for me, too."

We keep going, plowing through some basics, and I learn she was born in Little Silver, New Jersey, and is an only child. Her favorite childhood book is *The Phantom Tollbooth,* and her favorite dessert is something called halvah.

I tell her that I was born in Colorado, actually *in* my parents' bowling alley; that my favorite color might be brown—or maybe red or orange—but I'll tragically never know since they tend to look the same, thanks to my mild color-blindness; and that my favorite foods are anything that's not Chinese.

Then we get to the tougher questions.

"Duration and end of last relationship?" I ask.

"Ugh." Mia grimaces and drives her fingers into her curly hair. "People actually have to answer this?"

"This service *is* for people on the rebound."

"I suppose. But the question's kind of a downer, right? Anyway, my last relationship lasted a year, and ended about a year ago. You?"

I stare at the blinking cursor on my screen. A year ago? No one else since then? I don't know why, but that surprises me.

"Ethan?"

"What—oh. Two years for the duration, and it ended two months ago."

"Wow. Two years?"

"Next question."

"Touchy subject?"

I look up and see a teasing smile.

"You could say that." For a while there, I'd thought this day couldn't possibly get any weirder, but talking about Alison to a girl I slept-and-now-work-with is definitely leveling me up.

"Next. Question," I say. "Unless you want to watch me destroy an overpriced espresso machine."

"Number of sexual partners?" she says.

"What the fuck?" My eyes drop to the screen. Sure enough, there's the question.

"I believe the question pertains to how many. Not what."

"Christ. They really want to get to know you, don't they?" I roll my shoulders, feeling like I'm suddenly boiling. "Fine. Just don't judge, okay? This is a sensitive subject for me. Eighty-three."

Mia rolls her eyes. "In your *dreams*."

"Actually, then that number would much higher. Infinity, probably. If you want a real number, though, it's an even ten. And let me remind you that I was with one girl for two long-ass years, so you have to factor that into account."

I'm kind of expecting her to comment on the ten, but Mia says, "Two long-ass years, huh? Sounds like a good time."

"You have no idea."

"Actually," she says, "I think I do."

I hear sadness in her voice, and I'm tempted to ask her about her ex, but avoiding baggage wins. "What about you? What's your number?"

"Kyle makes four."

That puts my brain into lockdown for a little while as I process. *Four.* Four guys who've been with her. Four guys I don't know, but who I suddenly don't like.

Then I replay what she said. "So, with me, that's five, right?"

She gives me a *keep your voice down* glare and whispers, *"Four total,* because *we didn't."*

I lean back in my chair and cross my arms. "Oh, yes. We did. More than once, I'd say."

She leans forward, steepling her fingers and giving me a scrutinizing look. "And you think that why?"

"Well, for starters, your thong was in my toaster oven."

"Hey, it's a great place to store them. I might start doing that all the time. It could be the next big thing. Think about it. Thong warming drawers."

"Are we really talking about hot thongs right now?"

"Apparently. But a hot thong does not a sexual encounter make."

"Fair enough, but we did wake up naked in my bed."

"Still doesn't mean anything."

I put my hand to my chest. "That hurts. Okay, how about this: I've never been naked with a beautiful girl, in a bed, and *not* had it happen."

Hold up. Did I just call her beautiful? Yeah, I did.

Once again, Mia doesn't react. She's either used to being called beautiful, could care less that *I* just called her beautiful, or is hiding that she likes that I called her beautiful.

I catch my train of thought and want to beat the shit out of myself. *The job, Vance. Focus.*

"Let me think about this," Mia says. She taps her fingers to her chin and narrows her eyes like she's pondering the meaning of life. "So, you've been in bed with ten naked girls, and every single time, you've had sex with them?"

"That's right. I have a perfect record."

"And you're counting me?"

I spread my hands. "You were naked in my bed."

I remember the way she looked, all gorgeous curves, green eyes, and that wild curly hair. It's a damn good thing this desk is providing some cover, because I'm pitching a tent under it right now. Nice fucking timing.

Mia smiles and gives a little shrug. "Then I guess your number's only nine." She taps a few keys on her keyboard, changing it in my profile. "Sorry to spoil your winning streak."

But the sparkle in her eyes tells me she's not sorry at all.

Chapter 9

Mia

Q: Tell us about your family.

*I*mmediately upon arriving at Casa Galliano that evening, I am shoved onto a stool under lights bright enough to produce an x-ray, at which point a giant wooden spoon coated in something green is thrust at my face.

"Joe, you're in the middle of my shot," my mom complains, popping out from behind her Linhof Technikardan to adjust the lens, glare at my father, and shoot me a volley of air kisses. Her bottle-red hair is threaded with silver, and she's in grungy pink sweats and a black tank, so I know she's on a creative bender.

"Pearl," dad replies, "you're in the middle of my tasting." He turns back to me and winks. "What d'ya think of the pesto, Mia Moré? Good? Bad? Too salty? Needs more basil?"

Resistance is most certainly futile, so I take the spoon and taste— "Needs some chili paste, Jo-Jo, a little *spezia*"—then I wipe my mouth on my father's apron, finger-comb my hair, and strike a pose for my mom, which she immortalizes with a couple of quick shots.

"What am I this time?"

"The face of unchecked capitalism," she says. "I'm going to silk-screen you onto an eight-foot dollar bill. It's for an installation at the New York Stock Exchange."

It amazes me what they let my mother get away with, but when you're as famous as she is, you get to call the shots. "Really?" I tease her. "That seems so tame for you."

"Well . . ." She disappears behind the camera again, so I barely hear the rest, but I think I catch the word, "impaled."

I've had worse.

Looking around at the array of equipment and the wall-wide bulletin board cluttered with images, I think about how sure my mother seems to be, how all of her projects—as bizarre and otherworldly as they can sometimes be—seem so absolutely and perfectly *her*.

"Hey, mom," I say. "How did you . . ."

I'm not sure what I want to ask, exactly, and it always feels like cheating, somehow, to go to my mother for advice. Like taking a shortcut through private property. "How did you decide, umm—like what your artistic perspective would be? Like how to, I guess, see things the way you see them?"

"I just let myself play," she mutters. "I didn't hold on as tight as you."

I swallow, disappointed, and stare past her out to the sage scrub dotting the walls of the canyon beyond our backyard.

"Where's Nana?" I ask, changing the subject. "How's she doing today?"

"Good day," my mother says, but my father scratches the gray stubble under his chin and shakes his head. My mom's special gift—and curse—is seeing what she wants to see. It's great for art. Not so much for life.

I sigh, staring past my mother as she snaps a few more pictures.

Dad drops onto an original Eames that they treat like a yard sale find, completely heedless of the pesto that drips from his spoon onto the spongy yellow linoleum floor of my mom's studio. Luckily, my mom has the equivalent of Ethan's color-blindness when it comes to stains.

Which, of course, makes me think of him, of the things I'd learned during our mutual interview. I learned that he practically grew up in his folks' bowling alley and once missed a perfect score by one spare. I learned that his eyebrows swoop upward over his nose when he's deep in thought. And I learned—without him telling me—that he loves kids. His face shined brighter than my mom's studio lights when he talked about coaching youth soccer.

It doesn't matter. I know that. Though I suppose if you have to wake up next to someone after a night you can't remember and work with that person in your face every single day, it's better if that person is decent, smart, and sexy.

"How was your first day, kiddo?" asks my dad in that creepy way both my parents have of reading my mind. "Make any friends?"

"Great," I say. "Though it turns out I'm competing with another intern for a job there. And we're in marketing, which isn't my thing."

My mom clucks her disapproval, but my dad brightens.

"That's great," he says. "Best thing in the world is winning something you really fought for. And it doesn't matter if it's your thing. Make it your thing."

"I guess."

"Trust your old man on this one." He stands again. Since his accident—when an apprentice electrician turned off the wrong breaker, putting my dad in contact with a live wire, he's physically incapable of sitting for more than two minutes. He hands me the spoon and threads a precarious maze of light umbrellas, coiled electrical cords, and boxes of props that look like they come from a production of *Lysistrata* set on the moon.

Ducking behind my mother, he wraps his arms around her and nuzzles her neck. "This one said no to me about a hundred times before she gave me a yes."

"What are you talking about?" I say. "You got pregnant with me on your first date!"

"Yeah, but it took me a hundred tries to get to that date. No wonder we were so goddamn randy by then."

Laughing, my mom tilts her head up and draws him in for a kiss—my cue to gather up the shreds of my psyche and flee.

I grab my camera from the hall closet, where I've stashed it since some party guest of Sky's used it to shoot a highly meaningful vignette about his balls.

Heading through the sunny Tuscan kitchen to Nana's suite, I snag an apple from the basket, peek through the stacks of mail to see if anything's for me, and put aside my mom's copy of *Aperture* to steal later.

Nana's TV is set a notch past ear-splitting, so I knock vigorously and then open the door.

I find my grandmother in underwear and sneakers, trying to wrestle into silk pajama pants, the only thing she'll wear these days because, she says, everything else makes her legs itch. About a hundred bobby pins stud her wavy hair—also auburn out of a box—which means she's just had it washed and set.

"Oh, good, you're here!" she exclaims. Behind the thick lenses of her eyeglasses, her lively hazel eyes look clear, focused, and I'm thankful for that.

Sometimes, it feels like Nana's on a boat, and I'm on the shore, waving goodbye and watching her grow smaller and smaller in the distance. I can't swim out after her, and I can't bring her back. I can only capture the parts of her that remain in sight.

I shake off my gloom.

"Hey, Nana!" I give her a kiss on her cool papery cheek and then coax her back into a chair. "Let me help."

She lets me take off her shoes and then steps into the pajama pants, which I draw up her legs and then, lifting her from her chair, secure around her waist. I tug the drawstring tight, like she likes it, aware of how hollow-boned and small she feels to me these days.

"Is the top in here?" I ask, going to her closet.

But she just shrugs and gives me a look that tells me she's lost the thread. I find a soft cotton top in midnight blue with tiny white hibiscus spilling down the sleeve and help her into it, buttoning the buttons for her.

"I'm glad you brought that," she says, gesturing at the video camera I set down on her bureau. "They told me to film my things in case the girl comes back and takes them."

"What girl? Who told you?"

"The girl they have come help me."

She must mean one of her aides, though I can't imagine any of them stealing from her.

"Can we start?" she asks. "Bring me my purse."

I do and turn on my camera, focusing on her crisp bed linens to help me adjust the white balance and then opening the iris to let in a little more light.

She fishes around and pulls out a long strand of pearls with a diamond pendant in the symbol of a *chai*—the Hebrew symbol for life.

"Stan brought this back from Israel," she says, and I film her as she worries the beads, drawing them over and over again through her fingers. "He spent three hundred dollars on them, a fortune in those days."

"I guess he thought you were worth it, Nana."

She lets herself smile, though it collapses into a frown, and she shoves the beads at me. "Take them."

"Oh, no." I lay them in her lap, placing her hands back on top of them. "They're yours. You keep them."

She rolls them up and drops them back into her purse, which she snaps shut and hugs against her chest. "I just don't want that girl to get them," she says. "She comes in here and touches everything."

"She's probably just trying to clean or help you put things away." I make a mental note to ask my mom about this new person.

For now, though, I turn the camera back to my grandmother, try—but fail—to see her through the lens's more objective eye. I watch her, the wry half-smile on her lips telling me she's dreaming some secret dream—maybe about my grandfather or about being a young girl whose ambition brought her to the law and to fight for civil rights in the South.

I look around at her jewelry, at her books and dresses and me- mentos. Next to the photo of her standing shoulder-to-shoulder with Martin Luther King is one I love even more. She sits behind the wheel of an old car—a Studebaker, she told me—with one of my grandpa's cigars clamped, unlit, between her teeth. Her smile is ab- solutely dazzling, and she gives the camera a wink like the moment will last forever.

Something snaps to life inside me, and I realize I've found my way into my film. These objects—the photographs, the jewelry, the antique perfume bottles lining her ivory-inlaid dresser, all of these things she's kept through her adulthood, through the loss of my grandfather and her two older sisters, through her journey from an extravagant apartment in Forest Hills to this modest room clear across the country, they can tell her story for her. They can help me tell the world who she is.

"Tell me more about the necklace, Nana," I say and lift the camera once again.

Chapter 10

Ethan

Q: On a scale of one to ten, how would
you rank your physical fitness?

*H*ow the HR manager from hell wound up leading my team through warm-up drills is a mystery I will never solve.

One minute I was in Century City bumming a ride from Rhett Orland after work. The next, I'm on the Beverly Hills High soccer field watching him run my squad of under-nine boys through a third set of push-ups.

I've been standing here for ten minutes, and I still can't believe this.

"Come on, boys!" Rhett yells. He links his hands behind his back and paces down the line of groaning kids like a drill sergeant. "Put some *want to* in it! Backs straight, tails down! Feel that, boys? Can you feel the goodness?"

Unbelievable. *Feel the goodness?* The guy says some epically weird shit.

Tyler, my starting left wing, looks up from the push-up position, his nose scrunched up and his face red. "Coach Ethan, why do we have to do push-ups?"

It's a fair question. Nine-year-olds' arms are basically twigs, and I'm getting worried that Milo's are going to snap right before my eyes. Not to mention that upper-body strength isn't what I need from them. I need endurance. Core strength. Hell, I just need them to focus for more than two seconds at a time. But today things are different: my boys are helping me out with a little skill called ass-kissery.

"Because if you don't do push-ups," I say to Tyler, "*Coach Rhett* here is going to terminate me from my new employment."

Rhett stops his verbal assault and grins. "You're an intern, Vance, so legally I can't fire you. I can only *dismiss* you." His head whips back to the line of grunting kids. "Cameron, I *saw* you! You can get lower than that! Push 'em out, boys! Two more sets!"

This used to be the best part of my day.

I let Rhett finish warm-ups and then I get the boys running some drills. Juggling. Dribbling. Passing. These boys know what to do once they get moving. They're young, but it's a premier league team, with tryouts, tournaments, rankings. The whole deal. I made sure when I picked this group that they'd *want* to be here. I can deal with screwing around and nose-picking if they show some heart when we get down to actual soccer—and they do. My team has big-time heart.

When it's time to scrimmage, I join in, partly because it fires the boys up and makes them try harder, and partly because I can't resist the chance to touch the ball.

"Yo, Vance!" Rhett yells as he trots into the goal. I don't know when he did it, but he's gone to his car for biking gloves and a bright yellow, tight—even for spandex—shirt. His attempt at goalie gear, I think. He smacks his gloves together and drops into a baseball-ready stance, hands on his knees. Sweat rolls down his face and drips off his nose even though all he's done so far is yell, but Rhett's always overheated, even at the office.

"See if you can score on me," he says.

That makes me shudder a little. "Nah. I'm good, Rhett."

I feed a few balls to my forwards, Tyler and Milo, proud of them for getting past Rhett more often than not. Even prouder when they decide to start calling him Coach Sweat instead of Coach Rhett.

I pass to Tyler again, whose left foot is on fire today, but he sends it right back to me. "Come on, Coach Ethan! You shoot this one!"

"You go, Tyler." I'm not here to put on a show, so I pass it back to him. "Take it."

Tyler sends the ball to me *again.* "*You,* Coach Ethan!" he yells. Then he stops and lifts his twiggy arms in the air, champion style. "*Feel the goodness!*"

Well, shit. I can't say no to that.

I drive my foot through the ball, holding nothing back. The shot is a rocket, the ball plunging into the back of the net, exactly where I wanted it. It rolls to a stop before the kids even react, then there are celebration airplanes and chest-bumps everywhere, except for Rhett, who shakes his head.

"You got lucky, Vance! Come at me again! Bring it, baby!"

"Sure, Rhett," I say. "But I need a minute first. Can you handle this for a little while?"

Running around roused the beast that is my hangover. My brain feels like a water balloon jangling in my skull, and I need something to drink. Might as well take advantage of a short break and make the phone call I've been dreading all day.

Rhett genuinely looks touched. "Yeah, yeah. Anything, Vance. I got it."

"Thanks." I move toward the parking lot where I can still see the field and sit on the hood of Rhett's Mini Cooper, which is outfitted with a ski rack, a bike rack, and, of course, racing stripes.

Fishing my phone out of my pocket, I call home, hoping to catch my dad before the evening rush at the alley.

He answers on the third ring. "Black Diamond Bowl."

"Hey, old man. It's me."

"Ethan! How's my boy doing? They pick you for the movies yet?"

Dad's one of those people who sort of yells everything. Twenty years in a bowling alley will do that. He also thinks I'm harboring a secret desire to become an actor, since that's the only valid reason he can come up with for me to still live in Los Angeles post-graduation.

The crash of pins breaking fills my ear—a strike by the sound of it—and a wave of homesickness washes over me. What I wouldn't do to be there tonight, polishing bowling balls, un-jamming the vending machines and just hanging with my dad.

"Nope. No movies yet," I say. "How're things there? How's mom?"

"Good! She just called ten minutes ago from Arizona."

Oh, yeah. I'd forgotten. Mom drove with my little brother to U of A this week. I finished college just as Chris is going in.

Then it hits me: that's not going to make this conversation any easier.

I got a partial ride to UCLA for soccer, and my parents helped as much as they could, but I still had to take student loans in the amount of $28,000 to cover the rest. Now Mom and Dad have four years of Chris's school to pay and—

"Ethan?" my dad says.

"What? Oh—that's good, Dad. Chris is okay? He's getting settled in the dorm and everything?"

"Yep. They just unpacked the car, and they're heading to dinner."

"Cool," I say, and I'm out of words. I can't ask him anymore.

The thunderous smashing of pins grows quieter, and I know my dad has stepped into his office and shut the door.

I picture him there, watching his struggling business through the dusty blinds of the large window that faces lanes eight and nine. I picture the piles of bills on his desk—piles that aren't much different from the ones in the crate in my apartment.

"What's going on, son?" he asks, his voice growing gentle.

"Dad, I—I know this isn't a good time to ask this, but I need to borrow some money."

Silence for a few seconds. "How much?"

The back of my throat starts to burn. "A thousand? This job I got . . . it's gonna take a little while to see a paycheck."

"I see. Well. I can't lend you money, Ethan."

The words land like a punch to the chest. I stare at the grass by my feet, just concentrating on pulling in a breath and letting it out.

You always picture people who are completely broke pushing shopping carts full of trash, or sitting on a sidewalk with a sleeping mutt and a cardboard sign.

That's not me.

My cleats are worth $500. My education is worth over a $100K.

Two months ago I was signing autographs after my soccer matches.

"It's okay, Dad. I understand," I say. And now I'm wondering what he's dealing with. I know things haven't been good at the bowling alley for a couple of years, but what if he and Mom are in trouble?

"I don't think you do understand, Ethan. I'm not lending you money. You're my *son*. I'll wire three thousand to you this afternoon. Is that enough?"

The tightness in my chest doesn't really ease, but I find that I can breathe again. "Yeah, Dad. Thanks. That's enough."

It might not actually be enough to get me through the summer, but it's more than I should accept.

"Good!" he says, his voice rising back to its usual tone. "So, have you met any pretty girls out there?"

Mia's face pops into my mind. The afternoon is fading, and the sun-drenched trees on the south side of the field remind me of her eyes, all bright and green. "Actually, I did, but she, uh . . . she got away from me."

"Well, you've never been a quitter, Ethan. Go after her!"

I smile, shaking my head. "We'll see, Dad. We'll see."

When I get home from coaching, food aromas lure me to the kitchen, where I find Isis and Jason.

"Hey, E." Isis looks up from the lettuce she's chopping at the counter. "I'm making tacos. You hungry?"

I wrap my arms around her shoulders, hugging her from behind. "You're incredible, Isis."

"I'll take that as a yes," she says. "Good, because I'm baking chocolate chip cookies, too."

"Ditch this loser." I nod to Jason. "Let's run away together."

"Hands off my girl, Vance," Jason says from the table, without looking up from his laptop, "unless you want to suffer a periorbital haematoma."

"Actually, stay right here." Isis pushes a bunch of cilantro my way. "Wash your hands and chop this for me." Then she sends Jason a pointed look that finally gets him to look up.

On my way in, I noticed a few unfamiliar boxes stacked in the living room, and I'm pretty sure I already know what's coming.

Jason picks up the beer next to his laptop and takes a pensive sip. He sets it back down. "Isis is moving in. She'll pitch in for rent."

Translation: you should be okay with this because it's not that different than how things have been, and also, it's going to knock your monthly rent down a few hundred bucks.

"Jason!" Isis tosses a kitchen towel at him. It lands on his shoulder, but he doesn't even blink. My roommate is the most laid-back human being on earth. "You were supposed to *ask* him if it was okay," she says. "Not *tell* him."

Jason looks at me, and we both know this is fine. More than fine.

I like being around them. Isis is an aspiring horror novelist, with plenty of ink and pink-streaked hair. Jason was my teammate. We ruled the pitch together for a few years, as left and right strikers, but he graduated a year ahead of me. Now he's in his second year of med school at UCLA, on path to becoming an ER doctor. They seem like this really normal couple on the surface. Then you hear them talking about viscera and bodily fluids with true unbridled passion, and you realize they're made for each other.

After things ended with Alison, it helped me a lot to see their relationship. Jason and Isis are actually great friends, something Alison and I never were.

"It's no problem, Isis. Really." I make a sweeping gesture, encompassing our small apartment. "Welcome to our humble abode."

"Are you *sure* about this?" She moves to the stove and stirs the ground beef. "I don't want you to feel uncomfortable because I'm here. This is your place."

"I can handle putting the toilet seat down."

"I meant having girls over. That kind of thing."

Jason laughs. "Yeah, he looked real uncomfortable last night. Real inhibited." He shuts his laptop and grins at me. "What part was toughest, E? Was it hooking up with Mia in front of a packed bar? Or was it carpet bombing the place with each other's clothes?"

I take this in with complete fascination. "Could you be more specific about what you saw?"

His gaze narrows. "Come on . . . Are you telling me you really don't remember last night? You actually *blacked out*?"

"That's what I'm telling you."

Jason lets out a high-pitched laugh. "That's a tragedy, bro."

"I know. I think I might be scarred." I realize I've been taking my frustration out on the cilantro, which I've chopped down to green mush.

"I liked her," Isis says as she pulls the ground beef off the stove. "I didn't have much chance to talk to her since you were monopolizing her mouth, but she seemed cool. Are you going to see her again?"

"Yep. I'm going to see her tomorrow. And the next day. And the next day after that. She works with me."

Isis gasps. "*Seriously*? Okay, I need to know *everything*."

We load up our plates and sit down. As we mow through our tacos, I tell them what happened at Boomerang. By the time I take down a few warm chocolate chip cookies, Jason and Isis have me laughing at how bizarre the whole thing is, and I feel better than I have all day.

"Wow. Talk about full disclosure," Isis says, when I get to the questionnaires Mia and I filled out.

"Rest easy, my friend," Jason says. "You and Mia went all the way. We were practically witnesses to it at Duke's. You're at ten."

Isis reaches for another cookie. "I don't know about that. I'm with Mia on this. I don't think you did."

"I'm going to try not to take that as a personal affront," I say.

"You definitely shouldn't," she says through a mouthful. "Your masculine prowess was on display last night, E. You were rockin' it. I was *mighty* impressed."

Jason gives her a mock scowl. "What the frick, Isis?"

"I mean objectively impressed. As a completely impartial bystander."

"It's on, girl." Jason does the *my eyes/your eyes* gesture. "You and me. Mighty prowess. Later."

"Okay, love doctor, I'll be there," she says, before turning back to me. "Anyway, what's the big deal if you and Mia did or didn't last night?"

"Is that a serious question?"

"I just mean that you *work* together. Your story with her is far from finished."

"The fun part is. She's off limits. Company policy. We were given a strict warning to keep it professional."

"What do you think, Spicy?" Jason says, using his nickname for her. "How long until our boy here behaves unprofessionally?"

Isis stops chewing and looks at me like she just developed x-ray vision. "Two weeks."

"How sure are you?" Jason asks. "Twenty bucks sure?"

"Forty. And I get to redecorate the apartment when I win."

"Done," Jason says, and they actually shake on it.

"It's not happening, kids," I say. "I'm a man of my word. And I can't afford to screw up this job."

I finish my beer then toss the bottle and our paper plates in the trash. "Thanks for dinner, Roomie," I say to Isis. But even as I'm leaving, their debate continues.

"I'm going to lose, aren't I?" Isis says.

"Yeah," Jason answers. "He won't last a week."

"You suck, Jason," I call over my shoulder.

I pull the door to my room closed, shutting out the sound of his laughter. Then I kick off my cleats and nose-dive into my bed.

My pillow smells faintly sweet and floral. Maybe lilacs or violets? One thing I am sure about: it's not *my* smell.

The image of Mia smiling at me in the backseat of the cab fills my mind. Then Mia smiling from her desk at the office. Then I start putting my imagination into it, and she's right here, naked beneath me, her dark curls splayed around her face. Still smiling. Ready for me.

Shit. Jason might be right.

Chapter 11

Mia

Q: Guy-crazy or sisters-before-misters?

I'm in the shower, shaving my legs and plotting my strategy for the day, when Skyler barges in and sits down to pee.

"How's it coming in there?" she asks, and I peek around the Hello Kitty shower curtain to see her stretched out in a t-shirt, red shorts crumpled at her ankles, with a copy of *Vanity Fair* across her lap and a compact and eyeliner in her hands.

"Seriously, Sky?"

"What? I'm multitasking." She pulls back her white-blond hair and pencils around her eyes. "Plus, holding it can give you a UTI."

I finish one leg and squirt a line of lavender scented shaving foam on the other. "I feel like this whole moment falls into the category of too much information."

"Come on, it's one big vulva fest around here. You're not going to get squeamish on me now, are you?"

The next thing I know, Beth's also slipped into the room. "A what fest?" she asks.

"Oh God," I groan.

Beth shoves her hand into the shower to waggle silver-polished nails at me, and then I watch her silhouette move back and forth in front of the long vanity. The bathroom lights dim, telling me she's plugged in her hot rollers.

"Speaking of," says Sky. "You planning to break some rules with Jocky McStudpants over there?"

I'd told them about my first day at the job and Adam Blackwood's strict no-fraternizing policy. Which makes the prospect of my further hookups with Ethan even more tantalizing to them than to me. It's my future, but it's their *entertainment*.

"No, no rule breaking." I switch off the water and push open the curtain. "Plus, I don't think he's all that into me. Towel," I add, and Sky passes over an aqua bath sheet.

"Right," says Beth. She has half her hair in rollers in the time it takes me to dry off and step out of the tub. "Cause the guys all hate smart, pretty girls with big boobs."

"I'm not saying he hates me," I tell them, trying to push away the specter of my on-again-off-again-please-someone-shoot-me relationship with Kyle. "And it doesn't matter anyway. I want to get my film done, and I want that job. It's an awesome opportunity, and a way into the business."

"So's he," says Beth. "An awesome opportunity, I mean." She finishes her rollers, then hops up on the counter and starts to paint her toenails.

"There are other guys."

"When?" asks Sky, finally pulling up her shorts and flushing the toilet. She goes over to the sink, and Beth swings her feet out of the

way so Sky can wash her hands. It's pretty impressive choreography
for a seven-by-nine space.

"When what?"

"When are there other guys?" She turns to me and leans back
against the counter, arms folded. "You're letting *that tool* Kyle turn
you into Miss Havisham."

I laugh. "I am not Miss Havisham. For one thing, I don't have a
moldy old wedding dress."

"Laugh about it, but you're still letting him get under your skin."

I want to argue, but as usual, it's like she's read my mind. Not
that I think it's about Kyle. Not really. We were never a good fit
because he didn't have any passion. Not for me. Not for much of
anything.

But there's something else there, something that's kept me in a
holding pattern for the past year, something that keeps chafing at
me, a subtle wearing of my desire to put myself out there again.

The pebbled glass of the bathroom window flames orange as the
sun crosses to this side of our building. I better get moving.

"You know what it is," I say, just realizing it myself. "It's the
whole situation. I don't want to have to fight for anything. I don't
want to have to sneak around or prove I'm worth breaking rules for,
you know? I want someone who just wants me, without question.
And I want to want him back. And just go for it."

I don't say the rest of it, that I want the kind of love that feels
like an arrow snapping from a bow—sharp, inevitable, soaring. It's
too early for poetry, and the conversation's already making me feel
dumb and teary.

I want this job. I want to make my film. And I don't want anyone
who doesn't know whether or not he wants me.

Simple, right?

When I arrive at Boomerang twenty minutes early, I find Ethan's
chair still empty and extend a smug congratulations to myself for

beating him to work. I tuck away my purse, switch on my tablet, and sit there, staring at the space he'll soon occupy and reminding myself to treat him like a colleague, nothing more.

I turn in my chair, and something in the movement brings a sliver of memory back to me: swiveling on my barstool, my leg brushing Ethan's, a swooping feeling in the pit of my stomach. I taste sambuca on my lips and feel myself leaning in toward him, my hand on his thigh, my face turned up to his, and a kiss, light and warm, right there in a bar full of people.

I have a flash of pulling back and of him looking down at me with those blue, blue eyes, those long dark eyelashes, his face alive with surprise and amusement.

So, I made the first move.

Go, me.

"Now, there's the hustle I like to see."

I look up to find Adam Blackwood leaning against the long kitchen counter. He's all starched luxury and twinkle, his gray suit tailored to elegant perfection. How can someone so young, just a year older than me, look like he sprang from the womb in Armani?

"Thanks." Damn, I don't want to let that memory go, but— reluctantly—I do. "I, um, couldn't wait to get to work."

Smooth, Mia.

"Excellent!" He punctuates the comment with a clap. "We're gathered in the conference room. Want to join us?"

So much for being the early bird. "Absolutely."

"Great. Grab your tablet, and meet me in there. I'm off to round up the usual suspects."

He walks off, and I gather my things and head past his office to the conference room. Its walls are an opaque moss-colored concrete, and a glossy chrome boomerang serves as a door handle.

I pull open the door and find myself face-to-face with a room full of people.

And a wall-sized vista of a deconstructed pinup girl—an abstract mandala of dark hair and tawny flesh, red high heels, cherries, and sailor hats. It's more a pattern than a portrait, but I recognize the artist and the subject.

Because it's my mom's work.

And the pinup girl? That's me.

Chapter 12

Ethan

Q: Follower or leader?

"Thanks for coming, everyone." Adam takes a seat at the head of the conference table. His smile is so genuine, you could almost believe he doesn't pay us, his marketing team, to be at his beck and call.

Actually, he *doesn't* pay me to be at his beck and call, but that's going to change.

Day two on the non-job, and I feel a hundred percent better than yesterday. I got some sleep, I have cash in my wallet, and with Isis moving in, I might be able to stretch the money dad sent until late August, when the internship is up. Another plus was learning that Rhett lives in Brentwood, only five minutes from my apartment. I now have a ride to and from work every day, so goodbye road bike. So what if Rhett makes my ears bleed?

Things are starting to fall into place. I have a plan and it's going to work. Land this job, pay off some student loans, apply to law school. And this whole situation with Mia is going to smooth over.

I glance to my right, taking a quick shot of her profile. Green eyes. Wild, dark hair that corkscrews everywhere, slender chin and nose. She's prettier than I remember, and I remember her being really pretty, but that's irrelevant now. She's not going to faze me. She's not going to keep me from achieving my goals. Her scent—violets, I'm almost sure—isn't even that distracting.

"I brought you here to talk about DateCon," Adam continues, "the largest trade show convention in our industry, which is coming up in Vegas on . . ." He glances at the agenda in front of him. "When is it this year, Cookie?"

"Third week in August at the Mirage. *Like always*," Cookie adds, in a voice that sounds like frostbite.

Her whole look is sort of arctic. The pale blue shirt she's wearing has a jagged collar that looks almost as sharp as her spiked hair, and her makeup is all thick layers of silver. She looks like one of the capitol freaks from *The Hunger Games*.

"Yes, August. That's right," Adam says. "So that gives us eight weeks to prepare for what I want to be our best show yet. To that end, I'm doubling your budget this year, Cookie. I want a new booth. I want a party—and when I say party, I mean *the best* party at the show. I want every single attendee at DateCon to be talking about *one* online dating service: Boomerang."

"Is *that* all?" Cookie asks.

I don't know how she gets away with the things that come out of her mouth. Maybe Adam's hooking up with her? But when I weigh his easygoing attitude against Cookie's iciness, I can't see it. Besides, Adam strikes me as the type who practices what he preaches.

"No, there's more," Adam says. "I'm inviting our investors to the show. We'll hold our annual meeting there this year, and, it's too early to make any promises yet, but I'm looking at taking Blackwood Entertainment public next year, so it's imperative that everything goes off perfectly. I want you guys to blow the investors away."

He pauses and casts a relaxed look around the table that has ten times more impact than Cookie's icy stare. Adam *expects* excellence—which makes me want to give it to him.

"Okay," he says, "Cookie's going to run point on this, so—"

Rhett pushes open the conference room door. "Sorry, Adam, but I need you."

"Be right there." Adam stands and smiles. "This is a big deal, guys. Boomerang is on the cusp of breaking out and showing some real market dominance. And when it does, every one of us stands to benefit. I need *all* of you to put your minds to this show and give me your best."

When he leaves, Cookie takes over.

"Sadie, you're on party planning. Don't fuck it up, okay, sweetie? Logistics and scheduling with the venue and conference goes to you, Paolo. Do a good job and I'll consider putting in a good word for you with the INS. Investor travel arrangements and pampering is with you, Vanessa. You're good at kissing ass. This is your chance to be *great* at it. And booth redesign goes to the toads, Mia and Ethan. That's it. Now get to work."

The staff parts like cue balls after a killer break, disappearing through doors, but Mia and I are slower. I'm stuck replaying what Cookie said in my head to see if it makes any more sense.

Then Mia pushes up from her chair. "Cookie, do you have a minute?"

Cookie's hand hovers over the boomerang door handle. When her head turns slowly to Mia, I tense with the urge to throw myself in the line of fire to protect her.

"I can do the booth design myself," Mia says, "I mean—all the other tasks went to only one person."

She's taken the words out of my mouth; I was going to track Cookie down to say the same thing. I want a chance to shine. How the hell am I supposed to prove I deserve this job if Mia and I are working joint assignments?

Cookie takes a second to pull on a set of brass knuckles and throw down a quick shot of venom. "*You* are not a person. You are an intern, a toad, and so is he." She shoots me a glare. "Together, on your *very* best day, the two of you *might* equal one capable employee."

Jesus Christ.

"Go see Rhett for a company credit card," she adds. "The booth company is out in the valley. Winning Displays. I'm going to assume the two of you are smart enough to find it on your own. I want plans and a budget by morning. Get out there and make this booth happen."

"No problem," Mia says. "We'll take care of everything."

I have to give to her. The girl is good. Solid under pressure.

Cookie snorts. "We'll see about that."

I don't know if it's the attitude she's giving Mia, or just plain stupidity that gets into me, but something snaps inside me.

"Hey, Cookie. Hold up a second." Reaching into my messenger bag, I pull out a plastic lunch bag. "My roommate baked these last night. I thought you might like them." I hold the bag out. "For you."

She looks at me like I just offered her a serving of crap instead of chocolate chip cookies. Then she yanks open the door and marches out.

"Do you have a death wish?" Mia says under her breath as we head for Rhett's office.

"I wanted to see what she'd do."

"How the Cookie crumbles?" she says.

"Exactly. I was thinking that if she hurt me, maybe I'd get an offer of permanent employment as part of a settlement. You know, with fun things like benefits and paychecks."

"Hmm. Using guerrilla tactics, is it?"

"Can you blame me?" I say.

"No. I thought she was going to eviscerate me on the spot."

"I thought she was going to gouge my eyes out and feed them to the crows."

Mia stops just outside of Rhett's door. She rolls up onto her tiptoes and draws close, staring deep into my eyes. "Well, you're in luck. Looks like they're still there."

What's *still there* is my attraction to her. My pulse picks up, and I can't look away. I see the same richness in her eyes as I did yesterday, in the cab, and my mind fills with questions. I want to know more about her film and her family. I want to tell her my toaster oven misses her thong.

Someone comes down the hall and Mia settles back onto her heels, but I'm still locked in.

Come on, Vance. Break eye contact. You can do this.

I manage it, and my gaze drops to her sexy, lopsided smile, and then moves lower, and I'm picturing her the way she looked at my apartment. Naked.

Awesome, Ethan. Big improvement.

Behind me, I hear Rhett's office door swing open. I turn just as Adam steps out.

"Hey, Ethan!" Rhett calls from his desk. "I was just telling Adam that we're coaching together."

Mia shifts at my side. "You guys knew each other?" she asks me. "Before Boomerang?"

"No—we didn't." I know how this must look to her, like I'm brown-nosing. Maybe I *am* brown-nosing, but only because I need Rhett as my chauffeur.

"I hear you're very good." Adam leans against the doorjamb, slipping his hands into his pockets. "Four years at UCLA. Rhett told me about your records there. I'm impressed."

"Thanks. It was a good run." I resist the urge to see Mia's reaction. This is on the verge of getting embarrassing. I have no problem bragging for sport, but doing it to impress your boss is low. Coach Williams' voice pops into my head. *When it comes to showing your strengths, eyes over ears: don't tell them you're good, show them.* It's become my strategy, too.

"Do you still play?" Adam asks me.

"Just a pickup game on Saturdays with some of the guys who stayed local and whoever else jumps in."

"Hey," Rhett says. "You're letting me play this weekend. Right, E?"

I fight the urge to throttle him. Only my closest friends call me "E," and I don't want Rhett playing soccer with me this weekend. But with Adam here, my options for shutting him out are zero.

"Sure, Rhett."

"I used to play a little myself," Adam says. "Center mid."

Unlike Rhett, Adam's too cool to invite himself on Saturday, but I see a spark in his eyes that tells me his competitive spirit just kindled.

He wants to play.

Now I'm the one who's impressed. Guys who think they can hang with collegiate level players are either ballsy as hell, or idiots. Between Adam and Rhett, looks like both camps are covered.

"You're welcome to join, Adam. Anytime."

"Thanks," he says, clapping me on the shoulder as he leaves. "Count me in for Saturday."

Chapter 13

Mia

Q: How well do you handle pressure?

I spend a long, long elevator ride down to the parking lot, mentally rehearsing and then rejecting a series of withering comments I'm dying to make. Like, "How's that view from inside Adam Blackwood's butt?" and "Did you and Rhett fondle each other's *balls*?"

But I keep my lips clamped and my eyes on the elevator control panel. For one thing, Ethan looked like he wanted to crawl out of his own skin and beat Rhett with it, which tells me he's not exactly wooing the guy. For another, I'm not mad at Ethan, but at the whole let's-hoist-some-brews-after-a-sweaty-game-of-soccer-boys-club vibe of their little exchange. I've got the athletic grace of a puppy on Ritalin, so there's no way I'm meeting Adam on *that* level. Which means I have to find another arena, something *I* own.

That brings me back to the portrait in the conference room. Which I happen to know sold at auction for probably a decade's worth of paychecks from this place. So Adam's serious about collecting. And he likes my mother's work.

It gives me a pang of conscience to consider using this knowledge as leverage, but I file it away—for emergencies only, of course. I want to do this on my own, without hopping on the Pearl Bertram express train. There's no challenge in it otherwise. And more than that, zero satisfaction if I win.

When I win.

The elevator doors whoosh open, and we step into the sultry parking garage. The odors of baking asphalt and oil waft over me, a scent I weirdly love.

"So, what are we looking for?" I ask, sizing up the rows and rows of Lexuses and BMWs. I imagine Blackwood in something zippy, like an Aston Martin or a Bugatti. He seems like a guy who likes to go fast. But for a company car? I'm clueless.

Ethan's hair stirs in the breeze, revealing a tiny half-moon-shaped scar over his left eyebrow. Something about it seems boyish and endearing. But his blank expression tells me he has no idea.

He digs into his pants pocket for the key—a valet key, which he holds in a flat palm for my inspection.

"Wow, a valet key. I'm touched by Cookie's trust in us," I say, taking it. "Well, we know it's a Toyota."

"Thank God no one in LA drives one of those."

"Right. Thank God."

We stand there for a moment, looking out at row after row of cars, which stretch out toward the shadowy recesses at the far end of the cavernous garage.

I give voice to the unthinkable: "Should we go back up and ask?"

"Yeah, I definitely think we should do that," he says and sweeps an arm toward the elevator door. "After you."

"Why do I think you're going to shove me in and barricade it behind me?"

"You cut me, Curls. You really do."

I look up at him, into those blue eyes—electric and fathomless at the same time, slight creases turning them up at the outside corners. The shadows of the garage sharpen the planes of his face, making him look older and more ridiculously gorgeous—like a glimpse of the man he'll be in ten years.

"Somehow, I think you'll live," I tell him. Turning back to the rows of cars, I say, "Can't we just, you know, go around sticking our key in all the Toyotas."

"Yeah, if you don't mind leaving next Tuesday." He surprises me by grabbing my hand and tugging me back toward the elevator. "Come on, we'll do it together."

I dig in my heels playfully and tug back. "Oh, God, don't make me face that . . . that beast again! She's got a vicious streak a mile wide. I can't—I won't!"

"Where's your grit, dude?" Ethan teases, giving another tug that launches me against him. Then we're scuffling and laughing. And he's so close to me, I feel his warmth, the coiled energy of his muscles.

I try to grab the key back from him, but he holds it about a mile above my head.

"Come on, Curls," Ethan taunts. "Try and get it."

"You're going down." I make a suicide leap and nab it, but as I spin away, he grabs me around the waist, catching me in a firm grip.

I try to wriggle from his grasp, but I'm weak from laughing so hard. "Let me go, you jerk, or I'll feed your bones to that monstrous Yeti."

The elevator door opens to reveal Cookie, her eyes beaming roughly one thousand kilowatts of pure hate in our direction.

"Red Solara, dumbasses," she says, and the doors snap closed in front of her with magical swiftness, as if evil has a special velocity.

Ethan lets me drive, which comes as a surprise because no guy has ever let me drive. We put the top down and enjoy the golden clarity of the Los Angeles afternoon, the stirring of palm trees. It smells like tar and honeysuckle outside, and my hair pulls free of its braid and whips around my face. I know I'll be terrifying to behold by the time we reach our destination, but I don't care. The sun warms my skin; the 405 is miraculously clear; and we're moving toward an actual destination.

I holler over the roar of the engine and the fluttering of my blouse flapping in the wind, "What are you thinking for a theme?"

"Theme?" Ethan sits with his eyes closed, face turned up to the sunlight. His smile holds such contentment that I feel almost guilty bringing up actual work.

"Yes, for the booth. For the show. What do we want the design to be?"

He sits up and squints at me, shading his eyes. "How about something sports themed? You know, 'Have fun. Score big.' "

"Ew."

"Come on," he insists. "We're not eHarmony. It's not about life-long commitments. Nothing wrong with some fun."

"I know, but—"

"And we're *called* Boomerang. That's already sporty. How about, 'play hard, throw it back?' "

"Okay, that's even worse." I try to contain my hair so I can give him a solid glare, but it's no use. "And what exactly is the 'it' in that little slogan?"

He grins. "You know."

"No, sir, I do not. Because it *sounds* like you're talking about lady parts. Like, 'use them up and throw them away, boys.' "

"That's crazy," he protests. "It's lady *and* gentleman parts. You're free to throw *it* back, too."

I laugh. "So, that's the image we're unveiling for our investors? Sex organs whipping through the air?"

"It's genius. Give it time. You'll warm up to it. Seriously, though, why not something sports related?"

"I don't know," I say. "It feels shallow or . . . I don't know. Not everyone thinks of it as a game."

"But that's what Blackwood's selling, isn't it? Recreation? It's about having fun and then shaking it off at the end of the night, right? Live to score another day."

A sudden coolness creeps into his tone, and I wonder if he's thinking of that girl, whoever she was. The one who put him through two years of hell.

We pull off the highway and cruise along a few narrow residential roads. We're quiet now as we pass through mottled opaque shadows cast by lacy tree canopies.

"What's your idea for a theme?" he asks quietly.

"Well, of course I'd love to do a movie theme. Something funny, maybe. Like if Annie Wilkes had just used Boomerang, maybe things wouldn't have gotten so intense in *Misery*."

"Right," he says. "Or maybe Captain Ahab could have chased, um, a whale *and* a dolphin. Spread the love around."

I laugh. "And you act like you only know about sports."

"So, if I'm hearing you, Curls, you're saying that it's healthy to date a lot and that monogamy makes you dangerous. At least to writers and whales?"

I feel an itch of something—melancholy, maybe—but I give him a smile. "Something like that."

The GPS guides us down a row of squat warehouse buildings to a sign in the shape of a thumbs-up with "INNING DISPLAYS" in

1970s bubble type. I stop a few feet from the door, which is coated with a peeling layer of UV tinting.

"See," Ethan says, springing out before I'd taken the key—the valet key—from the ignition. "Inning Displays. It's a sign. Sports theme, for the win."

"It's a sign that Cookie's crazier than we thought."

I get out and do my best to smooth the snarled cloud of my hair, then dab on a quick coat of lipstick and make sure everything else is more or less in place. I wonder if Ethan feels like I do sometimes. Like I'm playing at adulthood. At being confident in totally strange situations.

Inside the building, row after row of display vignettes stretch before us, each with a different type of booth and elaborate signage. A slouchy dude with ear gauges and bushy sideburns sits behind a circular reception desk and mumbles a greeting in our general vicinity.

"Candy will be right with you," he tells us and gestures us to a plush leather sofa, which promptly swallows me whole. I struggle to sit up and hover at the edge.

After a few minutes, a towering blond woman comes clipping toward us, barking threats to others as she passes.

Ethan watches her, eyes wide. "No way. That . . . can't be . . . ?"

"You don't think—" But I can't even make myself process the sight.

She reaches us, and we leap to our feet like soldiers caught sleeping on watch.

"So you're from Boomerang?" She pumps my hand with mechanical precision and then moves on to Ethan.

"Yes, we're—" he begins.

"You're late," she barks. "My sister told me you'd be here at eleven." She executes a marching-band pivot and sprints away from us.

"Oh, God," I whisper. "Cookie and Candy." Never in the history of procreation have two less apt names been bestowed upon a set of human beings.

"You *do* realize you're supposed to be following me, don't you?" Candy fires over her shoulder. "I didn't realize I needed to spell that out."

"Sorry," I say. "We're coming."

We hurry to catch up with her, drawing close enough to hear her mutter "dumbasses" under her breath.

Chapter 14

Ethan

Q: Cotton sheets or satin?

*M*ia and I follow Candy past the lower budget booths to the primo setups in the back. We pass a booth for a suntan lotion company with a waterslide that lands in a clear-walled pool, a booth where the sides are made of rock wall, and then one with a fully stocked chef's kitchen.

When we reach a bedroom set complete with shiny satin sheets and fake flowers on the bedside tables, I lean toward Mia and whisper in her ear, "What do you think? Our competition?"

"Mattress distributor, asswipe," Candy says over her shoulder, then she stops and gestures to the booth on our right. "This is what Blackwood did last year."

I take in the white furniture and recessed lighting. The long white counter with a bank of computer screens, where I'm guessing people tried out the Boomerang website and member interface. Above the counter, there's a big purple Boomerang logo that's backlit.

"Wow. It's very . . ." It reminds me of a Virgin America airport terminal—style that's been watered down to accommodate the masses—but I'm not sure how much I should say with Candy standing right here.

Mia's mouth pulls into a grimace. "Blech? Uninspired?"

I nod. "Yeah. And predictable."

"And *generic*. It's almost *corporate*." Mia says the words like they're blasphemous, and I remember learning yesterday that her mother is an artist. A photographer. "And forgettable."

"Yep," I agree. "I can't even remember what we're looking at."

Mia shakes her head, getting more and more worked up. "I mean, what's the *message* of this?" She faces me. "Does anything about this make you want to have fun? Does it even remotely put you in a sexy mood?"

"No, but that bed does."

Mia's head whips to the mattress booth, her hair spilling over one shoulder. "Really? Even the cheesy satin sheets?"

"Hell, yeah. They look like a slippery good time to me." The fact that we're in a booth warehouse does nothing to deter my sexual imagination. I could *seriously* get down to some business on that bed with her. "What do you say, Curls? Should we throw some sex organs around?"

She breaks into a smile. "Well, when you make it sound so appealing."

Candy's hand snaps to her hip, the movement as sharp as a military salute. "What a lovely surprise," she says. "I thought neither of you would understand a single thing about booth design. Turns out you're both geniuses!"

She swivels on a heel and marches off, just like Cookie.

"Nice going, genius," Mia mouths accusingly as we follow. She gives me a playful shove on the shoulder, so I push her back.

And so it begins again.

We did this earlier in the parking lot and my arms ended up around her. I'm not sure what the deal is exactly, but my body seems to jump at any opportunity to touch her. When she pushes me the next time, I make a quick move, lifting her easily over my shoulder.

Mia gives the tiniest squeak, her body tensing, and I freeze, waiting for Candy to turn around, but she doesn't.

At this point a few things fire off in my head.

First and foremost is the fact that my hand is on Mia's ass. She's soft and curved in all the right places, and her weight feels amazing. Holding her feels amazing. I'm extremely tempted to make a break for the mattress booth and lay her out on all that satin.

Second is the concept of me flirting with the girl who could potentially take my job from me, which is a bit of a buzzkill.

And third is the security camera that hangs down from the ceiling. Whoever's watching on the other end, Mia and I are making their day.

I take a few steps like I'm carrying her off to bed until she gives me a solid jab to the ribs. Then I set her down reluctantly.

Through the thin silk of her dress, I feel her shape slip through my fingers as she slides down the length of me—the curve of her waist, and the groove of her spine, the angles of her shoulder blades—before she finds her feet.

For a long moment, we're pressed against each other and there's no hiding the truth, the physical truth of how I react to her. I am hard as steel for her, but the expression on her face isn't surprise. Mia knows she turns me on. What I see in her eyes is uncertainty. A kind of shadow pain.

We draw apart awkwardly, looking everywhere except at each other. Silently, Mia catches up with Candy, but I need a few seconds.

Not only to get my dick to calm down, but because I need to get my anger under control, too.

What did I do wrong? I definitely just crossed some kind of line. Did this internship get into her head? The fact that we're competing? Or is it something with her ex? But that can't be it. She's been single for a whole year.

Why the hell am I spinning on this anyway? I should be glad she has some kind of hang-up about being with me. I should be fucking *thrilled* about it.

Candy is waiting for us at a larger booth around the corner, her arms crossed, her foot tapping. She looks from me to Mia. Probably, she's sensed the shift in the mood between us, but I don't give a shit.

"This is the layout we're using for this year's show," Candy says, gesturing to a large booth that's shaped like a T. "Blackwood is paying for an end location—that means he'll have 180 degrees of coverage. We'll use the same color palette and furnishings, the same look as last year, but we'll divide the booth with a wall, keeping the lounge to one side, and the computer terminals to the other. That way the people who feel more inclined to linger and mingle can, while the ones who just want to see the website can log on, check it out, and move on. Any questions?"

Mia and I look at each other.

"Wait," she says, "you mean the booth for the conference is already planned? It's *done*?"

"No. It's not paid for yet. You did bring the company credit card?"

I've got nothing. It's all I can do not to start breaking booth shit right now.

Mia is quiet at my side.

Candy's face splits into a smile. "You didn't actually think my sister was going to let you two make a decision, did you?"

I still can't think of a single thing to say, and apparently Mia can't either.

"Oh, you *did*." Candy shakes her head. "That is so cute."

Chapter 15

Mia

Q: Are you a pouter or a problem-solver?

*W*e stop at a park to split a sandwich before heading back to the Boomerang offices. I watch as Ethan brushes leaves off a picnic bench for me, his dress shirt coming loose from his belt to expose a narrow swatch of tanned flesh.

Oh, Mia, I think. *You are so screwed.*

Because of his body, sure: the sleek solidity of it, the feel of him, pressed against me. Hard. The sensation of being exactly right, molecule-to-molecule, as he set me down in the display showroom.

But I can resist a body. I'm screwed because of his smile, because of that dimple that deepens when he laughs, his straight, even teeth, perfect except for one slightly turned incisor. I'm screwed because of his thick, serious brows, his perfect angular nose, and his eyes like a lake in the rain. I'm screwed, most of all, because of his kindness, which radiates from every pore. His passion, when he lets himself talk about things he loves. Because he insisted on paying me back for the cab and on paying for our sandwich. I'm screwed because of him, all of him. My body *and* my brain are conspiring against me here, but I can't let myself give in to them.

"What are we going to do about this Cookie situation?" I ask, swatting away a fly that's settled on the wax paper spread open between us. I move my half of the turkey and avocado sandwich toward me and pop open my diet Coke. It bubbles onto my hand, and I lick my finger then catch him watching me, which threatens to send me down another path of *truly* unproductive thinking.

"Situation?" he murmurs, raising his eyes slowly to mine like he's coming out of a dream.

"Yeah. Cookie. She's going to keep making it tough for *either* of us to get this job. Though I don't know why."

"Maybe an intern killed her mother."

I laugh. "Or her missing triplet, Cupcake."

Ethan takes a bite, chews thoughtfully. His strong jaw flexes, and I have to say, the boy even makes eating look good.

"I guess we can keep working on her, try to thaw her out a bit. But we probably need to get around her and go for Adam."

"And say what? His booth design sucks?"

He grins. "Something like that." Finishing his sandwich in two more bites, he adds, "Maybe I should do the talking, Curls. I've noticed you have some issues with diplomacy."

"Yeah, because your chocolate chip cookie gambit was so impressive." A seedpod spirals down between us, and I finger-punt it off the table. Even though I brought it up, suddenly I resent talking about work. "Maybe you can work on Adam during your soccer game this weekend."

As Skyler likes to point out, I sometimes have tone-modulation issues, and the statement comes out sounding more sarcastic than I intend.

"Hey," says Ethan, sitting back. "Adam invited himself along. I didn't want him there."

"Why not?" I strip the top piece of bread off my sandwich and sling it at a couple of squirrels darting around in the shade. "It's a good strategy."

"I don't give a damn about that," Ethan says, and his brittle tone matches mine. "I'm not trying to strategize. I just want to play some soccer. That's all I want."

"Clearly, you want more than that."

"Meaning what?"

"The job. You want the job." I fold the bottom half of the sandwich over and take a bite. Suddenly, I'm ravenous.

"And you don't?"

I swallow, and the sandwich wends a slow, painful path down my esophagus. *Chew, Mia. For God's sake.*

"No, I do," I say. "And I think it's okay to want it. So you don't have to act like every move you make is unintentional. You got Rhett and Adam to come play soccer. That's great for you. So just— it's okay to just want things."

Which makes me wonder if I need to be less squeamish about using my mom as bait. If it helps me get this job, what will it hurt?

He looks at me, and we're quiet for a long moment. I pick up my sandwich, just to do something. A breeze riffles the sandwich wrapper, and it skids across the table and onto the ground. I bend to retrieve it, aware that things have taken a really strange turn—and that I'm the one steering. Holy hell. What is wrong with me?

I march off toward a garbage can, failing to avoid the image rising in my mind. Kyle on our last night. The oceanfront cantina, where moonlight gave everything a magical glow, and his words almost disappeared beneath the insistent rush of the ocean. "I just don't know what I want, Mia."

None of which is poor Ethan's fault, of course. I take a few deep breaths— stupid to do over a garbage can—and return to the table.

"Sorry," I say. "I'm being unfair."

"It's okay," he tells me and gets to his feet.

He smiles, but it doesn't quite reach his eyes. What's there— curiosity, concern—makes me want to tuck myself into his pocket and just live there. Kyle would give me this panicked, checking-for-exits look any time I had even the slightest blip in my emotional baseline.

"Want to drive back?" I ask, and hold up the valet key.

"Sure."

We get in, and he starts the engine. "We'll figure it out."

"What?"

"The booth thing. Let's talk to Adam about it when we get back. We'll go in together."

"Okay."

He looks at me for a long moment and then takes off his tie and hands it to me with a smile.

"What's this for?"

"I thought you could tie it around your hair," he tells me. "Should have thought of it sooner."

I draw the silken fabric through my fingers, wishing he didn't make it so easy to like him. "That's really thoughtful." I pull my hair back and cinch it with the tie. The edges tickle the back of my neck, raising goose bumps.

"Ready?" he asks.

I nod. "Let's go."

Chapter 16

Ethan

Q: Blind dates: a chance for fun or failure?

*I*sis raps on the bathroom door. "We're leaving, E! Have a nice dinner with your new boyfriend!"

"Go easy on him, Spicy," Jason says. "The man is in crisis." His voice grows muffled and louder, like he's right on the other side of the door. "Ethan, sorry about that. Hey, almost forgot. I left your corsage for Blackwood on the kitchen table."

He can barely finish the sentence. No one's funnier to Jason than Jason. I listen to his laugh grow quieter until the front door shuts, and the apartment's quiet.

I swipe a stray drop of shaving cream off my ear, considering my reflection in the mirror. I look like I'm about to start a fight or hold up a bank—instead of join Adam for dinner.

It's Saturday night. I should be heading to The Reel Inn for fish tacos and beer with Jason, Isis, and the rest of the crew. Especially considering that Blackwood and Rhett came to soccer this morning. The pickup game was a success. Adam hung in there like a champ, and Rhett didn't die from heat exhaustion. I showed them both a great time. Shouldn't that be enough?

I jam the towel onto the rack and head to my bedroom. On a surge of hope, I grab my cell phone off my dresser to see if Adam canceled, but all I find is his message from an hour ago.

> **Adam:** I need you to come to a dinner tonight. I'll pick you up at 7.

What could I say except okay?

I check the time, seeing that I have ten minutes to kill before he gets here. I debate straightening up my room for half a second, then sit on the end of my bed and squeeze my hands into fists.

Why did he ask me? The guy was a self-made millionaire at eighteen. Aren't women lining up to spend a night with him? And why do I care? He's a good guy, and this is a positive sign for my career prospects. The more he and I connect, the better my odds are of beating—

Aw . . . Shit.

Mia.

An image pops into my mind. Her, smiling in the convertible with my tie looped around her dark hair.

That was Tuesday.

The last time I was alone with her.

The last time we were easy with each other, before a wall went up.

It's okay to just want things, she'd said that day at the park.

It'd taken everything in me not to say, *You're wrong, Mia. It's not okay for me to want you.*

All week I've been sitting across from her. I've learned she takes her sandwiches apart and puts them back together again before she eats them. I've learned she talks about her friends more than herself, and her family more than her friends. I've learned the film she's making is about her grandma, who has Alzheimer's. I've learned her hair is sort of like a barometer—a pretty good predictor of her mood.

And I've learned that I like everything about her.

Every. Single. Goddamn. Thing.

Before I can talk myself out of it, I pull up her name in my address book and send her a text.

Ethan: Hey Curls

My heart creeps into my throat as I watch the message post as *sent*. This is a bad call. Really fucking stupid. I'm about to toss my phone aside when her reply pops up.

Mia: Hey! What's up?

Okay. Time to make up a reason to have texted her.

Ethan: Big plans tonight?
Mia: Nothing much. Family night. You?
Ethan: Nothing as exciting as last Sunday.
Mia: You spent it with Adam at Duke's, didn't you?
Ethan: That night was all you, Curls.

There's a two-second pause.

Mia: Are you flirting with me?
Ethan: That would mean breaking company rules.
Mia: Yeah, but are you?

Ethan: Yes.
Ethan: I am.
Ethan: Speaking of
Ethan: what are you wearing?

I'm joking about that line, mostly. But I can't resist trying out a classic since I'm pretty much a sexting virgin. Alison balked at any flirting I did with her this way. She wasn't much for flirting, period.

I stare at my phone, waiting for Mia to put me in my place. Then her reply comes through and I almost fumble the phone.

Mia: Your necktie and nothing else.

Holy shit.

Ethan: Really???
Mia: No
Mia: ☺
Mia: You still there?
Ethan: Yes. Getting into cold shower.

The wood I'm sporting is going to require more than a shower. Awesome. Nothing like a supersized helping of sexual frustration when you're about to head out for the night.

Mia: You look good when you shower.

Jesus. She's trying to kill me.

I stare at the words, my mind firing off images of us together. Shower. Standing. Bed. Chair. Rinse and repeat. It's like the best kind of slide show in the universe.

I can't remember the last time a girl's gotten me this worked up.

Whether it's okay to want her or not has no apparent effect. I fucking *want* her.

I check the time. 6:57.

What did I do to deserve this?

> **Ethan:** I have to go. Ride almost here.
> **Mia:** Okay.
> **Ethan:** Have fun tonight, Curls.
> **Mia:** You too.

I sit there and reread our exchange until Adam texts me that he's
downstairs. I tell him I'm on my way then take a few seconds to pull
myself together.

Vomit. Car wrecks.

Vomit in car wrecks.

Okay. Good enough.

I reach for my tie, but stop myself and drop it back on the dresser.
Don't need that distraction hanging around my neck all night. A
white dress shirt is going to have to pass.

I find Adam waiting at the curb in a charcoal gray Bugatti. Getting in feels like climbing into a panther, all sinewy and low. I'm not
much of a luxury car guy—my idea of a sweet ride is a great off-road
truck—but Adam's car converts me on the spot.

"It's a little flashy," Adam admits as he pulls onto the street, "but
it was a symbolic gesture for me."

"Symbolic?" The smells inside are strong: leather upholstery and
a faint trace of motor oil. A badass combination. I breathe it in, my
head returning to a Mia-free zone. "How so?"

"I had two early investors in my first start-up. One was French,
the other German. Prior to going public, they tried to join together
and squeeze me out." Adam's grin is devilish. "They failed."

The dude is *a boss*. I feel a surge of optimism. Why was I bent out of shape earlier? I'm hanging out with Adam Blackwood. In a freakin' *Bugatti.*

"Did you buy the car after the IPO?" I ask.

Adam nods. "It was the first thing I did. Bugattis are French design, but the company is a subsidiary of Volkswagen."

"A German automaker," I say, filling in the blank.

"Exactly. This car reminds me to be careful about who I bring close." His voice drops, clouding with some dark emotion as he adds, "It's a lesson I've taken to heart."

He shifts into third as we merge onto the freeway. The car surges forward and we fall silent, that conversation over.

The way he navigates the traffic is defiant and a little vicious, like he's racing his own demons. But then we pull off the freeway and he smiles, and charismatic, cool Adam is back.

"I appreciate you coming to this with me," he says, the roar of the engine finally growing quieter. "I didn't want to pass up the opportunity. Having you there will relieve any awkwardness."

I'm totally lost. "Awkwardness?"

"Well, I *am* her boss."

No.

No fucking way.

I have to remind myself to breathe. "Adam . . . Where exactly are we going?"

"Didn't I tell you?" he says. "To Mia's parents' house for dinner. I'm a big fan of her mother's work." His gaze drops to my neck and his eyes narrow. "Check behind your seat. I think I have an extra tie back there. It's probably best to play it safe."

Yeah, that's a negative. Seeing Mia tonight is going to be the exact opposite of playing it safe.

Chapter 17

Mia

Q: Do you like to cook?

*A*pparently, the globe has tilted off its axis because my mom has decided to cook. Which means the homey meal I'd planned—my dad's special Lasagna Milanese—has turned into . . . well, I don't know what, exactly. It's blue; it smells like a foot; and it's somehow taken every pot and pan within a fifteen-mile radius to produce.

"He'll be here in ten minutes," I say, attempting to straighten as she creates, which is exactly as effective as sweeping up after a tornado. "Why don't you go get changed, Mom, and I'll . . ." I look at my father, who has gone into his usual wine-selection fugue state, and mouth, "Order a pizza?"

I really should have thought this through. I couldn't stand the idea of Adam and Ethan jocking it up together without my finding some way to even the odds, but now I feel as gross as I expected to feel in trotting out my mother. I feel guilty and frazzled, and Ethan's flirty text messages do *not* help.

I try my best to thrust that aside. Along with the image of him handing me his tie in the car, smiling at me across our desks at work. Standing in the shower, water making a slow trail down the contours of his abs.

My mom dumps a chopping board full of what looks like chives into something brown and burbling. I'm pretty sure there's an eye of newt in there somewhere.

"Pearl," says my dad. He plunks three bottles on the table—a Chianti, a Pinot Grigio, and a half-consumed bottle of Jim Beam I'm pretty sure is meant for him. "Let me take over for a bit. Go put on something nice so we can make the kid look good."

"Fine!" My mother shoves lids onto a few pots and heads out of the kitchen, untying her apron as she goes. "Don't let the messicant burn."

"What the hell is messicant?" My dad puts his arm around me and gingerly lifts one of the lids. Steam rises, forming the shape of a skull-and-crossbones before wafting toward the range hood.

Okay, not really, but it smells like death's armpit, and not one thing on the oven looks like actual food.

"Why did you let her cook?" I ask, mopping up Pollack-like spatters all over the slate countertops.

My dad pours a couple of fingers of bourbon and hands it to me. Then he pours a larger portion for himself. "Makes her frisky," he says, and clinks his glass against mine. "Salud!"

Kill. Me. Now.

The doorbell rings, and I consider diving out the window, Cowardly Lion-style, but I shove my bourbon glass into my father's hand. "Please, if you love me," I say, gesturing at the stovetop. "Do something with this."

Hurrying down the hallway, I smooth back my hair, brush the wrinkles from my peach linen dress, and slip back into the silver platform sandals I'd left near the front door.

I plaster a smile on my face and open the door to find Adam Blackwood there, a bottle of wine in one hand and a bouquet of pink daffodils in the other.

And Ethan beside him.

I blink, pretty sure I'm hallucinating, but no, it's Ethan. He looks absolutely devastating in a sharp white dress shirt and slim black tie.

"Ethan," I squeak. Clearing my throat, I try again. "Hey."

"Surprise," he says, with a small shrug.

Adam moves past me into the house. "Surprise?" he says, giving me a puzzled look. "I'm sorry. I phoned your mother and asked if it was all right to bring a colleague. She didn't tell you?"

Of course she didn't. "No, but that's—"

"It's all right that I asked him along, isn't it?"

"Sorry to crash," says Ethan, shutting the door behind him and stepping close. He smells fresh from the shower, and I am in *major* trouble. "I had no idea until we were on our way."

"No, it's fine." I seem to have lost all major motor functions and just stand there, gaping at him. "Um . . . Come on in."

We follow Adam down the short hall into the living room just as my mother enters from the other side. Dressed in flowing silk pants and a black kimono top, she extends an elegant hand to Adam. Now she's Pearl Bertram, noted photographer, not Pearl Bertram, mom and horrific chef. She's so smooth when she wants to be, and I'm such a dolt.

"Here's the colleague I mentioned," says Adam. He introduces Ethan to my mother and then to my father, who comes in with a charcuterie tray and wine glasses. Bless him.

"Ethan's got an internship, like me," I offer, forcing myself not to add how awesome it would have been to know he was joining this evening's fun. Now's not the time, and there's no point making Ethan feel even more uncomfortable than he clearly feels.

"Interns and competitors," Adam adds. "I like to keep things exciting."

Ethan and I exchange a look, and I stuff an olive in my mouth to keep from breaking into an idiotic grin. I'd say we have exciting covered.

I catch Ethan looking around, and I try to see our home from his perspective. An expanse of floor-to-twenty-foot-ceiling windows overlooking an overgrown English garden, sleek Danish modern furniture in shades of slate, brown, and tan. A Lucien Freud hangs above the fireplace, and a pair of Judy Chicago sculptures prop up travel books on the mantel. Everything opulent and polished, thanks to Bitsy, our long-suffering housekeeper.

Suddenly, it all feels ostentatious to me, like I need to apologize for my parents or for myself. Or like I'm not entitled to want things because I come from wealth.

I want to explain that it's because of my family's wealth that this job is important to me. My mother has her art. My father had a business he built from nothing. I want that opportunity to create something entirely on my own, to feel utterly entitled to everything I earn. I want to take this person that's so precious to me—my Nana—and immortalize her so that in some small way she'll live forever. And I want to spend my life making films. This job isn't only the best path; it's the *only* path available to me right now.

"Adam, Ethan, why don't I give you a tour of the studio?" my mother asks. "The light is gorgeous at this time of day, and we can finish our drinks out on the deck."

Thank you, Pearl Bertram, for pulling out the normal when necessary.

I turn to go, and then I remember that my dad and I stashed all the nudes in my mom's studio.

"Oh, uh, Mom, maybe you should just skip the studio."

"Nonsense," says Adam, rubbing his hands together. "I'd never forgive myself if I missed an opportunity to see your mother's work in progress. It's an honor."

Crap.

It's not so much that I don't want Ethan to see me naked. Obviously. It's that I don't want him to see me naked and sitting in what looks like a cocktail glass filled with blood. Or covered in eyes and nipples.

"Ethan, why don't you . . . uh, why don't you come meet my Nana?"

"Sure," says Ethan, giving me a puzzled look. "Though I'd love to see your mom's work too."

"I'm sure she'd be happy to bring out a few pieces to show you later," I say as I try to shoot a telepathic message to my mother not to humiliate me.

Ethan follows me down the hall to my grandmother's room but stops in front of a series of photographs my mother took of me—twenty-one of them, taken each year on my birthday. In each, I'm draped in white, my hair brushed back from my face, no makeup or other adornments. I love them, not because they're of me but because more than any of her other photographs, they communicate something of my mother's heart.

He stands there, looking at each one in order—baby to child to teen to . . . whatever I am today.

"These are amazing. Something in your eyes has stayed the same through the years." Ethan turns to look at me, and the hall light haloes his hair, giving it a liquid sheen. "They say a lot . . . Your eyes do."

"They do?" I ask. "What are they saying right now?" *Oh, Mia, I think. You are playing with fire.*

Something darts through my consciousness—Ethan wet, my hands in his hair. Our bodies bare, slippery. We're kissing. And laughing. What the hell did we do that night?

We're in dangerous territory here, standing inches apart in the hall, his sweet, thoughtful eyes locked onto mine. But right now, I don't care. I just know I want it again.

I step toward him. I can't help myself; his pull is too strong. The hell with the job. The hell with Kyle. I just need to wrap myself in his gorgeous beach-fire scent. I want to feel the length of him against me, want those soft, warm lips all over me again. And I want to remember it this time.

I take another step, and he watches me come toward him, his eyes half-lidded, lips moist and inviting.

And then Nana calls for me from the next room.

Chapter 18

Ethan

*Q: Grow old and gray with your partner at your side,
or blaze a solo trail into the sunset?*

I follow Mia down a long hallway, past a glass atrium with a modern stone fountain, telling myself I'm just imagining our chemistry.

She did not just look like she wanted to kiss me. And she does not look amazing in that peach dress. And I'm not losing my head over her.

Nope. I'm good.

Mia pauses at a door and knocks softly. "Nana? Coming in!" She steps inside and moves right to a sitting alcove at the far end of a spacious bedroom. The decor is modern like the rest of the house, but a little more elegant, with crystal chandeliers and white furniture, and light brown walls. I think. They could be in my color-blind zone and actually be red.

Mia kneels in front of a slender woman reading a book. She's in her late sixties by my best guess. I'm surprised by how young she actually seems, knowing she has Alzheimer's.

"Hey, Nana," Mia says. "This is my friend Ethan." She smiles up at me. "Ethan, this is my Nana, Evelyn Bertram."

Evelyn looks up at me with green eyes that are startlingly familiar until I notice that they're foggy, like glass that's been exposed to the elements for decades. Still, there's enough of Mia's humor and warmth in them that I find myself smiling at Nana like I've known her forever.

"Hello, Ethan." Nana extends her hand. "Call me Evie."

"It's a pleasure to meet you, Evie."

Nana beams at me. Then at Mia. Then back at me. "Well, sit down."

"Thanks." I sit in the chair facing her. Mia settles on her knees, her hand over her grandmother's, which rests on a book. There's love in Mia's posture and her smile. It's in her entire being. Maybe I'm inspired, being in the house of a famous photographer, but I want to snap a picture of her like that.

"Are you a university friend?" Nana asks me.

"No. Mia and I work together."

"Work?" Nana looks at Mia like she's lost, and I want to take back what I said. Suddenly, words feel a little dangerous.

"It's recent, Nana. I just started earlier this week. Ethan and I are coming up with marketing ideas for a company called Boomerang."

She talks steadily and slowly, but without patronizing, and I get the feeling she's told Nana all of this before. Then she glances at me, and the sadness in her eyes makes me hurt for her.

"Actually, Mia's coming up with all of the good ideas. I'm mostly there for support."

"You certainly look up to the task."

Mia lets out a small laugh. "What do you mean, Nana?"

"Look at him. He's cute."

"Thank you, Evie. And you're a beautiful woman."

Mia shoots me a look. "Are you flirting with my grandmother?"

"Yes, but she started it," I say. Then I notice the black-and-white photo in the silver frame on the table. "Wow . . . Is that you?"

I lean forward, seeing a young woman who I'm almost sure is Evelyn. The man on her right is her husband, I'm guessing, but the man on *his* right is what caught my eye. Martin Luther King Jr. Mia mentioned her grandma was involved in the civil rights movement in the sixties, but this is mind blowing.

"Where was this taken? What was he like in person?" The questions just pop out. I can't believe she was part of *history*. But the instant Nana looks at the photo, I realize I've made a mistake. There's no flash of recognition in her eyes. Only confusion.

"That was in . . . It was . . ." She bends a little toward Mia and whispers, "What was the name of the place?"

"Selma," Mia offers gently. "Selma, Alabama."

Nana nods, and I can tell she's disappointed with herself for not remembering. Then I see her make an effort to smile.

"Stan looks so young there. Doesn't he, Mia?" She looks past us, into the room. "Where is Stan? Isn't he coming to dinner?"

Aw, no. Mia told me her grandfather passed away when she was a kid.

"He can't come tonight," Mia says, squeezing her grandma's hand. "But we're going to have a great night anyway."

"What on earth could be so important that he can't come to dinner?"

"Nana, he's . . ." Mia bites her bottom lip. "Grandpa is . . ."

Watching this is brutal. What do you say? Your husband died years ago? How many times does this woman have to relive the death of the man she still loves? How many times does *Mia* need to watch her go through that?

"I'm sorry he can't be here," I say, needing to help somehow, "but it's a lucky thing for me. See, I came here dateless, and I'm hoping you'll agree to join me, Evie." I stand and extend my hand to her. "Will you come to dinner with me tonight?"

Nana's smile returns. "Yes," she says, taking my hand. "Thank you, Ethan. I will. But don't try anything. Stan gets jealous easily."

"I'll try to behave myself."

I loop her arm into mine and offer my free hand to Mia, who takes it.

As we leave the room, Mia lets go and I feel her arm come around me. She presses close, squeezing my ribs. "Thank you," she whispers.

And just like that, my night is made.

In the dining room, Adam and Mia's father sit at the table, deep in conversation. Adam swirls a glass of red wine absently as he listens. I'm a little envious of the attention Mr. Galliano is getting until I notice the sparrow perched on the back of one of the other chairs.

An actual real live bird.

It ruffles its feathers and does that quick head-tilt thing birds do, looking like it's just as surprised to see me.

"We leave the patio doors open a lot," Mia explains. She let go of my hand somewhere along the hallway, which sucked, but Adam's here. "Baudelaire sort of adopted our family."

"You have a sparrow named Baudelaire for a pet?" I ask, helping Nana into a chair. "How have you not mentioned this to me yet?"

"Shhh," Mia says. "He's very sensitive about that word."

"What word?"

"Pet. He finds it demeaning."

"Sorry, Baudelaire."

"He forgives you."

"Great."

I know we're both just making words. Prolonging this small moment where we're close and focused on each other. I can see her every eyelash. Her lipstick is peach, like her dress, and if I were to bend forward just a little, I could kiss her.

Mia licks her lips and a jolt shoots through me. We're thinking the same thing right now.

"What's for dinner?" Nana asks. "It stinks."

Mia jerks away, our connection severed. "Dad, dinner?" she asks, a little panicked.

Her father looks up from his heart-to-heart with Adam and winks at her. "Under control. Should be ready in ten minutes."

I don't see how that comforts Mia. Nana's right. Whatever we're eating smells like road kill, but she visibly relaxes.

"Drinks?" she asks, heading toward the bar. "Nana, the usual? Ethan?"

"Anything," I say, "but I was hoping to see your mother's studio first."

"Yeah, too bad about that," she says over her shoulder as she pours a glass of wine. "Maybe some other time."

I'm not sure I follow. "Why some other time?"

"How about now?" Mia's mom sweeps into the room. The woman has some stage presence, but Mia's father just keeps talking, clearly used to his wife's big personality. "Now sounds wonderful!"

She refills her wine glass almost to the brim, grabs the one Mia poured and tips her head, summoning me to join her. "Come along, come along! Next tour departs immediately!"

Adam breaks off with Mia's father and catches my eye. "You're definitely going to want to check it out."

At the same moment, Mia takes off like an Olympic sprinter, shooting past her mom and disappearing into the hallway. Two thoughts pop into my head. One, the girl claims she's not an athlete, but she can definitely move and she looks good doing it. And two, I'm obviously missing something.

"Thank you," I say, joining Pearl. "I was disappointed when I thought I'd missed out."

"Nonsense." Pearl hands me a very full glass of red wine. "This way." Then she loops an arm through mine.

"Whoa." I bobble my wine glass a little, but thankfully don't spill.

Pearl laughs. "Sorry. We're a touchy family. Sometimes, I forget it's uncomfortable for people."

"No . . . It's okay. I just didn't expect that."

Pearl smiles. "Unexpected things are my favorite."

I like unexpected too, but this night is starting to feel like I'm on Space Mountain: in the dark and totally unable to anticipate turns.

Pearl is short like Mia, but she walks briskly and I have to lengthen my stride to stay even with her and not spill wine. Also because everywhere I look are pictures, each one more interesting than the one before it.

"You know, Ethan," Pearl says, "Mia has told us a lot about her internship."

"It's a great opportunity." I don't add *for only one of us.*

Pearl stops in front of a carved wooden door that's different from the others in the house. It's all warped and weathered, like it was pulled up from a shipwreck.

She squares herself to me and grows very still. After a second or two, not even the wine in her glass moves.

I feel like it's the first time she's really *seeing* me and it's intense. I have to force myself to just stand there and take her eagle-eyed scrutiny. Retreating under her gaze would feel like losing, somehow.

"You have fantastic bone structure, a gorgeous Bernini-esque physique, and I'm absolutely *mad* for the cleft in your chin," she says.

What. The. Fuck?

I'm suddenly sweating like Rhett, but I manage to answer like I'm taking this all in stride. "Thank you."

"Don't thank me. Thank your parents."

"Okay."

"And probably your exercise regimen. Sports?"

"Soccer."

"Ah."

She nods, taking that in.

"I have not heard *a peep* about you from my daughter."

"I . . . didn't know that."

"Well, how would you?"

"Right."

Is she trying to mess with my head? I have never felt so wrong-footed around another human being before.

Pearl tilts her head like Baudelaire did earlier. "Do you know what that makes you, Ethan?"

"Unexpected?"

She breaks into a big smile, and I feel like I've just passed a huge test. "*Yes,*" she says, emphatically. "And *extremely* unique."

She swings the wood door open, leaving me with that little riddle to puzzle over. Thoughtful of her, since I didn't already have enough to try to contend with tonight.

I follow her into a huge studio space with soaring ceilings. One end looks like part laboratory, part factory, with a cluster of over-sized computer monitors and industrial-looking equipment that I can only imagine is for enlarging and transferring photographs.

Above the equipment, the walls are crowded with prints of all sizes. Amazing stuff. My eyes go to a shot of high heels with spar-kling sequins and a bow. I recognize them as the Wizard of Oz slip-pers, except they have a killer four-inch heel, the tip of which is pressing into a curve of smooth flesh.

It's the body part that's so arresting. I can't look away. I can't figure out if it's a breast or a back, or a calf, and that's how every single piece is. You look at it, and you want to know more. You *have* to.

The other end of the studio is much more open, with a drop cloth, a variety of backdrops, some props like wigs and umbrellas and angel wings, a few stools. Beyond that, huge glass doors lead to an outdoor patio and one of the most incredible views I've ever seen.

"Hey," Mia says.

"Oh, there you are," her mother says, whirling. Then she shakes her head disapprovingly. "Really, Mia?"

That's when I notice the sheets dropped over some frames resting against the wall.

"What are those?" I ask.

"Nothing," Mia says. "Nothing at all."

Chapter 19

Mia

Q: How do you handle a crisis?

*O*f course, my mother proceeds to whip the sheet off the frames like she's unveiling a new car. I don't even know why I tried.

The largest of them, and probably the most eye-catching, is a massive triptych my mom did, based on a Modigliani nude. I'm reclining on a red velvet chaise, arms up over my head, a white silk sheet weaving beneath my body to spill across my thighs. My skin looks burnished, almost amber. And because it's my mother, my body is sliced into thin spirals, like I've been through an apple peeler.

She pulls those away from the wall and sets them beside all the others I tried to hide: martini glass Mia, many-nippled Mia, avenging goddess Mia, with eight arms, a halo of detached eyeballs, and blue flames where one might normally locate my girl bits.

"As you can see," my mother tells Ethan. "My daughter's my muse."

From Ethan's perspective it probably looks more like shrooms are my mother's muse, though as far as I know she's never done a drug in her life.

But he steps back to get a better look at the pieces, and once again, I'm watching him look at me but a different version of me. Digitally manipulated, attractively lit, powerfully posed. *That* Mia.

"These are . . . extraordinary," Ethan murmurs, but I can't tell how he means it. Extraordinary, great? Extraordinary, bizarro? "I've never seen anything like them." It's dumb, too, but I feel a pang of jealousy, watching him admire her work.

"You see, my darling?" My mom captures my chin in her hands to plant a kiss on me. "Don't ever hide yourself." To Ethan, she adds, "She's beautiful, isn't she?"

"Mom!"

He glances at me, and his gaze is warm and considering, as though he's seeing me—real me, the one in front of him—for the first time too. "Very," he says.

"Let me show you what I'm working on now," my mother says, warmly. "It's a series called 'Foxes.'"

I groan. Those are the ones of me in different animal masks, taken in weird urban environments. Fox-mask Mia in a shopping cart under fluorescent lights. Cat-mask Mia crouched on a mall escalator, ascending into shadow. I'm dressed in most of them, but maybe we don't need to inundate the guy with our complete and utter weirdness?

"Mom, dinner's going to be ready soon. Why don't we head back to our other guest?"

"I really want to see them," Ethan says, grinning at me. Once again, I can't read the expression. Is he genuinely interested? Sucking up to my mom? Or just giving me tsuris, as Nana would say?

"Okay, but don't keep him too long, Mom," I say. I don't add, "And please don't tell him anything mortifying about yourself. Or me."

I start for the door, distracted, and catch the heel of my sandal on a snarl of cords on the floor. Flailing, I grab onto Ethan's arm and send his wine glass—filled with Chianti—splashing onto his face, his throat, and his beautiful crisp white shirt.

"Oh my God, Ethan! I'm so sorry."

He stands there, totally shocked, and then looks down at himself. A drop of Chianti slides down his nose and drops onto his shoe.

"Happy accident!" my mother says, clasping her hands like a Who on Christmas morning. "Mia, why don't you run and get a towel. And see if you can find him a clean shirt."

"I am so, so sorry," I tell him. "Stay right here. I'll be back in a minute."

More carefully, I flee the room, wanting to stop and bang my head against the wall a few times before I go. Why do I feel like a walking catastrophe around this guy?

I pass by the kitchen on my way to the linen closet. Looking in, I'm surprised to find my dad, Adam, and Nana sitting around the round table tucked into the window niche there. The two guys look like they've done some real damage to that bottle of bourbon already—though Nana still has her full glass of vermouth.

Adam sits back, resting his head against the wall, a strange expression on his face. "That's what they don't understand," he says hoarsely.

"How could they?" My dad tips back his glass. "That feeling like someone pushed a button on your life. And it's suddenly something new?"

"And something you didn't ask for," Adam replies. "Or want."

"Guys?" I say, coming into the kitchen. "What's going on? Everything all right?"

"Ah, my sweet Mia Moré." My dad waves me over, and I go. He threads an arm around my waist and squeezes. "The thing is, Adam," he says. "You have to find the thing that makes it worth it. That turns that life you didn't want into something you do."

Adam salutes my dad with his glass. "It's great you have that. Family."

"What are you talking about?" I ask.

Adam checks the remains of his bourbon for an answer but doesn't say anything.

"Jo-Jo?"

"Oh," my dad replies. "I told Adam here about my accident."

"Really?" He never talks about it. So, why to Adam—a stranger?

People always talk about the voltage when they talk about electricity. But it only took one amp to stop my dad's heart. He's got a chest full of shining pink scars to remind us of what happened—but I forget about the other wounds, the ones he carries inside.

"It's a good reminder that things go fast," my father says. "And nothing's guaranteed. You can only dig in and fight for your little share of happiness, *capisci*?"

"*Capisco*," Adam replies. Is there anything he doesn't know?

Glassy-eyed, he drains the last of the bourbon. For the first time that I've ever seen, he's a bit . . . askew. His collar droops on one side, and the knot of his tie's too tight, like he's been tugging on it.

"Maybe we should get dinner on the table?" I suggest. They could use some good bread to sop up the booze.

My dad lets go of me. Getting to his feet, he says, "Good thinking, sweetheart." He extends a hand to Nana. "Evie?"

Nana rises and smiles at me. Her eyes are her own again, green and sharp with humor. "Where'd that good-looking boy go?" she asks.

Oh, crap. I totally forgot about Ethan.

"I'll be right back," I tell them and explain about Ethan and the wine.

I dash into my parents' room, rifle through my dad's closet for a shirt, snag a towel from the linen closet, and rush back to my mother's studio.

"Hey, sorry about—" But the scene in the room chops the words off mid-sentence.

The studio lights blaze, and my mom stands back behind the camera, snapping pictures, calling out encouragement.

To Ethan.

Who's sitting atop a stool and posing for my mom—shirtless.

Chapter 20

Ethan

Q: Lights, camera, action—or do you prefer your fun in the dark?

*M*ia stops, a shirt in one hand, a towel in the other, and locks eyes with me. The moment stretches out between us, as we both try to process the situation.

I've been wondering how she'd react when she came back.

My top theory was with humor, a laugh, a joke of some kind, but embarrassment wasn't far behind.

The way she's looking at me, though—eyes wide, pink lips relaxed into a pout—isn't either. I've struck her speechless, which would be a massive turn-on if her mother wasn't standing ten feet away from me.

Actually. It still is.

Pearl lowers her camera and smiles at Mia. "Ah, you're back."

"Um, Mom?" Mia squeaks. "What are you doing?"

"Taking advantage of an opportunity," Pearl says. "I'd never have forgiven myself if he left this house and I didn't get a shot of that chin. Come look."

She messes with the back of the camera, and Mia moves to her, peering at the digital display that lights up.

Standing at the edge of the pool of yellow thrown by the spot-lights, they're mostly in darkness, but I can see Mia's mouth curve into a smile as Pearl scrolls through pictures.

In the seconds of silence that follow, I give myself a little pep talk. I'm secure in my own skin. Never worried about what a girl thought of me shirtless before because I know I have a decent build. Better than decent, actually, thanks to soccer. So why am I sitting here right now wondering what Mia's thinking?

"That one," Mia says, her hand stopping Pearl's. "That's the shot."

Pearl glances at me, then at Mia. "It's a different side of him. Darker."

And that clues me as to what they're seeing.

When Mia left, Pearl asked if she could take my picture.

I said, "No thanks."

She said, "Surely I can convince you."

What followed was some hardcore bartering wherein I agreed to sit for a few pictures in exchange for Pearl answering my questions about Mia.

I had a goal in mind like always, so I worked my angle of questioning to Mia's friends, waiting for the perfect moment to bring up her ex. I didn't want to know about him as much as what he did to screw up being with Mia. That was when Pearl told me what a fuck-wad the guy was, how he treated Mia, taking her for granted.

"Did he two-time her?" I'd asked.

"No," Pearl said, between snaps. "It was worse than that." *Snap,*

snap. "He toyed with her." *Snap, snap.* "He'd just disappear or lose interest sometimes, claiming some nonsense about needing to find himself." *Snap, snap.* "Then he'd come back and get her hopes up again. That happened 'til he drained the hope right out of her, the little prick."

I felt like tracking Kyle down and beating the shit out of him, and I'm guessing that translated as "Darker Ethan" in the photos.

"You should make some prints, Mom," Mia says now.

"Do you have a girlfriend, Ethan?" Pearl asks, and I catch a hint of wryness in her voice.

"Not anymore. Are we done here?"

"Dinner!" Mia's father's voice carries down the hall.

"My dinner!" Pearl pushes her camera at Mia. "Put that away for me, will you?" Her flowy pants flap as she breezes from the studio.

When she's gone, Mia sets the camera down on a table. "I feel like saying sorry won't quite cut it."

I shrug. "It's no big deal. I had to draw the line at full frontal, but otherwise it was fun."

"Prude."

"Hey, who's half naked here?"

"Sure, but have you looked around?"

"Actually, I can't stop." Pearl's images were already hard to look away from, but now that I know it's Mia in them, I can't stop staring. I can't believe I didn't recognize her right away, because the shape of her seems so familiar now.

We fall quiet for a moment, the spotlights buzzing loudly in the silence. They put off major heat, and I feel like I'm getting a sunburn. Thankfully the patio doors are open and it's a cool night.

Mia stands beyond the reach of the lights, but I can feel her looking at me.

"Mia?"

"Yes?"

"Shirt?"

"Oh, right," she says, looking down at her hand. She tosses the towel onto the table and comes over with the shirt.

"Here you go." Finally, she looks up at me. "I'll try to clean yours. Or replace it. With the other one I stole."

Standing, I take her father's shirt. "Thanks." I can tell just by looking that it's going to be too small. Not a surprise since I'm six-two, and Mr. Galliano is maybe five-nine. But what makes me hesitate isn't the fit.

I don't want clothes to be added to this scenario, I want them subtracted. I flash on an image of Mia's peach dress puddled at her feet, and the way she'd look under these lights. Under *me* under these lights, and I wonder . . .

I stare into her eyes, searching for the vibe I felt from her during our text chat earlier, or when she walked into the studio, but it's not there. There's no invitation from her, and I don't know if it's because of me, or the job, or her fuckwad ex, and right now, it really doesn't matter.

I need a solid green light, and I'm not getting it.

Adam's laugh echoes from the kitchen, like the call to retreat.

Mia says, "I guess we should go."

"Right."

I yank on the shirt. Just as I suspected, the thing is like donning a second skin. That's four sizes too small. Mia's laughing before I start buttoning it.

"Can you even breathe?" she asks.

"Barely, but I don't think I'll be able to eat anything."

"You're just trying to avoid my mother's cooking."

"No way. Sulfuric acid is my favorite." The higher buttons won't even stay closed, so I give up and look at Mia. "I wish I had some chest hair to complete the look. Got any gold chains I could borrow?"

She shakes her head, smiling. "You can't go to dinner flashing all that cleavage. Come here, I'll button it."

As soon as she touches my shirt, my hands frame her face, and I bend close, only inches separating us.

Mia doesn't tense or flinch in surprise, and I have this feeling she knew what I'd do when even I didn't.

We stay there, just breathing the same air for a few seconds, making a little pocket of shadow in the brightness that surrounds us.

This has to be our secret, or we could lose everything.

No one can know.

Neither of us says a word but the pact is right there, between us.

Then Mia's fingers close around my collar, tugging me closer, and I can't wait anymore.

I brush her lips with mine. This isn't our first kiss, but it sure as hell feels that way, and it seems important, somehow, to be tender with her.

That doesn't last long. I want more of her right away, and my tongue slides into her mouth. She tastes cool and sweet, like chilled grapes. When I feel her respond, kissing me back like she wants more, I wrap my arms around her, fitting her against me, and give it to her.

Mia draws back slightly after a moment, dashing kisses along the corner of my mouth. I take the opportunity to steal a glance at her from this close—she has the hottest body I've ever seen. I smooth my hand along her ribs, finding the curve of her breast. She sighs and presses closer, and the sound almost makes me lose my mind.

I need more. I hoist her up and turn, settling her on the barstool as I kiss her. Her knees are in my way, so I nudge her legs apart, pushing her dress up her thighs. Then I settle between her hips.

"You feel incredible, Mia," I say.

But the truth is she feels fucking perfect.

Chapter 21

Mia

Q: Do you like surprises?

I grip Ethan's taut biceps and ease my thighs further apart, pulling him against me. I can't get enough of his strong arm bracing the small of my back or his perfect fingers moving over my nipple, skimming the length of my body—familiar and new at the same time. I want more of his lips, soft and searching, and his delicious wine-warm tongue plunging against my own. We are locked in this world between the studio's shadows and the bright, all-seeing lights, and it feels like a dream, like a moment that already belongs to memory.

My hands wind into his hair, and I pull him closer still, wrapping my legs around him and crossing my ankles, trapping him. I feel him, all of him—his broad, solid chest, the heat pulsing between us, and the hard length of him against my lower belly, undeniable, insistent, and sending shockwaves through my core.

"Jesus, Mia," Ethan breathes against my lips.

I press against him, my lips and tongue needing to be every-where—on his lips, on the hollow of his chin, on his jaw, his throat, where I graze my teeth against the heartbeat throbbing there.

My lips stay there, exploring, while my hand slides down, down . . .

"Mia," my dad calls. His heavy footsteps thump in the hallway.

Ethan and I leap away from each other, and I'm off the stool and halfway to the door, my heart a furious piston, by the time my father appears.

"Dinner, honey," he says, and lightly bumps into one of the walls. He really *has* gotten into the booze. "Didn't you hear us?"

"Oh, sorry, no," I say, resisting the urge to smooth my clothes or my hair, which I know must be a crazed snarl. "Ethan and I were . . . um, talking. We'll be right there."

"I did what I could," he whispers. "But it's time to face the music."

"What?" Panic washes over me. Are we busted? How long have we been gone?

"Added some spices. Threw in some chicken and veggies." He shrugs. "Best I could do."

"Oh, right!" I exhale with enough force to blow out a candle. "Dinner. Right."

"Come on. It's getting cold. Or congealing." He executes a sloppy pivot to return to the dining room.

I breathe and peek back into the studio. Ethan leans against my mother's worktable, legs crossed, grinning in this way that's smug and charming and brazen and makes me basically want to burn the house down around us so we never have to leave this room.

"Dinner," I say. Though I want to grab his hand and slip out through the French doors into the coolness of the night.

"I heard."

"You coming?"

"In a minute," he smirks, glancing down at himself. "I've got a . . . umm . . . a *situation* to take care of here."

I follow his gaze. Yep. Definitely a situation.

"I'll leave you to it," I tell him. But because I can't resist, I steal over and throw myself on him again, give him one last full-on kiss and pour myself against the length of him. The situation becomes a full-on *incident*, and I dart away, laughing.

"You suck," Ethan calls after me.

I carry my idiot smile down the hall with me, thankful for the murmur of conversation and the strains of Béla Fleck that tell me that the evening is winging by comfortably without us.

I can't get the image of Ethan in my mom's photographs out of my mind. True, they portray a darker Ethan. Brooding, with that same intensity in his face that reminds me of the morning—less than a week ago—that I woke up in his bed. I want to know what moved through his thoughts in that moment.

My whole body feels light, untethered. Like I'm drunk or stoned. I slip into a chair across from Adam, who has gathered himself and sits with his usual air of crisp self-possession.

"Did you already do away with the competition?" he asks, grinning.

"Yes." I smooth my napkin over my lap. "He's been completely immobilized."

My mother waylays Ethan as he comes down the hall, and the next thing I know, he's staggering over with a serving dish large enough to hold a massive turkey. He sets it down and sits on the other side of the table, next to Nana. I'm afraid to look at him because I know I'll give myself away. But I do, and his eyes flick up to meet mine before focusing on his plate. A sexy half-smile plays across his lips, and I know he's entertaining the same thoughts.

Mom tugs off the lid of the serving dish, and I gasp. A surprised *what-kind-of-freakin'-alchemy-is-this?*-kind of gasp. Because the food looks, and smells, normal. Tantalizing, even. As a plus, it also resembles actual food—chicken in some kind of sauce. Things I actually recognize as root vegetables.

Mouths drop open in surprised "O's" all around the table. Except for my mom's, which presses into an exasperated line. My dad's in trouble, but dinner's saved.

"Wow, that smells different," Ethan blurts. He flushes and tries to recover. "I mean delicious."

Nana laughs and pats Ethan on the arm. "Nice try, young man."

Dinner is dished, and we all settle into comfortable conversation.

"What kind of things have you and Ethan been getting up to in the office?" my mother asks.

I almost choke on my wine but realize she means the *Boomerang* office. "Well, we've really only just started, mom. But we're working on a branding campaign."

"*Rebranding,* actually," Adam corrects. "I've asked Ethan and Mia to help push the Boomerang brand forward. They're working on boosting our presence at an upcoming trade show in Las Vegas."

"Speaking of which," Ethan inserts, smoothly, "Mia and I have been wanting to talk to you about the display design."

We focus on Adam while we give our pitch, but really it's like we're talking to one another, like we're a perfectly tuned machine.

"It could be so much livelier," I tell Adam. "Sexy and bold. It could really speak to the people you're trying to reach. The current design—" I look to Ethan for help.

"Just speaks to lazy people who want a place to sit," he finishes. "It's a lounge, sure, but like an airport lounge. It doesn't have real life. It's not —"

"Romantic," I say, warming up and doing half my speaking with my hands. "Or adventurous. Or new."

"Or cool," adds Ethan.

"Exactly! No matter what we come up with, or how we *want* to brand Boomerang, it's going to fall flat in that space."

"Like sticking the Mona Lisa on a shelf at a drugstore," says Ethan. His eyes have this keen, competitive gleam in them now. He's in his natural state. Relaxed, charged with enthusiasm.

Jesus Christ, I want him.

Adam laughs. "So the two of you are creating the Mona Lisas of media presentations? Is that right?"

"Damn right," says Ethan.

I nod. "We could, with a more inspiring backdrop. Let us do something else with the display."

"Whatever you have in mind better be worth the wrath of Cookie."

Ethan and I look at each other.

Crumbs. Cookie.

"I'm sure Cookie wants the best for the company," Ethan says. "And we want to make the most of this opportunity."

"Okay," says Adam, holding up a hand to halt the barrage. "I'm sold. New display design, whatever you want it to be. Within the budget, of course. Which is plenty generous. You split it down the middle—each take ownership of a half. The two pieces have to feel organic, but they also have to reflect you and your specific view of the Boomerang brand. Got it?"

"Perfect," I say, my mind already working over possibilities. This is going to be *fun*. "I know we're both up to the challenge."

"I don't doubt it." Adam dabs the corner of his lip with a napkin and then rises. "Speaking of challenges, you've reminded me of my plan for next week."

"What plan?" asks Ethan.

"Field research," he says. "Next Wednesday, you both start dating."

Chapter 22

Ethan

Q: How do you fight your battles:
cold shoulder or shouting match?

$\mathcal{W}$hat did you just say?" I brace my elbows on the table, feeling the seams of Mr. Galliano's shirt strain and pop.

Adam looks at me calmly. "Dates," he repeats. "To give the company product a test-drive, so to speak. A firsthand understanding of the service we offer. It's not mandatory, but hardly anyone passes on the opportunity. And obviously the commitment is only to spend a few hours with one of our matches, nothing more."

He keeps talking, going on about how he thought Rhett had told us, how it's something he suggests to all his single new hires, but my focus shifts to Mia. She looks a little pale, but it's hard to tell under the candlelight. Still, I can tell she's reacting to this way better than me. I have no doubt that Dark Ethan just showed up again. But what the hell kind of job is this? I'm already working for free. Now I have to surrender my fucking social life, too?

That's not even the worst part.

The worst part is the idea of Mia being subjected to spending a night with some of the scumbags I'm sure use Boomerang strictly for hookups.

Mother. Fucking. *Bullshit.*

Adam breaks off whatever he was saying. "Do you have a problem with this, Ethan? I'd never force an employee into an uncomfortable situation. In fact, I had my assistant Lena schedule your dates at the same location and time, thinking you two might find it easier, more like any other work assignment. It would allow you to compare notes afterward. And, I'll admit I'm a little old-fashioned on this point, but I like the idea of you keeping an eye on Mia."

Adam smiles, lifting his glass in her direction. "Don't take it the wrong way, Mia. I know *you* can handle yourself, but *I* would feel more at ease knowing Ethan is there."

"Having Ethan there is a *great* idea," Pearl says, looking at me with those sharp eyes.

"Yes," agrees Mr. Galliano. "That would ease my conscience too."

Uh-huh, I think. *You wouldn't be saying that if you knew I was parked between your daughter's legs ten minutes ago.*

Suddenly, I'm swimming in anger and lust. My eyes fall to the wine glass in front of me. I tip it back, needing something to chill me the hell out.

"Um . . . when is this all happening?" Mia asks.

"Wednesday night is the first one. I think there are two more scheduled later in the week as well."

"Oh—kay," Mia says. "That sounds—great."

"Three dates to look forward to!" Nana chirps. "How wonderful!"

Adam nods. "Could provide just the edge you two need to come up with the perfect displays for the conference."

"Oh, it'll definitely provide some edge," I say.

Mia shoots me a warning look, and then says, "Hey, did you know Ethan learned to play soccer in a bowling alley?"

That sends the conversation in a completely different direction. I was at the brink of letting Adam know exactly how I feel about his idea. Mia sensed it—and saved me.

Everyone is delighted when I tell them that I learned to shoot on bowling pins. How charming, they say. But really it was just a lack of options. I couldn't always afford to play in indoor leagues or traveling teams, so I played soccer where I could.

I know Mia meant well by bringing up this anecdote, but all I want to do is get up from this goddamn table. I don't even taste the food, but the wine goes down just fine.

Once our meal is over, I help Mia bring the dishes into the kitchen, then Mr. Galliano produces dessert—a crème brûlée that he torches at the table, which Adam swears is the best he's ever had.

Suckup.

Mia and I stand to take dish duty again, but as soon as we set the plates down, she grabs my hand and tows me into a little alcove, hidden away from the dining room. We share the space with a sculpture that looks like the discard pile at an auto shop.

"Are you okay with this?" she asks.

"The dates? Hell no. Are *you*?"

She shakes her head, but there's something in her eyes I don't like.

"What is it, Mia?"

"This job, Ethan. You need this job."

I'm not crazy about the way she says *need*. It hits too close to home.

I don't have a house like this. I don't own a pile of metal that's probably worth a million bucks in a special alcove. I literally don't even own the shirt on my back.

"You're right. I do need it. What about you, Mia? Why are you doing this? You don't need it for your grandma's documentary. You're obviously not strapped for cash."

Mia's mouth drops open. "Ethan . . . Am I supposed to justify myself to you? Just because I'm not desperate for the money doesn't mean this job isn't important to me. It could mean my career, something I build on my . . ." She shakes her head like she doesn't want to go there. "Look. I'm just confused by all this."

"I'm not," I lie. I don't know what I want anymore. I'm pissed. So fucking pissed. And the goddamn gallon of wine I drank during dinner is making my head spin. "There's no problem here, Mia. We got carried away earlier. We didn't do anything wrong."

"What do you mean?"

"We agreed we wouldn't have any romantic attachments with people we work with, and we haven't broken that rule. We messed around a little, but it wasn't anything . . ."

Wasn't anything *what*, Ethan? Amazing? Incredible? You fucking *liar*. It was all of that. *All* of it.

But I can't stop. I'm not her ex. I don't backpedal or waver on shit, and I'm not starting now.

So I try again. "What I'm trying to say is that what happened between us was nothing . . ."

"Nothing," she repeats flatly, but I see the hurt in her eyes.

"Nothing we can't bounce back from, I mean. We just have to get back to what we're both really after. The job."

I don't know what the hell I'm saying. I want to kiss her again. I want her against me. I want me against her against the wall.

I *do not* want her dating other guys.

A sick taste crawls up the back of my throat, and an ache builds in my chest that I haven't felt in weeks. In two months, to be exact, when I walked into Alison's apartment and found her in bed with her research assistant.

And I realize, suddenly, what's got me so fucked in the head.

I do not share nicely.

And I'm not putting myself anywhere near that kind of shit again.

Chapter 23

Mia

Q: Are you a lover or a fighter?

I march into the Boomerang office Monday morning like I'm going to war. I've got on an emerald bandage dress in clinging jersey, black leather stiletto boots, and my hair hangs loose, in glossy fat curls slicked into obedience by Skyler. I walk the rows of cubicles, carrying a gargantuan box of just-baked fritters and pastries that I dole out to my co-workers en route to my desk. I leave behind a trail of doughy sweetness and the groans of foodgasms.

Let the games begin.

Because he could have said anything. That's what I keep thinking. We've got this amazing language just *loaded* with words, phrases, even entire *sentences*. Ethan had a choice of thousands of them, a verbal cornucopia, and he said it meant *nothing*.

Our hot, dreamy moment in my mom's studio. The charge of *connection*—not just sex—that passed between us. The feeling of being *right*, in the right place, with the right person, doing the exact right thing—all of it.

Meant nothing.

Which translates to *I* mean nothing.

At least that's what I heard as I walked away, my throat squeezing around sudden tears I *refused* to shed. And after they left, when I lay on the sofa in the living room with my head on Nana's lap, that's what kept drumming through my mind: *nothing, nothing, nothing.*

To think I'd been within a breath of giving up this internship— for *him*. Because I wanted Ethan more than the job and because the idea of going out on "field research" dates made me want to puke into my purse.

Now, though, I plan to enjoy it. My life, post-acting-like-an-idiot-over-some-boy, is going to be a box of chocolates, and I'm going to take a bite out of each and every one.

Ethan's already at our desk, tablet open before him. He's wearing the same suit he dressed in for our first day of work, and my mind wants to shoot me right back to that morning, to waking in his bed, laughing with him as we tried to locate my clothes.

I clamp my mind shut around the images and hold out the box.

"Morning," I say, my voice as bright and fake as neon. "Bear claw?" That's all that's left, other than a nub of cruller.

"Good morning." He looks in the box and then up at me. His eyes are shadowed. "Thanks. I'm good."

I spin away and put the last pastry on the kitchen counter then stuff the Stan's box into the wastebasket, crushing it viciously beneath the toe of my boot. Returning to my desk, I settle in and switch on my tablet.

"Mia, look—" he begins.

At the same time I say, "Big day today."

We both say, "Sorry, what?"

"You first," I tell him, calling up my Boomerang profile and trying to decide if I need new photos. Maybe I should wear something sexier than the silk blouse I wore on my first day of work. Maybe get a little more cleavage going. And have Ethan take the pictures.

"Just . . ." He rubs the back of his neck. "What I said the other night? It came out harsher than—"

I put up a hand to stop him. It's bad enough I had to hear it in the first place, that I spent a weekend feeling dumb and miserable and used.

And I already know he's sorry. I saw it all over his face the minute he said it. But that doesn't matter. It's the seesaw I can't stand. The whole up-and-down, back-and-forth, endless torture of it. My heart just can't take the ride.

"It's okay," I tell him. "Really. You were right. We just—let ourselves get carried away, and it was fun, but . . ." I can't quite seem to look at him, so I focus on the spot between his straight, expressive eyebrows. "Let's just put all that in a box and tuck it away, all right?"

"All right," he says. "Great."

The hiss of the espresso machine fills the awkward silence for one long moment. I don't know what I wanted him to say. I do know it wasn't *that*.

"What were you going to say?" he asks.

"Oh, just that it's a big day today. We get to pick our first Boomerang dates."

"Yeah," he mutters. "Fun."

"It might be." I scroll through some of the profiles and land on the smarmiest-looking dude I can find—mirrored shades, giant margarita in one hand and his arms draped over the shoulders of straw-blond Amazonian twins. Who he kept *in* the picture. "Like, here's someone: 'RobbyDTF.' " I turn the tablet in Ethan's direction. "What do you think?"

"RobbyDTF," he says, giving me a look. "Subtle."

"Well, why bother with subtlety? Isn't that the whole promise of the site? 'Play hard. Throw it back,' right? Robby looks like the kind of guy who can play hard."

Ethan winces. Or maybe I imagine he does. "And weren't you the one talking about all the great experiences Boomerang members can have? The memories they can create? Does that guy seem like he's going to give you a great memory, Mia?"

"Oh, I don't know." I turn the tablet back around and pretend to consider. Robby's orange tan reminds me of a basketball, and his teeth have a menacing glint, like a shark's. "Maybe some nights aren't about making memories. Maybe they're just about hooking up and having fun."

Now we lock eyes, and I see hurt and frustration in his. But the snowball's already rolling downhill.

Paolo, the art director, comes over and drapes himself over the edge of my desk, back to Ethan. He's wearing black skinny jeans, rolled up to reveal white socks and red Converse. He's compact, with red-framed glasses, immaculate dark stubble, and golden-bronze skin that makes me want to take him out in the sunlight and film him.

"Dope fritters," he says and holds out his fist for a bump.

I laugh and touch my knuckles to his. This is his first visit to Intern Gulag, other than to pass by on his way to the coffeemaker.

"You better step up your game, son," he says to Ethan. "This one's gonna fritter you out of a job."

"I'll bring you a wedding cake tomorrow," Ethan says with a scowl. "What do you need?"

"It's more what you need," he says, and takes my tablet. "Really, Mia? RobbyDTF? Just. No."

"But look at that tan," I say, grinning. "And maybe he comes with the girls, too."

"Well, that *would* be a bonus. But no. Keep trying." He walks around to Ethan's side of the desk and leans over his shoulder.

"Seriously," Ethan pushes away from him. "What's up?"

"I'm here to help you pick a date, man!" he says. "It's like a rite of passage here. Your first awkward Boomerang hookup. I need in on that action."

"I think we've got it," I say. "But thanks so much."

"You don't understand," he tells me. "I work directly under Cookie. Do you know what that means? It means I get to have my ass chewed about twenty-six times a day." He loops his thumbs into his trousers, grinning. "I can show you the teeth marks."

"Not necessary," I say. "Though you have my sympathies."

"I should. So, what I'm saying is, you can't deny a man his small pleasures."

"Well then, by all means." Ethan hands over his tablet. "You pick." He drums his fingers on our desk and gives me a look. "Make her hot."

"Duh, dude. Of course." He takes the tablet, and I can see a reflection of the screen in his glasses as he scrolls through profiles. He stops on one and reads for a minute, his lips moving. "Oh, man," he groans. "Her."

Ethan takes a look and grins. "Definitely."

Turning the tablet in my direction, Paolo asks, "What do you think?"

The girl is all long willowy limbs, a redhead with brown eyes and a spray of adorable freckles on her nose. Her name's Raylene Powers, and her profile claims she's an avid rock-climber and helps build houses for the homeless. In one photo, she's actually standing between former president Jimmy Carter and Beyoncé.

I want to make a joke that he needs to find more of a go-getter, but my mouth feels packed with cotton. "Pretty," I manage.

"Score!" exclaims Paolo. "That's a winner." He reaches for my computer. "Let's do you now."

"For Christ's sake, Paolo," comes a screeching voice that turns my spine to ice.

"Shit! Cookie," Paolo whispers. He leaps to his feet, looking around for an escape route. "Hide me."

I'm seriously about to stuff him under my desk when Cookie comes clipping around the corner. She stops and stands there, arms folded, and drills a hole through Paolo's skull with her eyes.

"Paolo," she says in a tone that's terrifyingly pleasant. "Do you love this country?"

"You're on your own, kid," he says to me, and races away.

She aims her laser beam focus in my direction. "Did you want to offer *me* a pastry, Mia?"

I almost pee, she's so scary. "Well, umm, you didn't seem to want Ethan's cookies the other day."

She huffs away, and I watch her go.

Turning back to the screen, I sigh. "Oh, what the hell difference does it make?" I murmur, and launch my virtual boomerang at RobbyDTF.

Chapter 24

Ethan

Q: We all have a disastrous date in our past. What's yours?

Whoever invented the partner desk deserves a slow and agonizing death.

I can't look up from my tablet without seeing Mia's smile. Her lips. Her cleavage. She is literally in my visual "at ease" position. Right in front of me. Three feet away.

It's been torture all week, and it's not getting any easier.

I'm tempted to swap spots with the espresso machine and work at the kitchen counter, but that's probably what she wants. I have to be the reason she ramped up her clothes from work appropriate to drop-dead sexy. The way she looks in that black dress is destroying my focus. Just killing it. But no way am I letting her know that.

To try to distract myself, I pull up my date's profile.

Redheads have never been my thing since that hair color's pretty much lost on me, but she looks promising, even if she did go to USC. I can get past an intercollegiate rivalry and overlook her name, Raylene Powers, which is just . . . confusingly masculine. Paolo called her hot. That's a little generous, but she's no slouch in the looks department.

I try to picture myself having fun with her, maybe getting her back to my apartment, and end up with the memory of Mia naked in my bathroom, brushing her teeth with her finger.

Nice going, Vance. That worked.

Moving to plan B in my Mia Avoidance Strategy, I pull up the files I'm working on for the booth design. I've decided my entire approach is going to focus on movement, because it's what I know best.

For my graduating thesis in psychology, I did a study on the aftereffect of endorphins on athletes. Based on my survey, the sense of euphoria after a strenuous workout had a predictable outcome, with seventy-two percent of my test subjects choosing getting down as their most desired post-endorphin-rush activity. Which was surprising, in a way, since that runner's high feeling is similar to an orgasm afterglow, but hey. Can't have too much of a good thing, can you?

I guess Old Newton had it right. Bodies in motion tend to want to stay in motion.

I type up some notes on how to integrate all of that into a booth design, zoning out for a while, until Cookie's shrill voice explodes down the hall.

I glance up and find Mia watching me, her green eyes holding an undercurrent of sadness. I look down at my screen again, my stomach tightening. The things I said to her in the alcove at her parents' house come to mind, and I feel my face heat.

What a fucking asshole.

I pulled the jealous boyfriend card on her after one kiss. But, *Jesus*. What a kiss. And it wasn't just Saturday night. It was our first night, too. Mystery evening. In which I woke up with a hot, smart, funny naked girl in my bed.

Who's now my co-worker.

Who's also ironically making it hard for me to get any work done.

Christ. This has to go away.

The only real mistakes are failures to learn, Coach Williams used to say, and my ass is *learning.* I'm not going to let this girl ruin my plans. I'm not going to let her become an obsession.

Or maybe I am.

Jabbing at my keyboard, I pull up RobbyDTF's profile. Robby Down to Fuck. Excellent freaking choice, Mia. I shake my head, staring at his fake-tan mug. Zooming in, I notice he has bad teeth. Then I spend the rest of the day thinking of ways I can force him into much-needed orthodontia. Really, I'd be doing the guy a favor.

At six, I stand and sling my messenger bag over my shoulder. "So," I say to Mia. I've denied myself the pleasure of looking at her for hours, but the flipside is that now I feel like I'm starving for the sight of her. I rub a hand over my hair, trying not to stare. "See you tonight at Rock Sugar?"

"Wow," Mia says. "Time flies."

I almost roll my eyes. Time did not fly. Today time broke a wing and had to be put down. I've just spent four hundred and eighty minutes thinking about Mia, looking at Mia, and actively *not* thinking about and looking at Mia.

She shuts down her tablet and pulls her purse onto her lap. Usually it drives me nuts when girls can't find crap in their purses, but I'm a fan of this quirk of hers. Free pass to check her out. Which I shouldn't be doing, but screw it. A man only has so much self-control.

The girl is pure sex appeal, and those boots are *killer* on her. I'm picturing her with *only* those boots on when Mia comes up with her keys and stands.

"Do you need a ride?" she asks, scooting her chair in with her hip. "Ethan?"

"What? Oh, no thanks. I'm good. Rhett's waiting for me."

She nods, and I can't tell if it's disappointment I see in her eyes. "What about tonight?"

"Thanks, but I've got Jason's car."

"Okay . . . How's it going living with Isis?"

It's cool that she asked. I want to tell her, but things between us need to stay strictly professional. I drew a line in the sand on Saturday, and I'm not crossing it.

"Great," I say, using the mother of all non-answers.

"Great," she says, giving me a taste of my own medicine.

She pulls her purse over her shoulder. "I guess I'll see you later."

"Hold up," I say. "Should we have an abort signal or something for tonight? If it's awful, we should be able to communicate that, so we can bail each other out. What do you say?"

What I really want is to be able to step in if she needs it.

Mia shrugs, like she can't imagine Robby Down to Fuck being anything other than a complete gentleman. "Okay. How about we text the word Baudelaire?"

I shake my head. "Too hard to spell under duress. How about . . . Cookie?"

She smiles—a real smile—which guts me. I can't fuckin' win. She can be cold, or warm, or anything between and it doesn't matter. I'm screwed.

"Cookie it is," she says. "See you at eight."

"Okay," I hear myself say, but it's not.

Nothing about this scenario is okay with me.

I'm the first one to arrive at the restaurant, which is a bad call. Technically, Rock Sugar isn't Chinese food, it's Asian fusion, but my body can't tell the difference. The smell takes me back to that night two months ago with Alison, and a queasy feeling settles in my gut.

I grab a booth and take a moment to give myself a little pep talk about recommitting to the single lifestyle, which was the plan pre-Mia, and still *is* the damn plan. Land the job. Pay off some student loans. Apply to law school. All that stuff.

I open the menu and stare at it, wondering if I'm going to hurl before the food even gets here.

I feel Mia's arrival before I see her. I look up and sure enough, there she is, following the hostess through the restaurant. She's wearing a dress—red, I'm almost sure—that makes the black one from earlier look tame by comparison. Her curls are smoothed into long waves and she looks completely different but still the same— still unbelievably hot.

I watch as the hostess brings her to a table only a few feet away from my booth and says. "How's this?"

Mia does a double take when she sees me. "Oh . . . Um, this is fine."

Then she sits so that I have a perfect side view of her perfect body.

Awesome. Looks like I'll be spraining my peripheral vision tonight.

I pull my phone out of my pocket and check the time. Five minutes until our dates get here. Opening the menu again, I stare at lists of food, not really seeing anything but letters, until Mia crosses her legs. Then my eyes pull over like they're attached by a string.

She looks goddamn amazing. Couldn't she have worn sweatpants? A trench coat, maybe?

She catches me looking, so I clear my throat.

"Ready for the Robster?"

"Ready. You?"

"Yep."

We fall quiet but keep looking at each other. I wish it were awkward, but it's not. Looking into her eyes just feels right.

Mia looks away first, her attention shifting to the front of the restaurant, where a girl with a turquoise gift bag in her hands is speaking to the hostess. I recognize my date, Raylene. Walking up right behind her is RobbyDTF in the flesh, scanning the restaurant with the hungry look of a great white shark.

I get up from the booth, raising a hand so my date sees me.

"Ethan Vance?" she squeaks as she walks up. She does a mini-clap thing, then looks me up and down with such crazy excitement on her face that I want to make a break for it right then. "I'm Raylene Powers. My gawd! Aren't you gorgeous? How much fun are we going to have? Isn't this night already the best?"

I have no idea which question to answer, and I'm too busy focusing on the full-body hug Robby is giving Mia. He's practically lifting her off the ground.

"Nice to meet you, Raylene." I shake her hand, trying to ignore the way her inch-long fake nails dig into my skin. Then I wait for her to sit down before I take the opposite seat.

Raylene reaches for her dinner napkin. Her hand freezes, hovering there for a second, her fingertips trembling slightly. "Do you want me to sit next to you?" she asks. "I just sat here because it seems customary, but I can move if you want, so we're closer? What do you think? Too much or okay?"

Holy *shit*.

Holy. SHIT.

"What—no," I stammer. "I think we're good like this."

Raylene's shoulders sag, and I see my night going up in flames, with my career roasting over them, all because I couldn't survive a single date. Words tumble out of my mouth before I can stop them.

"Whatever makes you comfortable, Raylene. If you want to sit next to me, by all means. Please do."

"Great!" She scoots to my side. "That's *so* nice of you. Charming, actually. People say that chivalry is dead, but I don't know what they're talking about." As she speaks, she pulls over her place setting and straightens everything in front of her with total precision, like she sees only right angles. Then she straightens my fork and knife. Wine glass. Water glass.

"Perfect!" she says, when there's nothing left. "We are ready to go! Isn't this great? I'm already having so much fun. Aren't you?"

Suddenly, I'm having a hard time processing everything. Raylene claimed to be twenty-four in her profile, but I'm thinking she's ten years past that at least. The other thing is the way I can see white all around her dilated pupils, like she just saw a ghost. And won a new car. Then there's the way Robby is talking to Mia's rack, like her eyes are at chest level. It's really too fucking much to handle.

A bead of sweat runs down my ribs. I draw a deep, deep breath—then blow it back out as I see a steaming plate of kung pao noodles go by.

Too late. My stomach twists.

"Ethan?" Raylene says.

"Yeah?" I'm boxed in. The only way I get out of this booth is by climbing over it, and I'm actually considering it. There is a part of me that's dying right now. Dying and screaming *Cookie! Baudelaire!*

Raylene turns a little, hiding a smile behind her shoulder in a gesture that I think is supposed to be coy. "I brought you a little something. Don't worry, it's nothing extravagant. I wouldn't do something that forward or *slutty*. That's totally not my style. " Raylene's eyes go even wider and drop to my pants before coming back up. "I made triple-quadruple sure this was okay with the salesman at the store. He said this was the *perfect* thing for a first date. Not too much. Just right." She hands me the gift bag, which says Tiffany's on the side. "So, here. Open it!"

"Wow, Raylene. This is really nice of you, but I can't—"

"Yes, you can! Open it!"

"Excuse me, waiter?" I say, catching a busboy walking by with a tray of empty dishes. "Drink, please? Double whiskey, straight up. Raylene, do you want anything?"

"You *drink*?" She makes a face like I just told her I'm a pedophile. I must look terrified because she hurries to say, "It's okay, it's okay. We all have vices, right? Nobody's perfect. Open, open!"

I reach into the bag and pull out wads of tissue paper, half expecting to find a horse head or maybe a boiled pet rabbit, but it's just a small box. I take it out and open it, and inside I find silver cuff links, similar to what Adam wears.

I'm feeling a little dizzy at this point, but I can handle this. I have to.

"Raylene . . . These are great, but I can't accept them."

"But you have to! I can't return them." She takes them from me and holds them close to the candle. "They're engraved, see? EJV. Ethan James Vance. That's you! Aren't they the best? Here, let me put them on you."

I can't find a single thing to say, so I sit there, watching her long, shaking fingernails clip the cuffs onto my shirt.

"They look *soooo* good on you," she says once they're on. "My gawd, you are so handsome. I was so worried, signing up for a dating site, but you are such a catch. Gawd, I bet you're good in bed. Do you love them?"

"Um . . ." Still nothing. No words. My mouth is starting to fill with warm saliva. I feel like those animals that chew off a limb to free themselves from a trap. I would give my right hand to not be here.

"You can kiss me now if you want to," Raylene says. "I'm just saying it would be fine with me, as a way of showing your gratitude. I wouldn't think it was too forward."

Her hand comes down to my thigh, moving higher, and my dick literally retreats.

Right at that moment, Mia looks over to our table for the first time.

Chapter 25

Mia

Q: What's your idea of a perfect date?

*M*y brain attempts to absorb the picture in front of me. Ethan and his date sit side-by-side in the booth, about as close to each other as paint to a wall. And on the table in front of them is a box from Tiffany's.

I can't quite put it together.

Did that ginger giant *propose* to Ethan?

Taking a long and much-needed sip of my White Russian, I lean forward for a better view. Because judging from the location of her hands, she's not trying to put the ring on his *finger*.

"Oh, girl, look at you," says my date, eyeing my breasts with all the bug-eyed subtlety of a cartoon wolf.

I straighten sharply and exhale away my urge to stab him in his

Bettie Page tie with my fork. One thing he's got going for him: he's not afraid to make a statement.

And that statement is: I am gross.

Robby leans back and does this weird chest-massaging thing he's done about sixteen times in the last half hour. Like, *look at my shiny shirt, girl. Let it hypnoooootize you.*

Which would be effective. If I was Baudelaire.

"So, tell me," I say, working to get my mind off Ethan and Ms. Handsy giggling nearby. "Why'd you pick Boomerang instead of another dating site?"

Adam drilled into us that we're not allowed to let on that we work for the company, so I have to be careful about interrogating my date. Still, I need to get *something* out of this evening—other than a headache and a case of contact chlamydia.

Robby snaps his fingers at our server, and I want to leap across the table and break them off at the knuckle. "I'll take another one of these," he tells her, circling the ice in his glass. "What about you, sweetheart?"

"God, yes," I reply and down the rest of my drink in one gulp. "So, Boomerang?"

"Well, you know . . ." His eyes bounce around from my chest to his drink to a trio of girls crossing behind me to their table. He's been doing *that* all night, too—this weird visual triangulation, as though he has to remain ever alert for a more interesting opportunity. Like when he receives an invitation to some nearby orgy. "The DTF doesn't stand for 'Desiring True Friends.'

"Got it."

The server comes with a plate of pot stickers, and it dawns on me that we've only launched into the appetizer portion of the evening. A quiet groan of panic escapes me, but he doesn't seem to notice.

"Go on, honey," he says and pushes the tray over to me. "You look like a girl who can eat. Am I right?"

I freeze. "I . . . What?"

He gets a panicked look, and a blush creeps up his neck, turning his complexion from pumpkin to tomato soup. "Oh, Jesus, I didn't mean it like that. I'm not saying you're fat. You're not. You got some meat on you, sure. But it's . . ." He swigs his vodka tonic, like he can swallow down his stupidity. "I mean you just look like you know how to, uh, enjoy things. Like you're not one of those skinny salad-eating bitches." Another gulp, and his volume dwindles like a wind-up doll running out of crank. "Not that it's, uh, bad to . . . like . . . salads."

Would it be wrong for me to put my head in my hands and start keening? I hear Ethan cough and look over at his table to see the red-haired Mother Teresa brandishing a ceramic spoon in one hand and giggling.

"Oh my *gawd*," she says, brushing at his jacket. "Was that too hot? Did I burn you?"

Was she *feeding* him?

"Uh, no . . . Just shoved that spoon in a little deeper than I expected." He casts a look in my direction, but it's too dark in here to really read it.

"Oh, poor baby," she exclaims, and winds an arm around his neck. Lifting the spoon once more, she says, "Let me try again. I won't put it so far in."

Robby snickers. "That's what *he* said."

I rise from the table like I'm levitating. "I will return shortly," I say in a weird formal tone, like I've suddenly become a dowager countess. I'm pretty sure my synapses have misfired and that I'm about two minutes away from being able to smell colors.

Moving away from the table feels like the best thing that's ever happened to me. I want to stand in the middle of the restaurant and pump my fists at the sky like Tim Robbins in *Shawshank Redemption*. Even better, I want to bypass the ladies room entirely and head straight for my car, but I've learned exactly nothing from Boomerang Client #1, other than the fact that he, alone among males of the species, enjoys sex.

A giant woodcarving of Buddha hangs over the main dining area. I feel like lighting some incense and praying to him for a kitchen fire or an alien attack on the city. Instead, I move through the dimly lit space, passing one happy couple after another. The place is all sumptuous red upholstery, carved gold panels, and soft, sexy lighting, making everyone look absolutely fantastic and blissfully in love.

In the restroom, I snap open my purse and fish out my cell phone, hoping with every bit of me that I'll find a "rescue me" text from Ethan.

Nothing.

And no surprise. I have a close-up and personal view of how well things are going *there*. She's all over him, and he's eating it with a spoon. Literally.

Staring at my sallow complexion under the fluorescent lights, I make a pact with myself. If I make it through dinner without vomiting satay or drenching my date in White Russian, I can spend all day tomorrow in my pajamas, bingeing on *Dollhouse* reruns.

The door swings open, almost clocking me, and in walks Raylene Powers.

"Oh, gawd, sorry," she says, and flashes a bajillion kilowatt smile at me. She has pageant teeth and perfect alabaster skin, though under the unforgiving lights, I can see she's way older than twenty-four.

"No problem," I tell her, and because I'm a glutton for punishment, I ask, "You having a good night?"

"Oh, I'm having the *best* time," she says, moving into a stall and continuing to talk to me while she pees. "I got so lucky. You wouldn't believe it!"

"Really?" I look around for something I can use to hang myself with but come up short. "How so?"

"I let my friends make a profile for me on some dating site. And my first time out, I get this absolute hottie. I can't believe my luck!"

She keeps peeing, and I wonder if she has some kind of disorder.

"And he's nice, too," she adds. "A little quiet, but I think it's because he's into me."

Finally, she flushes and comes out again. At the sink, she washes her hands meticulously, soaping up to her elbows like a surgeon. I hear her singing under her breath.

"Dr. Oz says to sing 'Happy Birthday' twice while you wash," she informs me. Her eyes are a lively chocolate brown, but the whites glow a bit feverishly, like she's just had a face-to-face encounter with God.

"Good to know."

She eyes me. "You're with that cute guy, right?"

"Me?"

"Yes!" She gives me a wink and then leans into the mirror, like she's staring into infinity. "That good-looking guy in the purple shirt. You're with him?" She inserts a fingernail between her teeth, and says, "Got it! God, I think that was there since lunch!"

"Umm . . . Yeah, that's my date."

"Well, I hope your evening goes as well as mine is."

"And I *completely* wish you the same."

"Oh, I've got big plans for mine," she says and drills me once more with a look of low-level mania. "I'm going to drag him home and screw his eyes out." She flutters her fingers at me. "Ta!"

"Ta," I say, as the door swings shut in my face.

Chapter 26

Ethan

Q: Surf, ski, or another word that starts with "S"?

*W*hen our food arrives, Raylene launches into a discussion about her favorite vacation spots, Hawaii and the Desert, which I've learned is what people in Los Angeles call Palm Springs. Because LA is such a rainforest.

"We should go together!" she says, wiping every single bead of condensation off her water glass. "Either place. Or, oh my gawd—*both*! Not anytime soon, don't worry. Just someday. No pressure. It's only a suggestion, but wouldn't it be *so fun*?"

I take a moment to frame an answer that isn't flat-out rude.

"Actually, I'm not much for the beach, Raylene. I grew up in Colorado, so mountains are more—"

"I bet you look amazing in swim trunks." She sets the water glass back in its symmetrically optimal location and smiles at me, wrinkling her nose. "I thought I felt a six-pack earlier. Did I? Do you? Have one?"

The answer is yes. I've always had a strong stomach, but I will eat this entire plate of Chinese noodles—which I can't even look at—before I admit that. "Well, Raylene, I—*whoa*!"

I jam myself against the end of the booth as she reaches for my abs.

"Oh, I'm only playing with you!" She laughs. She retracts her claws and shakes her head like I'm being ridiculous. "Some things are so much better if you wait for them. Anticipation is the best, don't you think? Plus, I did feel a six-pack before when my elbow brushed against you, so I already know!"

As a psych major, I spent a whole quarter learning about the symptoms of shock. I'm definitely sweating. Can't cool down. Shortness of breath? Check. Confusion, anxiety, agitation? Triple check.

Raylene picks up her fork. "Do you also have those lower stomach muscles that sweep down? You know those V-shaped ones? My girlfriend Mona calls them dick indicators. What a name, right?" She covers a smile behind her hand. "My *gawd*! I can't believe I just said that, but I feel so comfortable around you! You're so nice, Ethan. This food is so good. But you're not eating very much. Isn't this night the best?"

"Yeah, the food is really . . . fragrant." The smell in here is going to kill me dead if Raylene doesn't take me out first.

As Raylene takes a few bites, I steal another glance at Mia. She's in professional mode, the expression on her face a little reserved, the intelligence in her eyes out in full, sparkling force. That means she's not into the Robster, which is the only item in tonight's *plus* column. But I hate the fact that he's put away four drinks in the past hour—and that he's still talking directly at her rack.

"Can you believe that, Ethan James?" Raylene says, scaling the walls of my mental fortress. "I mean, it's hard to imagine, isn't it?"

I missed the moment I became Ethan James.

"I, uh . . ." My mind does a little rewind and playback, searching for what I'm supposed to have a hard time believing. "Wow. It really gets to be a hundred *and ten* degrees in the Desert? I can't even imagine that kind of heat."

Which is a fucking lie, because I'm pretty sure that's my body temp right now.

Raylene nods slowly, a smile spreading over her lips. "That heat *exists*, Ethan James. I will prove it to you!"

I tug open the top button of my shirt and stare at my water glass, tempted to dump it over my head. Raylene has officially broken my soul.

It's an asshole thing to do, but as soon as she finishes a few more bites, I ask for the check. A glance over at Mia's table shows me that she and the Robster haven't even gotten their main courses yet, but I can't stay in this booth any longer. I will suffer permanent damage if I don't leave now.

"Aren't you eager?" Raylene says, doing her coy behind-the-shoulder smile. "Okay."

"Sorry, Raylene. It's just that I have work early tomorrow. But I had fun. Best night. And I'll walk you to your car. Jesus, it's hot in here, isn't it?"

Raylene looks at the button I undid and says, "*Very* hot."

"Okay, let's go!" I push her out of the booth, sort of gently, and catch our waitress, who has our bill. I sign my name somewhere on the receipt before she can hand it to me, and then make a beeline for the front door.

I'm outside in two seconds flat.

A steady flow of teenagers weave around me, talking about a slasher movie they just saw, but I just stand there, breathing like I'm in the Alaskan tundra. At the edge of the world. Free again.

Raylene hooks her arm through mine. "I am having so much fun,

Ethan James. So much! My car is this way. I found street parking, how lucky is that? Are you okay?"

She gets under my arm somehow as she talks. I can't imagine it's a very fun place to be as I'm approaching post-soccer match sweat.

"Yeah, yeah. Great." It's time to manage her expectations. "Listen, Raylene. I'm going to walk you to your car, and then I'm going to head home, okay?"

And for the first time, her deer in headlights eyes dim.

It catches me so off guard I almost trip on the curb.

"Okay. Yeah. That's okay. But we had fun, right? This is it right here. Wow. What a night, don't you think?"

She stops in front of a white Lexus SUV, and when our eyes meet, I think she must see the truth in mine because she looks down quickly at her purse. "I guess you don't want me to come over. That's okay. I understand. It's just that I got a sitter and everything."

"Raylene?" I say. "Can I talk?"

She nods. "I know I talk a lot. Okay. Your turn."

"Thanks." I rub my hand over my face, still trying to shake off the heat and stench of Rock Sugar. "Why are you doing this? The cuff links. Hawaii and The Desert. Why all of that? You barely know me."

"You were born in Fort Collins, Colorado, on August 11th. You're mildly color-blind. You played four years of soccer at UCLA, and your favorite book is *The Gates of Fire* by Steven Pressfield."

"Good memory, but that doesn't answer my question. Why all the hurry? Why me?"

Raylene's eyes well up with tears.

Aw, *shit*.

"Whoa," I say. "Raylene . . . I didn't want to make you upset. I was just wondering if you're actually okay."

And that's all it takes to break the floodgates.

"No," she says. "No, I'm really not."

Suddenly, she's sobbing and I can't understand a word she's saying. I manage to get her keys and open her car. I don't know what my plan is. All I know is that she's crying so hard she can barely stand upright, and the same basic instinct that drove me to flee the restaurant pushes me to help her. To give her some privacy while she breaks down.

I get her into the passenger seat then climb into the driver's side.

Rooting around in the backseat, I find a box of tissues. There's also a kid's backpack and a soccer ball back there, and I feel a lump rise in my throat because Raylene is a mom, and moms shouldn't hurt this fucking much. Just thinking about my mom crying like this makes me mental.

"I'm sorry, Ethan," she says between sobs. "I'm so sorry."

"Don't worry about it," I say, feeding her tissues. "This is actually easier on me than dinner was, so no apologies, okay?" That gets a watery laugh, which encourages me. "What happened? What's going on?"

"You really want to know?"

"Yeah." What else can I say? She needs help. "Yes, Raylene. I do."

So she tells me. For the next hour, I hear about the man who was her high school sweetheart. How they married at twenty-three, had a son, and spent nine great years together before, out of nowhere, he walked out on her six months ago. She tells me her heart feels like it breaks every day, every time she looks at her son, Parker, who has no father anymore, and how the divorce is nasty, and how she's too young to feel so used and tired, and how sorry she was again about putting so much pressure on me, on our date, but she'd been desperate for a night, just one night to get her mind off her troubles. To feel young and wanted again. And that all she really wanted was to laugh.

When she's finished, I sit back against the seat, processing it all. My eyes wander across the street to Mia's Prius, and I promise myself that as soon as I can, I'll head back to the restaurant to check that she's okay.

"Admit it," Raylene says as she smooths out the wrinkles of a used tissue and folds it back into its pre-used shape. "You think I'm a mess."

I shake my head. "No. Just a little surprised that we went from dick indicators to divorce so fast, but I'm adjusting."

Raylene covers her face with her hands. "Gawd. Sorry about that. It's just that it's been such a long time. And it feels so good to be able to touch somebody, and I guess I miss it."

I can relate to that. Since Saturday night, I haven't been able to get the five minutes I spent with Mia in her mom's studio out of my mind. I scan the steps leading to the mall for her.

"Well, then admit this," Raylene says, reassembling another used tissue. "Tonight is the worst date you've ever had."

"I'll admit it's a strong contender. But it's not my worst night."

"No?"

I shake my head. "No. Not by a long shot." But I'm not going there. I've experienced enough trauma this evening. If Alison comes into the picture, I'm going to need a straitjacket. So I turn things back to her.

"I'm sorry you're going through all of that, Raylene."

"I know you are. I can tell you are. You have kind eyes, Ethan. I noticed right away." She gives me a sad smile and stares at the refolded stack of used tissue in her lap, letting out a long breath. "What am I supposed to do?" she says, in that sweeping *what is life?* way.

"Let them dry for a day, then put them back in the box. They'll be good as new."

She laughs, and the sound brings a rawness to my throat, because it's a nice sound. And it's a goddamn shame it's so lacking in her life.

"Your son, Parker. Where does he play?" I ask.

"Oh." She glances at the backseat and smiles like he's there. "He was on a team in Laguna Beach, but I had to move closer to my parents so they could help out. So right now, nowhere."

I start telling her about my team, but she interrupts me. "Thanks, but he's not very good. He's used to be, but now he's scared of the ball. He actually runs *away* from it."

"This is my specialty, Raylene. Bring him by. Admit it: you trust me."

She smiles. "I'll admit it. I do."

I give her the details to my Dynamo practices. Then I unclip the cuff links and drop them into her open palm.

"Can you make it home okay?" I ask.

"Yeah," she says. "You're going back for the girl in the restaurant, aren't you? The pretty one with the curly hair?"

I don't know what to say. I'm too surprised she noticed anything earlier besides my stomach muscles and the exact geometry of our place settings.

"It's okay, Ethan. I just saw you look at her a few times. Is she an old girlfriend?"

"No, she's . . . someone I like."

The words sound intense coming out of my mouth, and I'm zoned out as I finish saying goodbye to Raylene, pissed that I've somehow made this thing I'm trying to wrestle down with Mia stronger by putting voice to it.

Someone I like.

Nice fucking going, Vance. Couldn't have said someone I work with, could you? Or someone I slept with. Or someone I split sandwiches with.

Jesus.

When Raylene leaves, I head back to the restaurant, taking the stairs two at a time. I spot Mia outside and instantly see that something's wrong.

"Really, Robby, I'm fine," she says, backing away from him. "I've got it from here. Thank you and good night."

Robby's steps weave as he advances on her. "Come on, sweetheart," he slurs. "It's only nine o'clock."

I walk up and touch Mia's arm. "Are you okay?"

She gives a tiny jump of surprise, then I see her relief. "Yes."

"Who are *you*?" Robby says, behind me.

I turn, making sure Mia's behind me. "Go home, man. Your night's over."

He pushes out his purple chest. "What the fuck is this? You brought *another guy* to our date?"

"He's right, Robby," Mia says. "You should go home."

"Are you kidding me? Bitch, I just bought you dinner."

I step forward, ready to beat the shit out of him, but he puts his hands up and steps away, retreating. "I'm leaving," he says, then looks past me. "Have a great night, you little whore."

I surge after him, but Mia's hand closes on my wrist. "Ethan, don't." She doesn't let go, and I'm dragging her with me as I move after Robby. There's no way I can get to Robby without hurting her. "Ethan, *stop*."

I look at her, but it takes me a second to actually *see* her.

"Are you sure you're all right?" I hear myself ask.

She hesitates. "Yeah. I'm okay."

I take her hand. "Let's get out of here."

I load her into Jason's Jeep without even stopping to consider it. Mia gives me directions to her place, and we're both quiet on the ride.

Part of me feels good about what I did with Raylene, like maybe

I helped her. The other part is pure self-hatred. What was I thinking, leaving Mia alone with that fucking idiot?

Finally, I can't stand the silence anymore.

"Did that shithead touch you?"

"Not really," she says smoothly, like she's been waiting for my question. "I mean he tried. I guess he did enough to shake me up a little, but you saw where we were. There were people around. He wasn't going to do anything . . . real."

For a while, all I can do is hang onto the steering wheel and make sure I don't get us into a car accident.

I lose time after that. I'm on the freeway, then I'm pulling into her parking spot. I cut the engine and stare at the steps to her apartment.

I can't stand myself.

I want to find Robby and hurt him. *Really* hurt him.

And I can't look at her.

She's about to get out of the car and disappear into her apartment, and my only chance of getting through that is by pretending the walkway in front of me is the only thing that exists.

Then I break my own rule and look at her, because tonight can't end like this. There's just no fucking way I'm letting that happen.

"Do you want to come up?" she asks. "Maybe we can hang out a little bit. You know—talk about tonight and—debrief?"

"Yeah. I want come up," I say.

But the truth is, I need it.

Chapter 27

Mia

Q: Do you like big crowds or more intimate settings?

Inside my apartment, I drag Ethan past the dog pile of friends and neighbors piled on my sofa watching *American Horror Story* and head straight for my bedroom.

Usually, I love my roommates, the warmth and chaos of living with this ever-changing tribe of friends and friends of friends. But tonight, I just want to seal myself into a quiet place, even if it's with a person who makes me ache just to look at him.

I switch on the bedside lamp and flop down on my comforter. Mashing all my pillows together behind me, I stretch out and gesture for Ethan to have a seat on the high-backed chair by my desk. What I really want is for him to come sit on the bed, pull me into his arms, and look at me in that way he does—like he *sees* me, like I'm more than just a pair of breasts and a socket in search of a plug. But that way madness lies, so I'm also relieved when he turns the chair around and settles into it.

I watch him take in the gossamer drapes, the white stenciled butterflies on the soft gray walls, and my video equipment stacked on a leather bench at the foot of the bed. Then his eyes come to rest on me, and emotions flit across his face quicker than frames in a film reel. It seems like he's taking this useless night as hard as I am.

He holds out his hand, and I can't help myself; I take it. It's warm and perfectly rough, and I can feel the life of him beating against my skin.

"You really okay, Curls?" he asks.

"I'm okay," I tell him.

But sitting here, so close to him, with Robby's ugly words churning in my head, I realize I'm anything but okay. A hard knot of resentment settles in my stomach, and I can't decide if it's toward Robby or Adam Blackwood or Ethan for giving me a glimpse of something so right and then snatching it away again.

I try to let that go, and say, "Guess we both picked winners tonight, huh?"

Ethan shrugs and withdraws his hand. "Raylene was okay."

I gape. "What? She was a lunatic!"

"She's just . . ." He runs his long slim fingers over the top of the chair, measuring his words. "I don't know. Lonely."

My face heats. Suddenly, the thought of spending another minute with him, rehashing the events of our evening, chatting like *colleagues*, feels as appealing as chewing sand. I don't want to marvel over how fair and compassionate he is. How kind. It's too much. I can't sit here so close to Ethan, in my *bedroom*, and know that I've got any number of RobbyDTF's in my future while this sweet, thoughtful person is completely off-limits.

Working to keep my tone level, I say, "I'm sorry. I know I invited you up, but I think I need to just chill here on my own."

His eyebrows lift in surprise. "I wasn't—"

"I just need to take a shower and curl up for a bit. I'm fine."

He shakes his head. "Can I get a word in here, Mia?"

"Sorry," I say. "Go ahead."

He gets up and comes over to sit on my bed, which makes everything ten times worse. I have to fight tears *and* the urge to throw myself on top of him.

When he looks at me, his eyes are soft and deep as night. "Listen," he tells me. "I need to apologize for the other night. I sounded like an asshole, and I didn't mean to hurt you."

You're hurting me now, I want to tell him. *Just sitting here and not being able to touch you hurts.*

"But it's the right thing," he finishes. "We both have a great opportunity at Boomerang. I don't want to jeopardize that. For either of us."

"I get it," I say. All this time I've wished for the opposite of *that tool* Kyle, someone who knows what he wants. Who makes a choice and stands by it. I should have been more specific. "And it's fine. I'll see you at work tomorrow, okay?"

I feel his reluctance to leave as a palpable force between us. But he stands and crosses to the bedroom door. "Okay," he says quietly. I feel his eyes on me, but I can't look at him. "See you tomorrow."

Cookie, Rhett, and Adam have flown out to Vegas for a pre-planning junket, which means Intern Gulag is now Party Central. True, it's at least partially my fault, as today's employee catnip came in the form of piping hot Fatburgers. What can I say? I'm the Pied Piper of food bribery.

Vanessa—from IT, I think—and Trent from Customer Relations have created a gnarly obstacle course of coffee filters and Styrofoam cups and compete, blindfolded and in rolling chairs, to reach the last burger, placed like a victor's trophy, atop the copy machine in the corner.

"You are my new best friend, Mia," Vanessa tells me, and tugs down one side of her blindfold to cheat her way through a hazardous switchback.

I get my little Canon Vixia out and train it on them while they bump each other off-course, laughing and grabbing at each other's chairs. Watching them stirs an inkling of an idea inside me, something I can use for the Boomerang booth presentation.

Maybe when I put the film together, I can slow down the scenes. Give it a dreamy, romantic quality. I'm not quite sure yet what I want to say, but maybe it's that fun can be meaningful, that something can be short-lived but still worthwhile.

I think of my mother telling me I need to "play" and turn the camera on Ethan, who clicks away—two-fingered—at his tablet keyboard. We're being careful with each other today, but mostly it's all right.

Without looking up, he asks, "What are you doing there, Curls?"

"Nothing. Just ignore me." I zoom in, getting a close-up view of his face, of the rare strands of gold-blond hair mixed in his with the caramel brown and of that little scar over his brow, curved like the indentation made by a fingernail. I move to his full lips and the dimple on his chin, which I see now is off-center by just a millimeter.

Even taken separately, every part of him contains this raw, imperfect beauty. I understand why my mom wanted to take pictures of him, though this Ethan is a lighter one, with sun from nearby windows haloing his skin and creating tiny sine waves on his sweeping dark lashes.

A mottled shadow fills my lens, startling me, and I pull away from the viewfinder to see Paolo grinning down at me. He hops onto the corner of my desk—the spot he's now claimed as his rightful habitat.

"How'd the dates go, kids?"

"Well, I guess I'd rank it right up there with the time you tried out that ménage-à-trois joke on Cookie."

He winces. "Oooh. Rough."

"Yep."

"Okay, I'm gonna hook you up today, Mia, and no arguing, got it?"

"Got it." I sign into my Boomerang account and hand him my tablet. A blind monkey couldn't make a worse choice than I did.

While he scrolls through my options, I walk around and shoot more of Vanessa and Trent, who have cleared off the long kitchen island and now seem to be using tiny Pippa from the Art Department as a kind of human curling stone.

"You won't fall, we promise," Vanessa assures her, but sure enough, she goes careening off the end of the counter on the third pass and ends up sprawled on a case of paper towels.

"Foul!" she cries weakly from the floor.

"She meant you won't fall on the *ground*," Trent says, and hoists her to her feet.

I get a little tingle of excitement because I'm starting to really see it now. Images like this. People playing, having fun, maybe being a little daring. Trying new things. I can film around LA, enlist Skyler and Beth.

Paolo gives a sharp whistle. "Yo, Mia, back to me."

I practically skip back to my desk, excited to start getting some of my ideas down, though less excited by the idea of another painful setup.

"Okay, I've got two options for you. Both primo."

"Lay them on me."

"First . . ." He swipes at the screen. "Brian. Film guy. Tremendous Whedon nerd like you, so total score. *And* he's got a band. Blues and alt covers. He uploaded a video, and it doesn't suck."

"Sounds awesome," I say. And I have to admit he kind of does. "Boomerang him."

"Do you want to look at his picture first?" asks Paolo. "He's a good-looking dude."

"Surprise me. Who else?"

"You go on, Frisky, dating two men at once!"

I smile. "No, I've got to do two more dates. You pick."

"What if you really like this Brian?"

I'm aware of Ethan's attention on me, the weight of his focus.

"I'll figure that out if I need to," I say, not risking a glance in his direction. "But, you know, for research purposes . . . I think it's important to experience, um, a cross-section of the clientele."

"For research purposes, of course." Paolo winks. "Then I present you with King."

"*King*? No."

"Okay, I totally get it. Douchy name. But trust me. He's a writer; you're a filmmaker. He's from New Jersey; you're from New York. I won't even get into the fact that he looks like he could be Drake's twin. I know you don't want to see him, but—"

"Pull the trigger," I tell Paolo. "I trust you."

"I wouldn't steer you wrong, baby," he says, and taps around on the screen a bit. "Okay, two dates, two weeks. You'll thank me."

"I'm thanking you now." Mostly for sparing me from having to pick for myself.

Paolo turns to Ethan. "Your turn."

Ethan pushes back from his seat and rises. "I'm good, man," he says. "Took care of it."

"You did?" asks Paolo.

He did?

"Yep, I'm all set. Thanks." He glances up at the clock. "Hey, Curls, can you give me a lift to soccer practice? My ride won't be back from Vegas 'til later."

"Sure," I say, knowing I'm doomed to spend the rest of the day wondering when he picked his dates and who they are.

Luckily, I actually find myself absorbed in making notes for the booth and talking to Pippa about some concept sketches. I see something cinematic, framed as a movie, but I don't know what style yet, what tone. They teach so many things in film school but there's that "it" factor, that mysterious, instinctive thing that can't be taught. A point of view. A singular way of seeing. I'm not sure I have it, and that terrifies me.

Before I know it, I hear the sounds of chairs squeaking back, people gathering their stuff. They drift by, dumping out their coffee mugs and rinsing them at the sink, gathering up leftovers from the fridge.

Ethan stands and gives his seat a sharp shove into the desk, toppling my camera, which rests on its rubber tripod atop my desk.

"Sorry," he murmurs.

Something's on his mind, I can tell. He gives off an unfocused, impatient energy, though maybe he just doesn't want to be late.

He's quiet all the way to the soccer field.

"At least you don't have to worry about Rhett clothes-lining some little kid today," I offer.

"That's football," he says, with a distracted smile. "But he's coming along later, after he lands."

He unfolds his long body from the car and gets out. "Thanks for the ride, Mia." He gives the roof of my car a little pat. "You have a good night, okay?"

"You too," I say, but he's already shut the door. I don't know what bothers me more: that he barely looked at me all day or that he called me Mia instead of Curls.

He jogs onto the field, and a glimmer of red catches my eye.

It's Raylene. There on the field. With Ethan.

She's in a tight yellow dress and black heels—on a soccer field. She races toward him like they've been separated for ten years and throws her arms around him. Watching them, my chest tightens like I'm in one of RobbyDTF's anaconda hugs.

What's she doing here?

She's got a little kid with her—pale with hair that's orange red to her deeper auburn. He's either her son or some kid she picked up so she could get closer to Ethan.

But that would be crazy, right? A person wouldn't do something like that, would they?

I don't know. Putting my car in drive, I know I better get out of there before I do something crazy myself.

Chapter 28

Ethan

Q: Team player or Lone Ranger?

*A*s I walk up to Raylene, who has a curly-haired kid glued to her hip, I try to gear myself up for the next hour and a half.

In the car the other night, I made it sound like I could help her. *This is my specialty,* I'd said. But what do I know about getting the lives of heartbroken thirty-year-old single mothers back on track?

"Hi, Ethan James," she says, moving in for a hug like we're old friends.

Instead of peeling away from his mother, Parker only slides to her side so he's buried under her armpit. It's the kind of thing you see toddlers do all the time, but he's almost nine.

"Hey, Raylene," I say, patting her back. "Hey, Parker. I'm Coach Ethan. I hear you played left forward on your other team?"

Parker turns away from me, so I'm talking to the back of his curly head.

"*Sorry,*" Raylene mouths.

"It's okay," I tell her. "I've got it from here. You can pick him up at seven."

That gets Parker to look up.

"What?" he asks his mom. "You're *leaving?*"

"Well, I . . ." Raylene looks at me.

"Team policy," I say. "The boys train better without parents around."

Parker throws his head back. "No!" he yells. "I'm not staying here!"

He goes from yelling to tantrum, which is my cue to leave. "I'll be on that field," I tell Raylene and walk away.

As I grab my gear from storage containers, I glance toward the parking lot, but Mia's car is long gone. I wonder what she thought of Raylene being here. Maybe it was close to how I felt earlier, hearing about the awesome dudes she's going to be meeting on her next two dates.

Fuckin' Paolo. The shit-disturber. But it's not like he knew it was torture for me to hear. No one at work seems to have any idea about Mia and me, which honestly is surprising.

I get the team going through warm-ups and stretches, keeping an eye on Parker, who sits at the edge of the fence tearing up grass.

"Where's Coach Sweat?" Tyler asks me. A few of the other boys chime in.

Rhett's an official coach now, cleared through the league, with his own set of keys to the storage lockers, his own team shirt, everything. When I told him he was in, I swear the guy got emotional.

Being around his level of energy can be overwhelming. It's like hanging out with a team mascot. Like he's a fire hose of enthusiasm.

But you can't keep someone like that at a distance for long. Sooner or later, they wear you down.

"He'll be here soon, Tyler," I say. "He's on his way back from the airport."

I'm moving the team into drills when Parker makes his way over and sits against one of the goal posts. I give it a few minutes before I go to him, which works out great, because Rhett's just bounding up, geared up like he's playing in the World Cup.

"Who's the new kid?" he asks, tipping his head toward Parker.

"Long story," I say, fully expecting that he'll want to hear all about it on the ride home.

I sit down next to Parker, who does his eye-contact-avoidance thing again.

He's a sturdy little guy, with wide shoulders, freckles across his nose and his cheeks, and a tough set to his jaw. He doesn't look like the kind of kid who's afraid of much.

"You worried she's not coming back?" I ask.

He scowls at me. "What?"

"Your mom? You keep looking at the parking lot."

"No," he says too forcefully. "I just don't want to be here."

"Yeah, but you are. For another hour."

"Who cares?" he says.

"About soccer? Me. About you? Your mom."

"So? I don't even know you. I don't even *like* soccer anymore."

I nod, absorbing his guarded body language, his defensive tone, and try to imagine what he's really feeling. Like his father doesn't care about him. Like his mother might do the same someday, drive off and never come back. Like there's no point to laughing and kicking a ball around because life is hard and unfair.

I don't know this kid. Not yet. But I actually *do* care.

I jump to my feet. "We're going to do this, Parker."

"Do what?" he asks without looking at me.

It's a good question. I don't really know. So I just say, "You'll see."

At seven, the boys are picked up by their parents. I introduce Rhett to Raylene, the only parent he hasn't met. Then he and I stow away the gear in the lockers, rehashing the practice. As I predicted, the questions about Parker come up on the ride home. I tell Rhett about the date with Raylene and how I offered to help her.

"That's real sweet of you, Ethan," Rhett says.

"I'm going to ignore the fact that you just called me sweet."

"But it is. You don't even know that chick. I mean she's hot and all, but you don't owe her anything."

"I know I don't. I just see something I can do. I watched Parker during practice. The kid's dying to play. I just have to find a way to get the rest of the boys to accept him. I think he's worried about being the new kid. The other thing is getting him out of his own head. Getting him to focus on something besides the fact his dad left and his life's probably in chaos. I'm going to schedule a team-building practice soon. We'll switch it up, do something different. It'll be good. Not just for Parker. The whole team could use . . ."

I stop myself because Rhett's giving me a strange look.

"What?"

"You have, like, a super-coach gear. Like a John Wooden mode. All philosophical and shit?"

"Uh-huh," I say, but the comment spreads through my limbs and into my lungs. I feel like I just drew a deep breath. Maybe I was channeling Coach Williams for a bit there, which is cool. A pretty good guy to channel.

Rhett takes a hand off the steering wheel and makes circles in the air. "Wax on, wax off, Ethan Miyagi."

"Whatever," I say, but I can't keep the smile from my face. A guy who quotes from *The Karate Kid* has to have some redeeming qualities.

Rhett looks at me. "Man who catches fly with chopstick can accomplish anything!"

"I bet that's actually true."

Up ahead on Sepulveda the light turns yellow. Rhett guns it, and the Cooper surges forward. As we fly through the intersection just under the red, his hand opens and he yells, "Clear eyes, full hearts!"

Aw, what the hell.

"Can't lose!" I shout, and give the man five.

At home, I find Jason and Isis curled up on the red or brown or orange couch they bought over the weekend. Neither of them has said anything about the bet they laid on me and Mia hooking up. Isis quietly accepted the win, slowly bringing in new pieces of furniture into the apartment. They've stopped heckling me about Mia completely.

I'm not sure how I feel about that.

"Sup, kids?" I say, kicking the door shut behind me.

Cabin in the Woods is playing on the TV, and a half-eaten pepperoni and mushroom pizza sits on the coffee table in front of them.

"Mandatory study break," Jason says. He's been hitting the books hard this week, and his eyes are almost closing.

"Joss Whedon marathon." Isis taps her rainbow-socked foot on the chair beside the couch. The girl is obsessed with socks, the weirder the better. "Join us."

"Yeah, join us," Jason says. I think he might actually be talking in his sleep.

Zoning out to a movie actually sounds great. But then I remember that Mia's a Joss Whedon fan too, and I don't want to be reminded of her right now.

"You'll have to manage without me." I grab a slice of pizza, eating it as I toss my messenger bag and soccer duffel in my room and head for the shower.

Which reminds me of Mia.

I check my phone when I get out, finding a message from Chris asking me what's going on, why did Mom sound worried about me when he talked to her?

I text him back, telling him he's doing college all wrong if he has time to text me and talk to Mom. Then I pull up Mia's contact information and engage in a very competitive bout of mental tug-of-war, in which I kick my own ass and win the prize of doing what I shouldn't do.

Ethan: All good there, Curls?

I type the message and then stare at it, my finger hovering over the *send* button. I want to know if she's in her room. Or hanging out with her friends, Skyler and Beth. I want to know anything. I just fucking want her.

But I can't break now, especially after I reaffirmed my commitment to our *co-workers only* rule at her place the other night.

I delete the message, then stare at my phone some more, not sure what to do with myself.

I need something else to think about besides Mia. A distraction.

Then it hits me. Maybe I've been looking at these Boomerang dates wrong. If I met another girl, someone cool, maybe that would push her out of my thoughts. I know the odds of that working are slim to none, but I've got nothing else.

Who knows? Maybe my next date will be the answer I've been looking for.

Chapter 29

Mia

Q: Is honesty always your policy?

$\mathcal{I}$'m going to blame it on a brain fog, because under normal circumstances, I absolutely would *not* tear away from the soccer field, drive back across town, and find my way into the Boomerang offices.

Under *normal* circumstances, I'd have zipped home, changed into my comfiest sweats, and flopped onto the sofa while Beth served me a heaping plate of her Poor Girls' Paella, the exact ingredients of which are kept strictly secret—even from me.

But clearly I've snapped some major twig because here I am, slinking along the dimly lit center corridor, on a weird kind of needy girl autopilot that just doesn't feel like me. Or like anyone who's not a cartoon character.

Still, I have to know. Who did Ethan choose for his next

Boomerang date? Raylene? Why is he being so tightlipped about it all? Why do I care? And how can I get off this ridiculous treadmill of clichés?

I can't. Not until I know.

A patch of light oozes from beneath the conference room door, turning the bamboo floor a milky white. Heart thudding, I tiptoe past. Someone's here, working late. Probably doing something more productive and reasonable with their evening. Whoever it is, I hope to hell I don't run into them. I already feel like an idiot.

Of course, that's not enough to keep me from slipping into Ethan's seat, imagining that somehow I can still feel the warmth of his body cradling mine. The oven clock ticks noisily, something I hadn't noticed before, and this little alcove seems especially shadowy and drafty at dusk.

I shiver as I glance around, listening for breathing or footsteps or the Ghost of Common Sense to come drag me out by the hair. And then I pull out Ethan's tablet and power it up. His wallpaper is an image of a soccer dude in a white uniform with beads of silver sweat haloing his head, caught mid-kick. Or mid-block. Or mid-something-intense.

I love the image. It's so Ethan. Beyond the obvious soccer element, it seems like him because it demonstrates someone's passion, his hunger to succeed.

Scrolling through apps, I tap on the Boomerang icon, which loads the site. Ethan's account is ready, the password already auto-filled. Which makes me wonder what I would have done otherwise. Gone home without prying maybe? I touch the screen, try to imagine what words make up that row of asterisks, wishing I knew him well enough to even attempt a guess.

I maneuver right to the "Game On" page and see that no, he hasn't chosen Raylene for dates two or three. This is worse. Date two—Carmen—is petite, deeply tanned, with full glossy lips and the brown limpid eyes of a baby deer. She's a nursing student, into crafting her own wooden jigsaw puzzles, and her profile is so funny and self-deprecating, I practically want to date her myself.

Date three: total disaster. She's beautiful, Asian, and a top-seeded tennis player. Every photo of her is fierce, shots of her on the court or hoisting a trophy, except for one where she's in a micro-dress and thigh-high snakeskin boots. She's arm in arm with another girl. They're making duck faces at the camera, and it's clear they're trying not to laugh.

She's still in school—pursuing a PhD in anthropology with an emphasis on migratory cultures. Someday, I'm sure, boys around the world will have screenshots of this girl on *their* computers.

It's a little tough not to admire Ethan's taste—especially the fact that he's picked girls with smarts as well as looks. And yet the thought of sitting across from him at a restaurant and watching either of these girls flirt and giggle and feed him hot soup is enough to make me want to scream myself raw.

Or, okay, it's enough to make me contemplate something a little evil. Not Cruella-de Vil-wearing-puppies-for-kicks-evil, but . . . Not. Entirely. Kosher.

The darkness seems to thicken around me, and I brighten the screen. Sitting, letting the plan solidify, I scroll through his matches, read over profiles. A part of me shrinks with every model-gorgeous, bright girl whose subtitle is a quote from *Anchorman*. They say LA is filled with beautiful women, but I never knew how many gorgeous, *accomplished* women there were. Holy hell.

If nothing's meant to come of my one night with Ethan and that one amazing kiss, fine. But the least I can do—for myself—is stack the cards in favor of him continuing to find Ms. Wrong. Spare myself the torment of seeing his love connection unfold right in front of my face.

So that's my answer, the sum total of what drove me here like a lunatic. I have to accept that he wants but doesn't *want* me. I don't have to accept that he's meant for someone else.

Judging by his sudden and inexplicable attachment to Raylene, I might want to bypass all the obviously crazy ones. What else will scare him un-stiff? Rodeo clown? Panhandling "freegan" who lives in her truck? I second-guess each one—rodeo clown equals adventurous; freegan equals resourceful and not bound by the trappings of materialism.

I rub my temple while I scroll through image after image, profile after profile. Somewhere in here must be a girl who is one thousand percent wrong for Ethan. An absolute catastrophe. Oil to his water.

Finally, I stop at a profile of a toned blonde in a perfectly tailored gray suit. She's beautiful, but her features seem overly refined, like the maker's tools kept chiseling just a beat too long. Her chin and nose are pointed, and her eyes are wide-set and the gray blue of glaciers. Something in them, an expression of haughtiness or distance, makes me feel like she could turn you inside out with a glance. From her stiff posture to her cool, burrowing gaze, she seems like someone who's never had an orgasm in her life. And doesn't want one.

I read over her details: works for her father's venture capitalism company, loves horses and haute couture, and has a quote from Kierkegaard prominent on her page: "There are two ways to be fooled. One is to believe what isn't true; the other is to refuse to believe what is true."

Uptight, quotes Danish existentialists. Daddy's girl.

I think I've found the *one*.

Chapter 30

Ethan

Q: Get mad or get even?

Everything good with you, E?" Rhett asks me as we hop into the Mini after work.

I have exactly half an hour to get home, change into casual clothes, and over to the Pink Taco—the location for tonight's torture session.

"Yeah. Fine," I say, stuffing my legs into the car.

"Cool, cool," Rhett says. He pulls out of the garage, but I know he's not through with me yet. Rhett picks up a lot more than you think he does. I know that's why Adam trusts him. It makes him great at his job.

"You just seemed preoccupied," Rhett says, making a left onto Santa Monica. "Not like your usual self, you know?"

What can I say? It's the truth. I was probably a bit of an asshole today, if I'm being honest. But I had no other recourse.

My day could have gone one of two ways: I could've worried about my dwindling bank account—and more importantly, the fact that Mia's going on a date with another guy tonight. Or I could've turned all that angry juice into something positive—which is what I did.

While Mia, Paolo, and Sadie played two truths and a lie, and then disappeared to a lunch where they probably braided each other's hair and traded best-friend necklaces, I put my head down and worked on my booth for the Vegas show. Complete professional focus, I've learned, is the only way I can stay sane while Mia sits three feet away from me laughing with people who are—well, who aren't *me*.

The result wasn't bad. I got a ton of stuff done.

"Just working hard," I answer Rhett. "Trying to get things lined up for Vegas." I adjust the air-conditioning vents away from me so they're blasting at Rhett.

"How's that going?" he asks.

"Good. I think I found a DJ for my side of the booth. A guy called Rasputin." Having music at the booth is part of my *movement* strategy.

Rhett makes a face. "You hired an old Russian dude to be our DJ?"

"I don't know if he's Russian, but he's definitely not old. He's only eighteen. Supposedly he's the shit right now. I think I've caught him at the front-end of a huge career."

"Sweet." We stop at a light. Rhett flips his visor mirror down and checks himself out. "And the video game?"

This is my favorite idea—a custom-made game where people can launch virtual boomerangs.

"Also locked and loaded. Jason's cousin, Zeke, designs games for Naughty Dog and he's setting me up. It's going to be super realistic. Projected onto screens so everyone can see it. It'll have a motion-sensitive glove, changeable targets, rankings, the whole deal. Zeke's pumped. I talked to him this morning and he'd been working on it all night."

Rhett grins at me, driving again as the light turns green. "You are gonna kill it, bro. The job's going to be yours."

"That's the goal," I say, but I'm not so sure. Mia's just too damn smart and creative to write off.

For the rest of the drive, Rhett and I talk about the Dynamos and our newest addition, Parker, but my mind is stuck on his comment.

The job's going to be yours.

It should've made me happier to hear that.

Half an hour later, I ask the hostess for a table at Pink Taco. *Specifically* a table. After Raylene, I've sworn off booths.

As she leads me past the bar, I see that Mia's already here—and that her date is, too. I slow down a little, taking a good long look at them, since neither she nor Prince Charming have spotted me yet.

For two days, I resisted the urge to pull up the guy's profile—my lame way of pretending he doesn't exist—but I can't do that anymore. He's right there, on a barstool that's turned toward Mia, a pitcher of Sangria between them.

He's a decent-looking guy. Olive-skinned. Tall and lean, with longish wavy hair that I'm sure girls dig. He's dressed in a dark tailored suit, which makes me wish I hadn't changed into jeans and a casual polo. But, seriously. Who wears a fuckin' suit to grab a burrito?

Mia is still in the floral dress she wore to work, but she's changed her earrings from the small gold stars I noticed earlier. While diligently ignoring her. She changed her hair, too, pulling it into a braid that hangs like a dark rope over one shoulder.

With her hair that way, her small chin and her bright eyes stand out more. So does all the smooth, perfect skin along her neck. She looks delicate—and that makes me want to wrap myself around her.

Or watch her share a pitcher of Sangria with some other dude.

Fuck. These dates are going to kill me.

I shake off the tension in my shoulders, catch up to the hostess and sit my ass down. Then I pull my phone out of my pocket and fire up my Boomerang app. What's interesting about all of this, I think, as I furiously search for Prince Charming's profile, is that I have never been the possessive type—and yet, when it comes to Mia, the girl who isn't even mine, I *am* that guy.

There.

Found him.

Brian Bergren. Originally from Scottsdale, Arizona, plays in a band, and is also currently the personal assistant to an Oscar-winning director who I've never heard of. Brian is looking for dates with someone funny, smart, and interested in the arts. On and on it goes, like a freaking joke. Like I'm reading a list of Mia's ideal characteristics in a guy.

I scroll down to the *Dealbreaker* column, where people usually list things like smoking, drug use, criminal records, but ole' Brian's answer is just adorable.

Dealbreaker: Stanley Kubrick. I can't date anyone who doesn't have at least a superficial knowledge of his work. I wish I were kidding, but I'm not.

How great for Mia.

She's just met herself in attractive male form.

"Ethan?"

I almost drop my phone.

Mia stands across from me, hands resting on the back of a chair.

"Hey—what are you doing here?" It comes out sharp, but she just busted me doing recon on her date. I think.

"I'm on my date." She looks over her shoulder, at Brian Freakin' Kubrick, who's watching us from the bar.

"I can see that. I meant here at my table."

"Oh." Mia looks down at her hands for a second. When she looks back up, her green eyes are a shade darker. I know I'm being a dick. But I can't stop myself. I'm a derailed train. "Well, I got a text about your date. There was a complication or something."

"A complication?"

"A cancellation. Late. A late cancellation." She kneads the back of the seat as she talks. I'm not sure why. Mia doesn't get nervous around me. "Cookie sent me a text, though, and, um—they set you up with someone else. She should be here any minute."

"Great. Thanks for the message, Mia."

"You're welcome. Have fun tonight, Ethan." My attitude's finally getting through to her, because her tone of voice really says *you're an asshole.*

"Oh, I *will*," I say, like I'm planning to take my super-hot un-known emergency backup date up against a wall first chance I get.

Mia cocks her head to the side, her eyes narrowing on me. "Huh," she says. "So will I."

"Awesome. Great."

"Yeah . . . Great," she says, meeting me toe-to-toe.

"So, I'll see you at work?"

"Sure. See you at work." Mia gives a tiny shoulder shrug. "I might be a little late, though. You know. If things go well."

"Ah," I say, nodding. "Nice, Curls. Thinking about going for number six tonight, are you?" I hear myself say. It's actually amaz-ing that I haven't lost my shit right now. Truly amazing.

"Well, it's too early to call. But he'd actually be number five, since you and I never happened."

"We happened, Curls. I guarantee it. Not just once, either. We happened a few times. *At least.*" She rolls her eyes and walks away, but I'm not done. "I'm your number five, Mia!" I yell, like a complete fucking lunatic. "*I* am your *five!*"

A family in the next table looks over their sizzling fajitas at me, but Mia doesn't stop. I watch her join Brian Kubrick—who keeps looking over like he's trying to figure out whether he should be worried about me or not.

I send him a silent message, clearing that right up.

It was stupid of me to worry about her dating another Robby. The guy was an asshole, but he never stood a chance. Brian Kubrick, on the other hand, is a real threat. He has the potential to screw everything up.

If I allowed myself to care, which I do not, I remind myself.

Right. Keep telling yourself that.

The waiter comes by, taking my drink order. He's barely walked away when my awareness shifts to a blond knockout weaving through the tables. She heads my way, looking right at me, and—

The blood drains out of my skull, and my vision grows spotty around the edges, like I'm about to pass out. But I don't. I only watch as she walks up to my table.

Alison.

My ex.

Is here.

"Hi, Ethan," she says, her mouth tugging up in a one-sided smile.

Seconds pass. Lifetimes. Millennia. And I still don't have the capacity to grasp what the fuck is happening.

Alison pulls out the chair Mia had just stood behind and sits down. Her smile fades, and I see two years of memories emerge in her teary blue eyes.

"Thank you, Ethan," she says. "Thanks for giving me a chance."

Chapter 31

Mia

Q: Do you ever feel awkward in social situations?

I walk away from Ethan, one billion percent sure that this little social experiment of Adam Blackwood's is going to turn me off both food and boys for life. A lead weight sits in my belly, and the air inside the restaurant seems suddenly hazy, thick with the cloying sweet-sharp scent of sizzling onions and peppers.

Ethan made me mean, and I *hate* to be mean.

Okay, he didn't *make* me, not exactly. He just brings it out in me—chafes all the raw bits until I want to curl into a protective ball.

I slip back onto my stool next to my date Brian and give him a smile that feels fleeting and phony.

"Everything okay?" he asks. He's got one of those square, boyish faces with ruddy cheeks and a fantastic nose that looks like it's been broken a time or two. His eyes are an almost reddish brown—like cacao plants—and they drink you in, slow between blinks as though afraid to miss a single thing.

I like him.

The thought registers with a rocklike thud in my brain and promises to go absolutely nowhere. Poor Brian.

Reaching for a chip, I nod, swirl it around in a stone mortar full of chunky guac, and stuff it in my mouth with little thought to the effect that garlic and cilantro will have on my breath.

"Yeah, fine," I finally say. "Just a co-worker. Had to, um, chat about some work stuff."

"Seemed pretty intense," Brian says, and gives me this watchful look—all curiosity, no judgment. It makes me want to tell him things. "It also looked like he wanted to rip my head off." He picks up the pitcher of sangria and pours some into my half-filled glass, and then he tops off his own.

"Oh, that's just his face." Even the joke makes me feel dumb and disloyal. Because it's not true. And because it's such a beautiful face.

Jesus, I have to pull myself together. But I feel wired, unsettled. I remind myself of Baudelaire, mincing along the edge of a chair, twitching, a second from flight.

I breathe out, try to come back to the moment, try not to think about gorgeous, jerk-face Ethan.

"What made you sign up for Boomerang?" I ask Brian in the least subtle attempt to change the subject ever.

Out of the corner of my eye, I see a ripple of blue and look up as an absolutely stunning blond girl slinks by. She's in a blue halter dress with a jeweled collar that circles a pale swan neck. Her gray Louboutin pumps cover the distance between the front door and Ethan's table in about five steps.

And then it dawns on me. I'm looking at *her*. My precious ice queen.

Suck that, Vance, I think, dying to swivel on my stool so I can watch the whole awkward evening unfold. I feel guilty for the setup but less than I did before he acted like a jerk tonight.

Brian's eyes flick over for a couple of beats but then dutifully return to me. I like that too. He doesn't pretend not to notice a gorgeous human being. But he's not all ogly and gross. Like Robby. And, I allow myself to admit, like Kyle. That *tool*.

"It seems safer, somehow." It takes me a second to realize Brian's answering my question.

"Safer, really?"

He dips his head to catch a glob of guacamole before it slides off his chip. "Well, to use a filmmakers' analogy, maybe it's like narrowing the aperture a bit." He makes a frame of his hands and looks at me through it. "Like it's less pressure to say, 'I'm focused on this one night, this one date, rather than the first night of what we're both hoping will be an entire lifetime.'"

It seems like a fair answer. A good one. But I can barely home in on it. I know there's a juicy drama playing out behind me, and I'm dying to see for myself.

Brian asks, "What about you?" at the same time that I suggest, "Hey, want to move over to a booth?"

"Sorry." He grins. "Sure."

We tell the bartender. Brian grabs our glasses and pitcher, nodding at me to nab the chips and guacamole. I follow him as he weaves between booths and places us, miraculously, in the perfect spot.

Only my date slides into the booth facing Ethan and the Ice Queen, leaving me to either sit with my back turned to them or slide in next to him, which feels like a signal I don't want to send.

I hover there dumbly for a second, the stone bowl of guacamole growing heavy in my hand.

If I sit next to Brian, I'm saying I want to get close, snuggle up to him.

But I'll be able to see Ethan.

If I sit across from him, I won't come across like some desperate goof with boundary issues, but I won't be able to see the action. Which is kind of the whole point.

Suddenly, the idea of decades more of this dating crap makes me want to smother myself to death in the guacamole bowl.

I set down the bowl and chips and smile at him. Nodding in the vicinity of his lap, I ask, "Hey, mind if I . . ."

Lucky for my ego, he lights up immediately and makes room for me. "Sorry. Of course. I mean, I didn't know if you think it's awkward."

Yeah. It's definitely awkward. I mean, it's not like I'm a trout with eyes on the side of my face. I don't get why people do it. And now I'm one of those people.

I slide in, turning toward Ethan's booth at the exact moment a server comes to stand directly in my eye line, blocking my view.

Come on!

"Dinner, kids?" the server asks. He's got a white-blond televangelist's pompadour and two stylized red "X's" tattooed above his eyebrow, which I realize with some dismay, is actually the Dos Equis logo. I'm guessing he's going to regret that in roughly . . . well, now.

"What do you think, Mia?" asks Brian. "Want to split something? Fajitas, maybe?"

"Sounds great." I try to employ my x-ray vision to see through the waiter's scrawny chest, but sadly don't seem to have them charged up this evening.

Finally, we get through an excruciating process of choosing protein source, flour or corn tortillas, vegetables and other sides until I just want to scream at him to put some goddamn food on a plate and bring it to us already.

He moves away, and my attention zeroes in on Ethan and his date.

I expected to see the untouched drinks, to see Ethan's frown, his posture of disaffection. And I do. He looks miserable. The girl looks

miserable. But it's the wrong kind of miserable. It's—intimate somehow. They lean their heads toward one another. The girl's long pale
fingers rest there, close to him, suggesting she wants to touch him.

"Why are *you* on the Boomerang site?" Jason asks, and the question feels stale, like it's part of a conversation I had sixty years ago.
"What are you looking for?"

I tear my gaze away and murmur, "Good question." But I don't
know what I want except to stop sitting here, burning with curiosity
and miserable at seeing Ethan with another girl. Even a girl whose
company he clearly does not enjoy. "I guess I just want to be . . . I
don't know. Authentic?"

Nervous about tipping into dangerous territory, I gulp the last of
my drink. "I just want to be able to look at a person and say, 'I want
you.' Or 'I really like you so much.' It's like none of us—not me, not
any of my friends, no one I know, will ever just put themselves out
there and say, 'I want to be with you.' We're all scared of giving up
the power of being the person who cares less."

"Well, that's—" Brian begins, though what can he really say to
that?

Ethan slides out of the booth and stands. He snaps open his
wallet and throws several bills on the table. When he turns away, his
eyes lock onto mine, and there's something so sad and tortured in
them that I actually gasp.

"What's wrong?" Brian asks, alarmed.

"Nothing. Just . . . My, um, colleague seems upset."

Ethan stalks past me, and I'm shocked to see the girl—the Ice
Queen—rise and rush after him. Only, as she passes, I can see her
face is blotchy and that tears glitter in her eyes.

"What the hell is going on?" I half hear myself say.

"Lovers' quarrel?" Brian suggests.

But that's impossible. They've never seen each other before.
Have they?

Chapter 32

Ethan

Q: Do you forgive and forget, or hold a grudge?

Alison follows me outside.

"Ethan, what's going on?"

The tone of her voice is so familiar, it sends chills down my spine. I should keep walking. I don't owe her a fucking thing. But she's so confused. Something's not right about this. About her being here tonight.

I stop. "Did you plan this, Alison?"

"No. I thought you did." She appears in front of me, but I keep my eyes on the passing cars. A parking valet across the street catches a set of keys in the air and jogs around the corner.

"I only got your name a few minutes ago," she says. "I got a message with the details for the date. I thought someone was playing a joke on me at first when I saw your name. Then I started to hope you'd finally decided to talk to me."

I look at her for the first time. She's beautiful. It was the first thing I noticed about her years ago, and she hasn't changed. She's beautiful the way an icicle is. Cool and sharp. Not half as fragile as she appears to be.

I swallow and draw a breath and swallow again, trying to figure out what the hell to say.

"So you came here to meet someone else," I say, and suddenly I'm fighting back images of Alison sitting on her bed in her bra, sheets tangled around her, eating takeout Chinese food with another guy. Since that night, she's called and texted me a hundred times. I managed to avoid her. I thought it was over. Until now. "I can't say that surprises me."

Alison winces. "Ethan—" She pushes her long blonde hair behind her ear. "I don't know how this happened. I promise you, it wasn't something I did. But I've been wanting to see you so much. And if you'll just give me a chance, and listen to me . . ."

She falls quiet, wrapping her arms around herself.

A remote part of my mind finds this interesting. Alison doesn't get nervous or flustered. In situations where she *should* be nervous, she becomes ruthless. Lethal. She's like a snake that way.

The valet pops up beside us, out of breath and smiling, his bowtie crooked. "Are you two waiting for your car?"

Alison looks at him. "No," she says. One word but it packs a punch. There's the girl I know.

The valet retreats so fast he practically sends up sparks on the pavement. Then we're alone again.

"Are you dating, E?" she asks, throwing me off. "I guess you are, if you're using Boomerang."

I shake my head. "No. I work there. This is work for me. These dates."

"Oh." Alison actually looks relieved. Her arms loosen around her stomach. "Me too. I work for my dad now. I'm looking into Boomerang for him. He's thinking about becoming an investor."

Alison's father is an investment banker and he's loaded. Big-time loaded. He makes Adam look like a pauper.

I know I should be considering what she's saying strategically. I could bring Adam some inside intelligence. But all I can think is that I told this girl that I *loved* her.

What a fucking idiot. I didn't love her. I loved the fun we had together. I loved the vacations we took. I loved having a girl that every guy wanted on my arm. And at the year mark, if you don't say those words, something's not right. Which it wasn't. But I said them anyway. Now I wish I could take them back. The fact that I gave them to her so carelessly pisses me off.

A breeze sweeps past us. Alison's shoulders give a small shiver. It's a cool night, but I don't feel it. I don't feel anything right now except the desire to leave.

"Ethan . . . I haven't seen anyone since you."

"I don't care what you do, Alison. I stopped caring when I found you in bed with Carl."

"Craig."

"Don't care."

"I messed up. I know I did. And I'm sorry. I'm so sorry."

I draw in a deep breath and hold it, trying to let the rational part of my mind weigh in. What I want is for this to *end,* so I form an answer that will get me there.

"Okay, Alison. You said it. You can go on with a clear conscience now."

"That's not what I'm trying to do. We spent two years together, Ethan. Most of it was amazing. If this is the way it ends for us, then we're throwing away all that time. And I guess—I guess I want to see if we can salvage some of it. I don't mean get back together. Not that I think we would—or that you'd consider it after what I did. But it's like all that time never happened. And I don't like the way it feels to regret so much."

I've had the same thought a number of times. For a while, I was constantly having to edit my past to remove references to her. Anything could trigger a memory I didn't want. The smell of cinnamon reminded me of the holidays with her—Alison always dusts her coffee with it. Other times it was Jason and Isis breaking off in the middle of a story—something the four of us had done together. Even flipping channels, seeing a glimpse of sport fishing, surfing, kayaking, reminded me of the trips I took with her family.

It hasn't been as intense lately, since summer. Since Boomerang. Not by a long shot. But I do get what she's saying. I know how it feels to want to erase your past so it's not there for you to hate. What I'm not clear on is what she's asking for.

"What do you want, Alison?" I ask. "For us to be friends? Is that it?"

Hope flickers in her blue eyes. "I don't know, exactly. I'd like a chance to remake us. I screwed up, Ethan. And I guess I just don't want to lose everything."

Chapter 33

Mia

Q: What scares you?

*L*ight blazes from every window of my parents' house, and the front door stands wide open to the night. A sharp blast of adrenaline punches my solar plexus. I leap from the car and run toward the house without really knowing for sure that I stopped the car or turned off the engine.

"Nana?" I call as I cross the threshold and hurry through the front hall.

I rush through the house, calling to her, starting with her room, which looks as though it's been ransacked. Bureau drawers are pulled out, some even onto the floor. Her closet stands open with piles of clothes puddled beneath pristine satin hangers. Books lie scattered on the floor, and I almost trip on an overturned teacup. But she's not there. Nor is she in my mom's studio, any of the three bathrooms, or in my pop's workshop downstairs.

"Nana! Come on," I call to her, opening and closing the doors of every guest room and of the darkened media space with its half-dozen plush leather recliners and wall-wide movie screen. Everything feels lifeless, empty. I shudder as I head outside through the back door. Foreboding weighs on me, slowing my steps, giving my movements a dreamy sluggish feel.

The palm trees circling the dark garden twinkle with ropes of fairy lights, but they hit me as cloying and artificial, not sexy and festive as they normally do.

I stand there in the hush of night and peer into the shadows, listening.

"Nana?" I whisper, and my voice lifts onto the suddenly stirring breeze. My throat pinches as I shift through the shadows, toward the edge of the property, which drops off steeply down to the canyon below.

A sound off to my left halts me. Branches cracking underfoot. I follow it, sprinting around the koi pond and squeezing through the narrow gap between two poplars to move around the side of the house.

There I find Nana wandering through the yard in her nightgown and robe. The satin sash dangles from a nearby bush, twisting in the evening breeze.

My relief makes me want to ball up and vomit. It also makes me want to punch something in the face.

"Nana, Jesus." I rush across the lawn to her. "What are you doing?"

She doesn't spare me a look, just keeps wandering across the yard, red hair glowing the color of blood in the hazy moonlight.

I'm late, I know, but my parents can't have been gone for more than forty minutes. What happened here? How did she get in this state?

Gently, terrified of frightening her, I tug at the sleeve of her robe. "Nana?"

"Don't just stand there," she demands. "Help me find it."

"Find what? What are you looking for?"

"That girl took all of them," she mutters. "Every last one. She left me nothing."

The girl again. I forgot to ask my parents, but now I'm really concerned. Could she have done that to my grandma's room?

"What did she take, Nana?"

"All the prettiest ones," she replies, and of course that doesn't help.

Again, I think of the steep drop through tree branches and sharp rocks. I think of coyotes, out hungry and roaming in packs. Guilt and shame consume me, not because I leave most of the worrying to my parents but because a deep part of me, the selfish little girl inside me, wants to run away from this as fast as I can. But I don't.

I touch my grandma's shoulder gently but with enough pressure to bring her eyes around to me. They look small and fevered, birdlike and sunken into the wan skin surrounding them.

"It's so dark out here, Nana," I tell her. "Whatever you're trying to find, we'll have better luck in the morning."

"But what if they're gone by then? What if the girl takes them all and goes back on that train?"

Takes what? What train? I want to scream a million things at her, but I know she's confused, that she's overlaying events in her mind. She's in a waking dream so much of the time now that it's so hard to know what's real.

I guide her back into the house where I help her get washed up and changed into a nightgown that doesn't have dirt clinging to the hem. Then I bundle her into bed. In the dim light cast by her bedside table, we talk about her life as a young woman, meeting my grandfather, giving birth to my mother. I can't save her, but I can offer her some touchstones on nights like these.

"I'll find out where the girl put your things," I tell her. "And we'll get them back." All the pretty things—whatever they may be.

I spend a little time reorganizing her room so she's not frightened by its condition when she wakes in the morning. After straightening the house and switching off most of the lights, I bring her a cup of lavender tea and honey, but she falls asleep as soon as I set it on her ebony nightstand.

Her red hair coils in the hollow between her chin and shoulder, and there's something coquettish about the way her face softens in sleep—but strong too. Like the face of Joan of Arc, if Joan fought her battles in Selma, Alabama, and 1960s Manhattan instead of Orleans, France.

I put a few more things away and then sneak from the room, leaving the door cracked open just an inch, the way I liked it when I was a kid. I turn out all the other lights on that side of the house but keep a dim hall light glowing in case she gets up and needs to find her way.

Finally, I sink into a kitchen chair and light the cluster of candles resting in a copper votive holder on the table. Their flames sputter and give off a plastic, chemical scent, but their three golden points warm me and help my bones unknot.

I put my head in my hands and tears come. Just a few. That boat feels farther away than ever, my nana the smallest speck on a gray horizon.

After a minute, I brush at my eyes. She's still here, I remind myself. And with my camera, I have the power to hold her, to keep her with me in some form and share her with others.

That makes me think of Ethan. Before I know it, I've taken out my phone. It's ridiculous, but I miss him. I want the connection. And I want to know what the hell happened at Pink Taco tonight. Who *is* that girl?

>   **Mia:** Hey, everything okay?

The candle flames shrink and stretch. Approximately sixty thousand minutes pass before his response appears.

>   **Ethan:** Define okay

No joke. No, "Hey, Curls."

>   **Mia:** Umm. You're safe, sound, and in one piece?
>   **Ethan:** Two out of three. No way I'm sound.
>   **Mia:** What's going on?
>   **Ethan:** That girl tonight?
>   **Mia:** Yeah?
>   **Ethan:** That was Alison. My ex.

Suddenly, it's like I've gone farsighted. I have to hold the phone
out, concentrate really hard on the blue bubbles and the white type.

How is that even possible? How could I have scanned through
dozens and dozens of profiles and found his freakin' ex-girlfriend?
What are the odds? It feels like it would be easier to go outside and
be hit by a meteor.

Hysterical laughter bubbles up in me, but I pass my fingers
through the candle flame a few times, looking for a little sting
to settle me down, help me make sense of what absolutely defies
sense.

My phone chimes.

>   **Ethan:** Still there, Curls?
>   **Mia:** Yeah. Wow. That's crazy.
>   **Ethan:** Not as crazy as I feel right now.

Mia: Sorry. Should I call?

Ethan: Nah. I'm beat. Want to pretend it was all a bad dream. Or a bad joke. Which reminds me.

I wait, and when nothing more comes, I say:

Mia: ???

Ethan: I'm going to kill Cookie for pulling this shit on me.

Oh, *crap*.

I start typing an answer to Ethan, telling him that *I* switched his dates, that it wasn't Cookie but me. But each time I try, it sounds crazy—like something a psycho jealous girlfriend would do. It doesn't seem like me, and it sure doesn't seem like something he'll understand. At least not right now.

I'm on my fifteenth effort when another message comes through.

Ethan: I'm out. Doing breakfast with the ex, but get there early for the show. Cookie's going down.

Mia: Don't do anything crazy.

Which could mean either seeing his ex again—why would he do that?—or antagonizing Cookie, who didn't have a thing to do with this. Both paths seem like bad, bad choices. And both paths seem like ones I've laid for him myself.

Chapter 34

Ethan

Q: Do you live more in the past, the present, or the future?

I manage maybe two hours of sleep, then I meet Alison for breakfast at John O' Groats, where I push some food around while we both act like we can do this. Remake ourselves. Or whatever the fuck it is we're doing.

Alison asks me about my parents and my brother. She asks about the Dynamos and Jason and Isis. She chips away, getting me to talk about the people and things I care about until I start to relax in spite of myself.

Then she asks about Boomerang.

"What's Adam Blackwood like?"

"Mixing in a little work, Alison?"

She smiles, a little guiltily. "I was just curious. Dad's trying to get a read on him." She takes a sip of her latte—dusted with cinnamon—and picks at her egg-white omelet. "Do you like work-ing there?"

"Yeah, I do. I've met some really good people."

My mind does a stop and pivot, suddenly one hundred percent focused on Mia. On her green eyes and sweet smile. The way she felt the night I kissed her in her mother's studio. She was so responsive, so turned on. I want that again. I *need* that.

Alison must sense that I'm distracted because her eyes narrow on me, then take on a resigned sadness. She looks down at her latte. "It means a lot to me that you're here, Ethan."

"I almost blew it off."

"I probably would have if our situation was reversed."

"Maybe not," I say. "Give yourself a little credit."

She continues to stare at her coffee, but her eyes begin to fill with tears, which shocks me. Prior to this Remaking Us campaign, I've only seen her cry once, when her horse, Zenith, broke a leg and had to be put down. I pull a napkin out of the holder and hand it to her, flashing back on Raylene. This is starting to become a habit for me.

"Thanks." Alison takes it, but she tucks it beneath her plate. She's already gotten herself under control again. No hour-long cry for her.

"How's your mom?" I ask, because it feels like I should.

She looks up and pastes on a smile. "Oh, you know. Raising mil-lions of dollars for charity. Doing lunch. Getting Botox. The usual."

Her mom is a piece of work. She's the most self-absorbed human being I've ever known. I don't know what to say next, but I'm saved when her phone buzzes.

"It's my dad," Alison says, fishing it out of her purse and declin-ing the call. "I told him I was seeing you this morning."

Okay. This is awkward. "Tell him I said hi."

"You know him. That's not going to cut it. He'll ask me a hundred questions about you, then decide to call you himself. He wanted to call you weeks ago when we—ended. I swear, he almost disowned me. He misses you."

I smile, because the idea of her dad missing anything except making money is hard to imagine. He's a shrewd entrepreneur like Adam, but where Adam seems to have fun in business, Alison's father is ruthless. Graham Quick and I have nothing in common, which makes me both nonthreatening and interesting to him. Plenty of times on trips it felt like he wanted to spend more time with me than with Alison.

That is one screwed-up family, but I got along with them okay.

"Well, tell him he can call anytime," I say.

"He'll probably ask you to golf with him."

"That'd be great. I'd love to school him again."

"He'll keep inviting you until he wins."

"Then we're going to be playing a lot of rounds."

Alison's smile fades and her long fingers flatten on the table. "You bring out the best in people, Ethan."

I can't believe what I'm hearing. And I can't take this non-Alison character any longer. I have to call her out. "You're pretty different, you know that?"

She shakes her head. "No . . . I'm not. Only with you, Ethan, believe me. I guess I have nothing to lose and everything to gain." She straightens her back in a familiar gesture. It reminds me of all the times I've heard her mother harp on her for slouching even when she wasn't. "And I mean what I said," she continues. "About you. I think that's why I held onto you so long."

"Because I was your life coach?"

"No. Because you were my life preserver."

I'm emotionally beat up by the time Alison drops me off at work. I need time to think, to process, but as the elevator rises to the seventeenth floor, my numbness wears off and I remember how Alison happened. Mia's words at the restaurant last night come back to me.

Cookie sent a text. . .

I take off like a horse out of the blocks as soon as the elevator doors open, barreling through the lobby, down the hall and straight into Cookie's office.

I find her sitting at her desk, signing a stack of documents with a sleek silver pen as Paolo watches on.

"What the hell are you trying to pull, Cookie?"

My entire body pulses with anger.

The silver pen stops, and Cookie looks up. "*Excuse* me?"

"I know what you did. If you didn't like Mia and me going around you to Adam about the booth, fine. But that was a *low* way of fighting back."

Cookie rises from her desk in slow motion, her eyes the same color as the pen clutched in her hand.

"Mr. Vance," she says, sounding more professional than I've ever heard her. "I don't have any idea what you're talking about."

"Come on . . . Are you trying to tell me what happened was a *coincidence*? Don't pile on the BS now."

Paolo has turned pale at her side. For an instant, I wonder if I've made a mistake. That maybe some crazy glitch happened, where my original date canceled and the Boomerang algorithms kicked in and reassigned my ex to fill the gap.

But there's no way that happened. This shit did not happen organically. Cookie was pissed about Boothgate and found her perfect weapon in Alison. She's probably been planning it for weeks.

"O-kay," Cookie says, in a forced chipper voice. "No more piling on the BS. Understood, Mr. Vance. Oh! Speaking of coincidences, it's simply perfect that you're here because I had something I wanted to tell you. About the show? Your booth budget has been reduced. Effective immediately. That's all me, not Adam—God forbid I *BS* you anymore. You'll have to eliminate your precious video game from your plan. Now get out before you upset me, you irrational little peon." She drops back into her chair and starts signing again.

Before I do something *really* stupid, I force myself to leave.

I knew it. This is war.

Word spreads around the office at lightning speed. No one says anything to me, but I can feel that everyone's heard. Whenever anyone comes by the kitchen, there isn't the usual chatter. They just grab coffee in silence and go.

Mia is quiet too. She keeps her focus on her work, barely sparing me a glance. As the hours drag by, I get the impression I've disappointed her somehow, and that's the part that sucks the most. Her checking in on me last night was the only thing that kept me from losing my mind. Just knowing she was thinking of me, even if it was just for a small part of her night, made a difference.

Now I feel like a villain in her eyes and in this office—exactly the opposite of what I've been working toward. I've given my best to this company, and I know I'm doing good work. It's unbelievable that one below-the-belt attack by Cookie could screw up everything.

Three months ago I had all this forward momentum. College graduation. Dreams of landing this great job and paying down loans before moving on to law school. Now I'm somehow doing this backward slide and I can't find a way to pull myself out of it.

I don't realize it's noon until Mia stands and grabs her purse. "Can I take you to lunch?"

"Sure," I say, before I can think about it.

We walk to the garage and climb into her car in awkward silence.

"I'm not hungry," I say. "So whatever you want is fine. I'm just along for the ride."

Mia's hands come off the steering wheel. It's dim in the underground garage, and I can only see the contours of her face, but I know this look of hers. A mixture of understanding and warmth.

The tension lets out of my shoulders, and I realize that's all I've wanted all morning. To see her look at me with that expression.

"It'll blow over, Ethan," she says. "You know how Cookie is. But I'm sorry about the video game."

I make a mental note to strangle Paolo for being so accurate in his gossip spreading. "No need to be sorry. I'm still doing it."

"You're . . . What?"

"Cookie approved the funds for the game already. I'm not calling Zeke to cancel it."

Mia shifts so she's facing me. She's wearing a tight white dress that hugs her every curve, and I kinda want to thank her. Her hotness is a welcome distraction from all the life crap I'm dealing with.

"Ethan, are you sure?"

"Yeah. I'm sure. It feels like Cookie is—I don't know—hazing me or something. Anyway, there's no way I'm backing down." I smile. "You should be celebrating. The job's pretty much yours now, Curls. Congrats, winner."

Mia leans back against the headrest. "No . . . We'll fix this, Ethan. I'll help. I promise."

A weird emotion claws up my throat. My hands fist with how much I suddenly want to hold her. If I could just hold her right now, none of this would fucking matter to me. Not Alison or the goddamn video game that's going to get me fired. Yeah. Holding her would "fix this," and I have to bite the inside of my cheek not to ask her for that.

I set the rules, after all. We're coworkers. Coworkers don't cuddle.

So I play-punch her on the shoulder instead.

"Hey," I say. Time to lighten the freakin' mood. "Want to go bowling with me and eleven nine-year-olds tomorrow night?"

Chapter 35

Mia

Q: Are you the sporting type?

No one should look this good in a pair of bowling shoes, but of course Ethan looks like a god. Like he should be in a loincloth, flinging a discus instead of hefting a sapphire-blue bowling ball and staring down the pins as though they've personally insulted his mother.

The alley is neon-lit and retro. Every server looks like Rosie the Riveter or an escapee from a swing band. They circle with heaping platters of wings and bowling-pin-shaped beer glasses.

I drift around for a bit, filming the couples there on dates, the single-girl bowling leagues checking out the single-guy bowling leagues. But time after time, my lens finds its way back to Ethan.

All around him, a squirming battalion of nine-year-olds wrestle, knee-bounce on the fake leopard skin and vinyl benches, and gener-

ally create a moving cloud of pandemonium while Rhett tries unsuc-
cessfully to marshal them into teams.

"Come on, guys," he says. "Let's see a little discipline."

He's already made the mistake of letting them enter their own
names into the computer for scoring, which means that my bowling
compadres have names like "DUCK LIPS" and "MR. BUTTS."

Ah, nine. Such a precious age.

Ethan rises up on his toes, lunges forward a few steps, and fires
a missile down the alley, practically shattering the pins. A strike. Of
course.

"Way to go, Coach!" says a husky kid with a white-blond faux
hawk.

Ethan swivels and grins. Jerking a thumb at the pins, he says,
"You're up, Butts." Which of course makes the kids hysterical.

For now, it's just Ethan, Rhett, the kids, and me. Most of the
kids, that is. I don't see Raylene's son or Raylene yet.

I need to head out early to make one of Skyler's concerts, but
I *have* to tell Ethan that I'm the one who switched the Boomerang
date. The guilt is chewing away at me, and I've already spent three
whole days watching Ethan commit professional suicide without
being able to cough up the words.

I take a deep breath. Then two more. Then give myself a pep talk
along the lines of "Mia, don't be such a chicken," and then I part the
sea of sticky boys, most of whom smell like fried food and ozone.

I can totally see why Ethan loves what he does. They're awkward and hilarious and think calling someone a "Pooptart" is the
funniest thing ever. Which it kind of is, especially when a tall Asian
kid changes Rhett's name on the computer to just that.

Ethan's got one of the kids, this one with a light-brown buzz cut
and huge ears, in a head lock and is giving direction to the blond
kid—Mr. Butts. "Stand back. Keep your shoulders square to the foul

line. When you swing the ball forward, release it about two seconds before it's parallel to the floor. Got it?"

"We'll see," says the kid dubiously.

Ethan releases the other kid—Buzz Cut—and fishes in his pocket for a couple of dollars. "Shit."

"Coach Vance!"

"Sorry, *shoot*." He looks up at me, frowning. "Can you chip in a few bucks? I want to get them some pizza or something."

I practically throw two twenties at the kid, overjoyed to put something back into the good karma column, even though it's a pretty meager offering.

"Cool! Can I keep the change?" asks Buzz Cut as he starts off toward the food counter.

Ethan nudges him in the backside with his black bowling shoe. "Don't be a smart guy. Get a couple—one plain, one pepperoni. And some lemonades or something." He points at another kid. "Tyler, go with him. I'm putting you in charge of bringing Ms. Galliano her change. Got it?"

Ms. Galliano makes me think of my aunt or some other mature person who isn't standing around waiting for an opportunity to confess to doing the dumbest, most impulsive thing ever.

The kid gives me a shy look and nods, though he seems to be rendered speechless.

"Tyler," Ethan adds, exasperated. "Go with him means, you know, actually *go with him*."

"Right," says Tyler and promptly trips up the two carpeted steps to the main floor of the alley. Even with the neon amber tingeing his skin, I see his deep splotchy blush as he scrambles to his feet and hurries away.

"Hey, Tyler, get me a beer, will you?" says one of the other kids, and he and his buddies fall over themselves laughing.

Ethan smiles. "Who knew that taking them off the soccer field would make them lose their minds?"

With the sound of pins crashing all around us, we watch two kids go up side-by-side in neighboring lanes and await their turns to bowl. Each follows Ethan's directions, squaring his body, bouncing gently on the pads of his feet. Politely waiting for those nearby to take their turns.

I'm going to lose my mind if I don't do this thing.

Clearing my throat, I say, "Hey, Ethan—"

But the kid on the left swings his arm back, and the ball flies out of his hand, crashing into the throng of nine-year-olds goofing around over the ball return.

One of the kids screams, "My foot" and topples over, knocking another ball out of the hands of the kid nearby. That ball rolls away, toward a family with three little girls who scream when they see its slow advance, like it's a freight train bearing down on them.

We split like seven and ten pins, me to rescue the ball before it gently nudges the tiny foot of a five-year-old girl and Ethan to conduct triage on the Gordian knot of writhing boys.

The dad of the other family scoops up the ball and hands it to me with a smile, then wisely shuffles his girls off to sit on the bench farthest from us.

"Thanks." I return to help restore a bit of order though anyone looking at my life at the moment could tell you this is *not* my area of expertise.

Ethan sets the one kid—Milo—down on a bench and kneels in front of him to untie his shoe. "Okay, buddy," he says. "I'm just going to take a look at your foot and see if anything's broken, okay?"

Milo nods, and Buzz Cut, who's returned from his pizza-ordering mission—plops down to hang over his friend's shoulder and watch.

"Oh, *Gawd*, what happened now?" asks a voice from behind us. I look up to see Raylene hovering over us, her red hair teased to super mall heights. She wears a white denim wrap dress and stiletto heels that are most certainly not lane-approved.

"Hey, Parker," Milo says, and some of the other boys murmur their greetings as well. I can see right away that they're being gentle with him in that surprising way kids sometimes have of being protective where it would be easy to be rough.

Parker eases out from behind his mom to approach the injured party. "What happened?"

And then Rhett comes up, chest puffed out strangely and, I swear, an extra button unbuttoned on his skin-tight bowling shirt. His scarily angular face is all softness now though, and his eyes sparkle in a way that I've only seen when he's scored a soccer goal or fired someone.

"Just a soldier down on the field of combat," he booms, and Raylene laughs with all the teeth going, and it's clear these two are going to end up together sooner rather than later, which makes me happy, relieved, and curious to know whether they'll destroy small villages in the heat of their lovemaking.

Ethan moves the kid's foot around and squeezes a few toes. "Nothing broken," he says. Then he slips the bowling shoe back on and gives it a pat. "But this foot's a whole size larger now."

Milo grins and slides off the bench. "I'm gonna change my name to Big Foot!" he exclaims and rushes over to the computer.

Ethan looks after him, a sweet smile on his face, and then turns to me. "Crisis averted," he says, as he rises.

One of them, anyway.

"Hey, can I grab you for just a second?" I ask. "Before everyone else comes?"

"Sure, what's up?"

"Just . . ." God, I'm going to look like such a jerk. Fitting enough, I guess, since I am *actually* a jerk for doing what I did. I suck in another couple of breaths and wave him over a few steps away from everyone, moving us closer to the crane machine and the tiny arcade near the front door.

He keeps looking back at the kids. "I can't go too far."

"I know," I tell him. "This'll only take a second anyway. I just feel like I need to—"

But his eyes move away from me, and something unreadable passes over his face. "Uh, hold on," he tells me and starts away.

"Wait, Ethan."

"One sec, I'll be right there. Keep an eye on them, okay?"

He hurries away, and my stomach tumbles when I see the reason why.

Apparently Alison has come to bowl too.

Chapter 36

Ethan

Q: Box of chocolates or bag of chips?

I'm jogging over to Alison when it hits me: of all the dumb ideas I've ever had, bowling with my soccer team, my ex-girlfriend, and Mia definitely wins the prize.

It's going to be a hell of a night.

"Hey, Alison. You're here." I lean over the pink baker's box in her hands to give her a hug. "What's this?"

"Just a little surprise I had made for the team." She opens it and does a little flourish with her hand. "Ta-dah."

More than a dozen cupcakes are packed inside, white frosting crisscrossed with chocolate lines to make them look like soccer balls. Only one at the center is different and my mouth starts watering the second I see it. Chocolate hazelnut turtle cupcake. My favorite.

The gesture is vintage Alison, so I'm not surprised. She's always been one for giving, sometimes extravagant things. In the past there was always a trace of desperation to her generosity, like I was a skittish animal that might vanish into the mist without a steady diet of custom Nikes and designer shirts and expensive dinners out. But these cupcakes feel different. I see it in her eyes. She doesn't expect anything back except my gratitude, which she has.

"These look great. Thanks." I nod to the boys. They've formed a line behind the foul line, all except Cameron, who's swinging a bowling ball back and forth, about to toss it through a tunnel formed by ten pairs of spread legs. Somebody's going to get hurt again, maybe castrated, but thankfully Rhett stops Cameron just in time. "If it's okay with you, let's hold onto these until the end, otherwise they could go atomic."

"I think that's wise," Alison says, her eyes going wide at my team's antics.

"Okay." I hesitate for a second. When she texted me this afternoon asking if we could talk again, I figured we could do it here: a nice, loud public place that's about as unsuitable for heart-to-hearts as you can get. I'm fine with talking again, surprisingly, but I have zero interest in putting myself in any situation with her that feels remotely intimate. That shit's never going to happen again. Ever. But I didn't think this through very well. With the team here, I won't be able to talk to her for another hour. "I'm tied up for a bit, but—"

"It's okay, Ethan. Go ahead," she says, waving me away. "I'll grab a drink and hang out until you're free."

"Okay." Once again she's unrecognizable to me. This girl is a hundred times more easygoing than the one I dated. I'm half expecting her to unzip her skin like a Scooby Doo cartoon.

As I head back to our lanes, I look for Mia, wondering what she'll make of Alison being here. I find her kneeling in front of Parker, tying his bowling shoes. She's comfortable right in the middle of the chaos.

For the moment, Rhett's got the boys in some semblance of order, so I sit next to Parker. Mia glances up, catching my eye for a split second, before she turns back to her double knot.

"Everything okay, Parker?" I ask.

"My mom forgot to double-knot my bowling shoes even though I told her three times to do it but it doesn't matter because they feel like they're too big anyway," Parker says. Then he does this exasperated exhale thing that makes his red bangs float up for a second.

"You want me to get you a smaller size?" Mia offers.

Parker shakes his head quickly.

I smile, remembering how it feels to be that age. A pretty girl already makes you mute, though it's years before you realize why.

"My dad, Shep?" I begin, thinking of a story that might help me get Parker past his reluctance to bowl. "He owns an alley in Colorado, where I grew up, and—"

"Tyler told me," Parker interrupts. "He said you learned to shoot goals there. In a bowling alley."

I smile. This is a good sign. Parker was my main motivation for putting this night together. He's been coming to practices, but he hasn't joined in yet. He's only watched, which is also what he's been doing tonight. Or so I thought. Tyler's my ringleader, and if he's starting to talk to Parker, accept him, then things are looking up.

"Yep," I say. "That's true, but back to my dad. He thinks too many people rush through their approach—the steps you take just before you bowl. He says when you're wearing shoes that are too big, you have to slow down so you don't trip. He has this theory that most people end up bowling better in big shoes."

Parker is quiet for a moment, staring at me with too much intensity for a kid.

"Is it the same thing with soccer?" he asks. "Would big shoes help? I mean big cleats?"

"Help what? Score lots of goals? Kick with lots of power?"

I sense Mia smiling in my peripheral vision. I want to look at her, but I don't dare break eye contact with Parker. He's listening to me. He's finally *hearing* me.

"Power," he says. "I want to kick hard and far. Like you do."

I cross my arms and gaze across the lanes like I'm thinking about it. "How about adding accuracy to that list?" I ask. "Power and range don't mean much if you can't kick where you're meaning to."

"Yes," he says before I've even finished speaking.

"All right, sure," I say. "I can teach you that. No special shoes required. But you'll have to keep coming to practices. You'll have to *participate*. Not just watch. And you'll have to work hard."

It's not the most rousing speech I've ever given, but fancy words aren't what he needs. If I'm right, Parker just needs to believe that I won't make him promises and then disappear—and that he has a place in the Dynamos that's his, no matter what.

"Fart Knocker?" Rhett yells, breaking the little cocoon that's surrounded us. Rhett squints at the scoreboard, then looks around. "Guys, listen up. Hey, guys! Does anyone know who Fart Knocker is?"

Parker jumps up. "Gotta go." He stops at the ball return and turns around, locking eyes with me. "But yes, Coach. Okay."

Mia straightens and slips into the seat Parker just vacated. She's wearing a smile on her face—I feel it even without looking at her.

"You look mighty proud of yourself, Coach Ethan."

"Yeah . . . I like that kid."

"Is he your favorite?"

"If by favorite you mean that he's the one I think about the most, then yes. He is." *That definition would also make you my favorite girl,* I think. Then I mentally beat the crap out of myself. "Parker's just had a tough time, you know?"

Mia shakes her head, her curly hair shifting over her shoulder. "No. What happened to him?"

I lower my voice, though there's no chance anyone's going to hear us with the noise. "His dad walked out on him. On them," I say, nodding to Raylene. Only then do I see that Raylene is sitting with Alison. Two glasses of white wine sit on the table in front of them. It's like I've stepped into an alternate dimension.

"That's sad—poor guy," Mia says, her brow creasing with concern.

My eyes drop to her lips, to the soft pink shine of her lip gloss. It'd be so easy to just bend down and taste her. My willpower disintegrates when I'm this close to her, so I lean back a little and focus on my bowling shoes. "I can relate to him, in a way."

"I thought your parents were together," Mia says. "You told me they're still crazy about each other."

"They are," I say, noticing that she remembers the things I say almost verbatim. I wish I hadn't noticed. Knowing that isn't going to make my life any easier. "I just meant that I know what it's like to have someone you trust disappoint you in a big way."

Mia blinks at me. "What?"

"Nothing . . . Never mind." I don't want to bad-mouth Alison—especially since she's here. I grab Mia's hand and pull her to her feet. "You're up, Ms. Hubba Hubba."

Her eyes lift to the scoreboard above. "Hubba—what? That's not me. One of the boys entered that."

I grin. "Wonder which one." I tow her out to the lane, stopping to grab her bowling ball on the way.

"Ethan, I'm allergic to sports," Mia says, as she tries to squirm out of my grip. "I told you this! I even carry an EpiPen."

"Just try it. It's not going to kill you." I hand her the bowling ball, which tips her forward as she absorbs the weight.

The boys have all stopped what they're doing. They stand in a line, as still as they've been all night. Then Milo catcalls, "Coach

Vance is touching his *girlfriennnnd*," and suddenly they're all snickers and nudging elbows.

"I'm serious, Ethan. I could gravely injure you." Beneath her smile, I can tell she is actually concerned. "I break windows when I try sports. I break *bones*."

"It's okay. You're in the hands of a professional." I fix her grip on the ball. "You're going to bowl a strike, right here, right now." I take her hips and turn them a bit. Then I walk around her and adjust her arm, then pull her shoulders back. The boys start chanting, "Mi-a! Mi-a!"

"Are you done?" she asks, looking miserable. "Can I go now?"

"No, you're all crooked."

"You just put me in this position!"

"Yeah, it didn't work. Relax, Curls. We got this." I step behind her, thinking I'll help her the way I learned, with my dad guiding my motion. But the instant my body lines up with hers, I know I've made a mistake. A big one.

Her incredible violet smell invades my nose and throws my body into immediate chaos. Heat shoots through me, and I'm suddenly doing everything I can to not think about how good she feels against me.

"You hold it this way." I wrap my hands around hers to show her how to hold the ball, but less than one percent of my mind is still thinking about bowling. I'm getting hard for her right here, with people everywhere, but I can't talk my goddamn dick down when I'm pressed against her ass. There's just no way it's happening. I keep talking, because what the hell else can I do? "Swing straight back and straight forward. You're going to want to let go right when . . ."

"Ethan," she says.

Just that. Just my name, but it's like a plea and a demand rolled into one.

"Yeah?" I say, my voice sounding hoarse and deep. There's something so familiar about this. About her pressed against me this way.

"What are we doing?"

She's turned into a statue in front of me. A statue with soft curves that are driving me insane.

"Not what we want to be doing," I answer.

The words spill out of me at the speed of truth.

Mia darts away like I've stung her and chucks the bowling ball. It lands in the gutter with a crack and bounces into the next lane, where it begins the slowest roll imaginable. Eventually, it makes it to the end of the lane and disappears.

The boys fly into hysterics, but Mia looks up at me. I hate the hurt and anger in her green eyes. It sends me crashing from the high I was on moments ago, with her body against mine. I get the feeling I should apologize, but I'm not fucking sorry. What just happened felt too good for me to regret it.

Without a word, she hops off the lane and heads over to Rhett—who's standing with Raylene.

I can't go after her right now, so I force myself to get back into coaching mode. I spend the next hour trying to keep the boys from breaking fingers and toes, with the occasional success of actually sending a ball down the lane.

My mind never completely bounces back though. I keep thinking about the hurt look in Mia's eyes. Since that night at her parents' place, I've fought off desire for *weeks*. Tonight, desire fought back and it kicked my ass. By touching her the way I did, I violated the understanding we had—the one *I* championed—to be friends and coworkers, and nothing more.

Yeah. Regret just showed up after all. Bastard.

As seven o'clock approaches, I gather the boys to say a few words like I always do at the end of practice. Past the elbowing, fidgeting boys, their parents stand in a semicircle. Mia is there. She doesn't seem angry anymore, which loosens the tension that's been coiled in my shoulders for the past hour. It's only then that I remember she wanted to ask me something earlier, just before Alison showed up.

Alison is back there too, holding the baker's box, and Rhett stands next to Raylene. My eyes snag on them for a second, seeing the unmistakable signs in their body language, and my mind makes a calculation. Rhett plus Raylene equals *whoa* . . . How did I not see that coming?

I lean on the ball-return machine, bringing my attention back to my team. "So, guys. What did you learn today?"

"I want to have my tenth birthday party here."

"The pizza here is so good!"

"Mr. Butts bowled two strikes!"

"Okay, okay," I say. "Anything else?" I look at Tyler, praying the kid will give me a break.

"Yeah," he says. "Being on this team rocks. But I already knew that."

"It's a good thing to learn again, isn't it?" I ask. "A good thing to be reminded of?" A few of their heads bob, telling me I've got them where I want them. "What do I always say about being on this team?"

"That it's less about *me* and more about *we*," Cameron offers.

"That's right. You guys play as much for each other as you do for yourselves. I think we did a good job of working on *we* today. What do you boys think?"

A chorus of shouts rises up around me. "All right. Good job to-night, Dynamos. Go see Alison before you leave for a cupcake and remember to say thank you."

Usually it's a jailbreak at this point, with kids stumbling over anything in their path to get going, but no one moves.

"It's all paid for, boys," I say. "If you turned in your shoes, you're free to go."

Milo, who's sitting cross-legged on the floor, reaches into his soccer bag and pulls out a ball.

A *soccer* ball.

He rolls it my way across the shiny floor. I know what they're going to ask me before I trap it. As usual, Tyler speaks for the group.

"I asked my dad to talk to the bowling alley owner, and he said it was okay. That you could do it. But just once and just you."

I look at eleven faces, trust radiating from their eyes. As much as I don't want to do this here, in this place that's so much like home but isn't, there's no way I'm disappointing them.

I hear a few squeaks of excitement as I bring the ball to the foul line and back up.

As I check in with how natural this used to feel, recalling the right amount of power, the right pin to aim for, quiet falls over the lanes around me and then farther, until all I can hear is the pulsing beat of a Rolling Stones song piping through the speakers.

I have an audience, but that doesn't rattle me. It never has.

I explode forward and drive my foot through the ball. It sails down the lane, and in an instant, nine pins go flying into the backstop. The number ten pin does a slow, teetering spin, and for a second I think I've blown it. But, finally, the pin topples over and the boys go ballistic behind me.

A perfect strike.

And it felt *awesome*.

I turn, looking for Mia, smiling before I even find her. But I don't find her because she's not here. Mia is gone.

Chapter 37

Mia

Q: Are you generous with your friends?

I wind my way around tables at Maxi's Café and slide in next to Beth just as Skyler takes the stage. The crowd hoots for her, and she flashes a smile and gives her cello a twirl before settling onto a stool, fluffing out her long butter-yellow dress, and resting the instrument between her thighs.

Usually, I love this moment before Sky starts to play. People look at her and see your typical manic pixie dream girl, with her babydoll bangs and willowy frame. They don't expect what they get: a musical beast with a ferocious percussive style that shakes the windows.

Tonight, though, I can barely settle into my chair, and my pulse roars like the ocean in my ears.

I ran away from Ethan, away from the truth of what he said and the deeper truth of his hands on my body. He put his arms around me on the lane, his taut body pressed against my back, and a flood of memory rocked me to my brown-and-black bowling shoes.

We're wet—I still don't know why we're wet. *But he's behind me, lifting my dress over my head, flinging it off somewhere. We're in his kitchen, lights off and laughing, my whole body weak with it and with one too many shots at Duke's.*

I brace against the cool stainless steel of his refrigerator as his hands come around me, cupping my breasts, thumbing the silk of my bra. He brushes aside the heavy curtain of my wet hair and breathes warmth against my neck. His lips move over me, his fingers slip down my body, heating my chilled flesh. The contact makes me shiver, a slow delicious shudder.

I feel like I could dissolve on the spot. My molecules feel like helium, like embers shooting off a sparkler. I press back against him, wanting to turn, to feel his lips on mine, but he holds me there, one hand firm on my stomach, his tongue teasing my skin, lips moving down my shoulder. He's so hard against me, the feel of him scoops my insides, turns me to liquid.

"That's not fair," I say, and my voice feels like it's drifting down from a far-off cloud.

"What's not?"

"You're still dressed."

And that's when I pulled away and slung my bowling ball into the other lane like I was throwing a softball pitch.

After that, I couldn't get away fast enough. I hate that I didn't say goodbye to the kids or to Rhett, but I just didn't have it in me. I couldn't have those images looping through my mind, couldn't stay there, so close to him. But not *with* him.

Skyler fires up her drum sampler and launches into a power-house version of "Purple Haze," her blond hair swinging forward and a look of pure joy lighting her face.

Not what we want to be doing.

Ethan's words ping-pong around in my brain. It's true. What I *want* to be doing starts with a replay of that snippet of memory and ends with him naked in my bed. What *I* will be doing is forcing it into my own thick head that I can't have that. Even though he slipped tonight, he's made his feelings clear.

And he's got Alison now, thanks to me. Which is okay because I have Boomerang and the Vegas trip in just a few weeks. I have my film and my friends and family. That's plenty, I tell myself.

Really.

Skyler launches into a bossa nova "Bitter Sweet Symphony," her bow flying over the cello, hands slapping at the fingerboard to create this beautiful chop that's her signature sound. She's on fire, and her passion incites me.

I've seen so many friends graduate with no idea who they are, really, or what they want. Nothing drives them. So they drift, shifting their discontent from low-wage job to low-wage job.

I'm lucky enough to know—to have always known—where I'm meant to be. I have to stop taking that for granted. I have to attack it the way Skyler attacks that cello. I have to find out who I am and dive deep.

And I will.

For the next hour, I watch my best friends: one of them onstage, transported, in love with what she's able to do; the other here with me, wearing an avid expression that tells me she's dreaming of her own turn in the spotlight. I want to thank them both for the awesome gift they give me every day. The gift of being kickass beautiful girls.

Skyler starts in on "Seven Nation Army," my favorite, and the music lifts me. I want to thank her for giving me that, for dragging me out of my self-pity into a place of inspiration and gratitude.

A mental light bulb pops to life. At the break, I dig in my purse for my cell phone and find the phone number for Brian, my Boomerang date from the other night.

Mia: Hey, want to meet an amazing girl?
Brian: Another one, you mean?
Mia: ☺ Maybe **THE** one.
Brian: You bet.
Mia: Maxi's Cafe. Half hour?
Brian: See you there.

"What's got you all smiley all of a sudden?" Beth asks.

I drop my phone back in my purse and give her a smile. "You'll see," I promise. And for the first time in a few weeks, I feel certain I'm right.

Chapter 38

Ethan

Q: Are you good at facing the music, or do you dance away?

*W*hat are you saying?" Rhett jerks the steering wheel, almost hitting the car to our right as he pulls into a parking spot in the underground garage. He cuts the engine and the blasting A/C shuts off, leaving a coating of frost on my dress shirt and tie. "I know I didn't hear you right."

Ten minutes ago, we were laughing about how close we came to disaster last night when Milo picked up Raylene's Jack and Coke instead of his drink. Now we're on Alison somehow. I don't know how Rhett got me onto this, but I'm learning that he can do sleight of hand with words.

"You heard right," I say, forcing myself to sound casual. "I'm going to Colorado with her this weekend."

Rhett's features go even sharper with a scowl. "Your *ex-girlfriend*?"

"Yes, Rhett. My ex. We went for sushi after we left and—"

"Damn . . . Bowling to sashimi." He shakes his head. "That offends me for some reason."

"Yeah, the whole night had more twists than a bag of pretzels. Speaking of which"—I push his shoulder—"What's with you and Raylene?"

"Nothing." Rhett's eyebrows snap together, and he's suddenly serious. "She's a nice lady, that's all."

I grin. "Definitely not all, Rhett."

"It's not what you think." He makes a dismissive motion with his hand. "We talked divorce lawyers. Alimony. Stuff like that. Trust me, youngster. Things get complicated when you're an old dog in your early thirties."

"Dang. And here I was enjoying the simplicity of my social life now."

"My point exactly, Vance. Going away for the weekend with your ex-girlfriend is a *very* bad call. Sorry, man. I try not to meddle. I haven't said anything about the stunt you're trying to pull with Cookie—"

"You know about that?"

"You mean the seventeen-thousand-dollar video game you're developing without her approval? Yeah, I know about that. Guess who's covering your ass?"

A combination of embarrassment and anger spreads heat through me. I can't let Rhett take the fall for me. "I didn't ask you to get involved in my business."

"Your business is the same as mine, Ethan. And it's too late, I'm already in, but that's not what we're talking about right now. Going to Colorado with your psychotic ex is like launching a grenade into your personal life."

"Alison's not psychotic."

"See? She's already breaking down your defenses."

"She is not. We've—accepted each other in a new way. We put the past where it belongs."

Rhett's scowl deepens. "She has you speaking in *greeting card*, bro. You can't reduce life to a pithy statement."

"You sound a lot smarter when you're pissed."

"You commit to stupid shit when you go to sushi with your ex."

"I retract my last statement."

"Retract your weekend plans too. She's reeling you back in. Can't you see that?"

Sitting across the table from Alison last night, she seemed so *different*. So vulnerable and honest. She doesn't want me back. Not in the way Rhett thinks.

"No," I say. "She's letting me catch a ride on her private jet so I can see my parents. Her family owns a ranch an hour away from my house, and my dad's birthday is this weekend. And my brother, Chris, is coming home from college—" I'm starting to sound like I'm asking for permission so I wrap it up. "It's a convenience thing, that's all."

Rhett stares at me in that human resource-ey way, all perception and insight.

"Definitely not all," he says finally.

"Whatever." I grab my messenger bag and jump out of the Mini, shutting the door harder than I need to.

Rhett and I are silent on our way into the offices, but I'm done being judged by him. What does he know, anyway?

I won't spend the weekend watching Jason and Isis cuddle on the couch while I try not to think about Mia. About how she felt against me. Or remembering the way I hurt her. I need to get out of town or I'm going to lose my fucking mind, and if I want to go home to Colorado, then I'm goddamn doing it.

Rhett's wrong. Nothing's going to happen with Alison.

I'm getting a free ride, and that is *definitely* all.

Chapter 39

Mia

Q: Can your friends tell you everything?

*T*hrough elaborate machinations involving cupcakes, a promise to film a bridal shower for Paolo's cousin, and a little bit of extra sweet-talking of anyone I know won't narc me out to Cookie, I have commandeered the Boomerang production studio so I can shoot Beth for the convention booth. I've also commandeered Paolo, who'll act the part of Beth's dates. I plan to have them improvise some datelike chitchat, maybe hold hands or make out a little, and then I'll play around with backgrounds and settings in post. Brian offered to help, and I may take him up on it, since effects are not my thing.

The equipment here is so high-end it makes me salivate. Some of it's nicer than the stuff we used in film school. Guess that's yet another benefit of working for a big-time media mogul. I doubt eHarmony has a full-scale editing bay in *their* basement.

Just being around all of this piques my hunger for the job. The money is one thing. But all of this—the resources, the equipment, the creative trust that serves Adam across all of Blackwood Entertainment—makes for a ridiculously rare opportunity. An opportunity I really, *really* want.

"Okay," Beth says, settling onto a green-painted cube that will become a divan or a high-backed cushioned chair or, who knows, maybe the captain's seat on a spaceship. "Before your friend comes down, you *have* to talk to me about this Colorado situation. You're being too calm, girl. It's freaking me out."

"It's fine," I tell her, though my throat closes around the words, making them sound strained. "It just means I can totally shut the door on all of this nonsense."

What is there to say? From the minute Paolo stuck a mug of latte in my hands and laid the news on me about Ethan's big trip, I've felt sick and deflated. If I let myself think of them together in that way— the way we were, in my mother's studio, in the back of the cab, in the cool shadows of his kitchen—I won't be able to accomplish a thing.

She folds her arms across her chest and raises an eyebrow. "Which nonsense is that? The nonsense where you're totally into him? Or where he's totally into you?"

"The nonsense where he clearly still cares about his ex. The nonsense where I have much better things to do with my life than kill my career to go grubbing around after someone who's not into me. Again."

"You said he couldn't keep his hands off you—even in front of his ex."

"Exactly." I take a reading of her face and adjust some of the reflectors to bounce more light in her direction. "The problem's not physical."

"Not with that rack, it ain't."

"Ha. Ha."

"Seriously, what *is* the problem? Enlighten me."

I kneel down next to her and smooth the simple flowered dress we borrowed from Sky over her knees, then spend some time playing with her hair until she slaps my hands out of the way and fixes it herself.

"We've already talked about this."

She rolls her eyes. "You mean the 'I need to be chosen' bullshit?"

"How is it bullshit?"

I start to rise, but she clamps two hands on my shoulders and stares me down. "Let me ask you something, okay?"

"What?"

"When you wanted to go to film school, how did you go about doing that?"

I sigh. "What's your point?"

"I'm just wondering if you waited around in your house for film school to come to your door and say, 'Mia, we choose you.' "

"It's not the—"

"And when you wanted this swanky gig here, what did you do? Did you wait for baby Ryan Gosling to call you up? Or did you storm the damn castle and get yourself a job?"

"An internship," I remind her. "That I have to *share*."

"It'll be a job at the end of all this," she says. "You know how I know?"

"No." Because I don't know anything of the sort. Except that I've accidentally stacked the deck in my favor by putting Ethan and Cookie on a path to the apocalypse, something I still *have* to fix.

"Because when you want something, girl, you don't screw around. You go for it. You've never waited for me to *choose* to do the dishes or give you back stuff I've borrowed. Or for Skyler to *choose* to pay the light bill. You don't wait around for anyone or anything. But with boys, you act like goddamn Sleeping Beauty. Like they're the *only* ones with choices to make."

"That's not fair." I twist away from her and get to my feet.

Though I busy myself looking through my camera viewfinder, tears threaten, and I blink them back.

"I'm not about being fair right now. I'm about being real."

"Well, spare me, okay?"

She gets up, blowing all the work I just put into arranging her, getting the lighting just right.

"Damn it, Beth," I start, but she takes the camera gently from my hands and sets it on the table beside us.

"Listen to me, honey," she says. Her voice is warm and melting, which is just not like her. And her expression is kind enough to undo me on the spot. "You know how we always call Kyle *that tool*?"

I nod.

"Seems to me that you're the one acting like a tool. Like you're something that gets to be picked up or put down whenever some boy wants. You know?"

I put my face in my hands because I feel the truth of it, sizzling along my every limb, rooting my feet to the floor. I wasted so much time with Kyle, waiting for him to see me for who I am, someone who has value, who deserves to be picked. I waited without asking myself if I actually wanted *him*.

Oh, hell.

Just then, Paolo slides into the room. "Date time!" he exclaims, and I've never been so happy for an interruption.

"Yep," I say and lift the camera once again. "Why don't you both take seats?"

Beth hesitates for a second, but I give her a cool end-of-discussion smile, and she flops back onto her cube.

"Awesome," I murmur, though nothing about this feels awesome at all. "Let's get started."

Chapter 40

Ethan

Q: Does the truth set you free, or does it set you on fire?

So what happened to your parents?" I ask Alison. "Didn't you have big plans for the weekend at the family cabin?"

She looks at me, her eyes hooded in the dimness. The small window behind her frames a circle of a sky that's fading from blue to black. It's Friday night, and we're thousands of feet in the air, somewhere halfway between LA and Loveland—the private airfield we're flying to outside of Fort Collins.

Alison takes a careful sip of her vodka tonic and sets it down. "Something came up. Two somethings, actually. My dad had to fly to New York for a work emergency, and my mom had a social emergency."

"Social emergency?"

She smiles—something I know she does to mask her disappointment. "A bridal shower she happened to remember right when my dad had to cancel. It's that middle-school maneuver. You know . . . *You can't break up with me because I'm breaking up with you first?* He's too busy for her, so she's *way* too busy for him."

"Sorry," I say, but it's typical of them. I know she's used to it.

Alison's smile goes a little wider. "It's okay."

In the faint light of the cabin, her teeth are too white, too perfectly straight. She looks down and gently shakes the ice in her glass. It's still half full, but mine is empty. No more vodka. No ice. Even the lime looks sucked dry.

"You could've canceled, Alison. You're going all this way to spend a weekend by your . . ." I cut myself short, because I know why she didn't cancel. I know why she's here. She didn't want to let me down again. "Listen, Alison, I don't—"

"It's okay, Ethan. I don't expect anything. I don't want to make you uncomfortable. I just couldn't say no to the chance to be with you again—even for a few hours. And I didn't want you to miss your father's birthday."

"Why don't you come out to dinner tonight?"

As soon I say the words, an odd feeling settles over me, like I'm betraying someone. But I push it away before I can examine it. I don't have to answer to anyone, and Alison can't hurt me again. The *remaking us* campaign has actually done me a world of good. Emotionally, there's nothing there anymore. Nothing drawing me toward her.

"Aren't you going to dinner with your family?" she asks.

I nod. "Yeah, but it's all right. They'll be happy to see you."

"Really?"

"Absolutely," I say. Then I unbuckle my seat belt and move to the small bar console, where I make myself another drink.

"What the hell are you doing, E?" Chris grabs my elbow and tows me toward the bar at Jimmy's—our family's favorite pub. "How could you bring her to Dad's birthday dinner?"

I take a long pull of my beer and consider my little brother. College has changed him for the better. It's subtle, in the way he holds himself, his shoulders a little squarer, his voice a little deeper, but it's there. I freakin' love the kid. It's so damn good to see him, but I don't need him playing mother hen.

"Drop it, Chris. It's done. No need to make it a huge deal."

Dinner with the family—and Alison—is behind me. Two hours and three Jack and Cokes later, and I'm still alive. Feeling the booze, definitely, but otherwise no worse for the wear.

"It's obviously not done, Ethan. She's still here." Chris leans closer, and I realize he's taller than me now. That sucks. "None of us like her. And we sure as hell don't like her after what she—"

"You're ruining my buzz, Chris." I'm swaying a little, my head too light. Which is the opposite of how my stomach feels. The ribeye steak I put away at dinner has settled like an anchor in my stomach. I lean my back against the bar, and now the crowd blurs behind Chris, all rust-colored flannels and jeans. Everything looks faded and worn compared to LA's sparkle and shine.

Chris assesses me like he's making a forensic analysis of my clothes, my face, my posture. I don't know what he sees, but judging by the worry in his eyes, I'm guessing it's the opposite of the growth and maturity I just saw in him.

"What's gotten into you?" he asks, lowering his voice so I almost can't hear him above the bar noise. "Is it because you're not playing ball anymore?"

He's dead-on about me feeling off kilter, but it's not because I miss soccer. At least I don't think so. And I know that I don't *want* to know. The whole point of the vodka, the whiskey, and the beer in my hand is to get away from *knowing*.

"Please shut up, bro." I take a sip, almost missing my lips. "I'm asking you to—just stop."

Across the crowded bar, I see Alison rise from my parents' table.

As soon as she turns her back, my parents and their closest friends, the Davises, exchange looks of relief.

At dinner she mentioned wanting to take my family to Palace Arms in Denver sometime—a restaurant that's ten times fancier than where we were. It was a passing comment, but it was enough to put a damper on things. My mellow working-class parents don't see things the way she does, like there are quality ratings on everything. They were just happy to have us all together.

Beside me, Chris lets out a muffled curse when he sees Alison coming. "Great . . . The Anti-Christ cometh."

As I watch her thread toward us through the crowded bar, her tight body wrapped in designer leather and denim, it occurs to me that both Rhett and Chris are convinced that Alison and I are hooking up again this weekend. Then it occurs to me that the thought would *never* have occurred to me otherwise.

It wasn't anywhere in my thoughts.

But now it is.

And I wonder.

What if we did?

Beside me, I feel Chris looking from me to her. "Well, this sure looks like it's going to end well. It's painful to watch. In fact, I'm not doing it. Give me your phone."

"My phone?"

Chris holds out his hand. "My battery's dead and I'm trying to get ahold of Jake and Connor."

His high school buddies. I fish my phone out of my pocket.

Chris takes it and then snatches the beer from my hands. "I'm taking this too. Your judgment's already impaired."

He leaves to join my parents, who are now laughing and doing Jell-O shots with the Davises, happier than they've looked all night.

"Hey," Alison says. "Did I interrupt something?"

"Nah, he was just leaving." It's crowded, and I have nowhere to stand except either behind her, or wedged right beside her. I take option two, because option one would bring Mia instantly back into my thoughts, and that's the last thing I need, remembering how she felt at the bowling alley, or how she looked at work today in a green dress blouse that matched the color of her—

"Ethan?"

"Yeah?"

"I asked if you'd have champagne with me if I ordered a bottle?"

I glance around me. Jimmy's isn't a dive, but it's not a place for drinking champagne either. Not by a long shot. But then this is the girl who got a manicure before she went on safari.

"Sure," I say. "Why not?"

The bartender gives Alison a mildly irritated look when she orders and leaves the bar to retrieve a bottle from their stock in the back.

"So," Alison says, smiling at me.

We're getting pressed in from all sides, so our legs are smashed together.

"So," I say back. I've got nothing else. I don't want to talk to her. A dark, primal urge to just get her naked hits me. It slams into me, but it's gone in a flash. I know how she feels. I was with her for two years, but she's not who I want. Alison never made me feel the way Mia does. No one makes me feel the way Mia does—except Mia.

Fuck. So much for numbing my brain with alcohol.

Suddenly it feels like the rib-eye steak is sprouting thorns in my stomach.

"You okay, Ethan?"

"Absolutely."

Not.

The bartender sets an ice bucket down in front of us with a clank. He hands me two champagne flutes filled with bubbling liquid, the rims spotted with dishwashing soap. I hand one to Alison, sweat breaking out along my spine.

"To new beginnings," Alison says.

I repeat the toast, or maybe I don't. The bar is spinning in one direction and my head is spinning the other way.

As I bring the flute to my lips, someone jars Alison from behind. She jerks forward, and her champagne spills over my shirt.

"Watch it!" she snaps over her shoulder. Then she looks at me, her hand settling on my chest. "Shit. I'm sorry, Ethan."

I can't look at her. I can't look up from my shirt.

The memory of Mia spilling red wine on me in her mother's studio flashes before my eyes. But then the sweet smell of the champagne reaches me, and it takes me further back. Opens up a door that's been shut in my mind for weeks.

This, I realize. This is what happened between us.

My mind is barraged by images, tastes, and smells. Champagne and Mia's sweet violet scent. The feel of her curly hair in my hands, her soft lips kissing my jaw. My hands exploring every inch of her.

"Alison, I need some air," I say.

It sounds like an excuse, but it's the truth, and then I'm moving through the crowded bar and out into the street.

I need a place where I can be alone, where I can let myself remember, because it's here. It's all coming back to me. Mia, and what we did after we left Duke's. Finally, I remember our first night.

---------- *Chapter 41* ----------

Mia

Q: Dancing queen, or dancing fool?

$\mathcal{M}$y plans to lie in bed all weekend and treat myself to a cinematic pity fest (*Love Actually; Pride and Prejudice; (500) Days of Summer*) are thwarted by my two best friends, who seem intent on torturing me, even though I am *always* sweetness and light with *them,* in addition to respecting their private time and their need to marinate in their own emotional juices every now and then.

Tonight's torment: Operation Get-Mia-Off-Her-Ass-and-Out-to-the-Club. Its first stages included shoving me into a gold sequined tank and black mini, teasing my hair to ceiling-scraping heights, and loading my purse with condoms.

Yeah. No.

Its second phase, now in effect, includes the bar at Club Tonga, a drink the size of a fish bowl, and Skyler's super subtle efforts at matchmaking—repayment for Brian, I think, which consists of slinging dudes in my direction and saying, "This is Mia. She's hot, right?"

So far I've scored general—if confused—agreement, except for one gay guy who says, "Oh my God, *so* hot," and tries to feel me up. An act I shut down by offering the analogy that being a dog person does *not* give you the right to molest cats.

Miffed, he bounces away, and Skyler gives me a sharp nudge to the ribs. "Be nice."

"Ow. I am." Just not nice enough to give strange men a free thrill. Sue me.

"No, you're not. You're putting off a stink cloud of bitchiness."

Drink straw clamped between her perfectly veneered teeth, she watches the parade of guys, no doubt looking for further opportunities to humiliate me. Her eyes light up, and she starts to slide from her seat, gaze riveted on a slouchy actor type with a well-trained five o'clock shadow.

I jump up before she can move in for the kill. "Let's dance." Beth's been on the dance floor for an hour, and suddenly that seems like a much more appealing place to be.

Lifting my drink, I push the straw aside and go for a full-on gulp. Okay, several gulps, until I drain the giant glass and thunk it back on the bar like I've just proved some point.

The liquor burns on the way down and then spreads a soothing heat through my belly, warming every bit of me and giving me a pleasant buzz, like my brain's been coated in cotton candy. This might be exactly what I need.

"Come on," I say and grab Skyler's hand, almost pulling her out of her striped oxford kicks.

The crowd pulses around us, and I'm hit with rolling waves of body heat, Axe cologne, and fruity perfume. I feel enveloped, buoyed, and I get a sharp visceral pull to be in the middle of it, moving to the thump of the music that throbs inside my own chest, becomes part of me.

We push through the crowd, and I'm hazy, body tingling in a way that feels turned on but not. I'm hungry for the closeness of people but not one person. I want to dive into a sea of flesh and lose myself.

I push into the tight knot of bodies until I reach the center of the music and the chaos. Of course, that's where I find Beth, shaking it hard, oblivious to the people around her. Eyes closed, she gives me an ecstatic smile, like she's got some kind of best-friend sonar that tells her I'm close.

The base shakes the floor, which feels spongy and far away. I start to dance, and I feel my problems lifting out of me, flying up to the laser-hatched ceiling, flying up and away into the night.

No more Boomerang and Adam Blackwood.

No more competition.

No more famous mother who has seen and done things I may never get to do. And no more Nana, with her fading memories, her frantic paranoia. I'm all brightness inside, all thoughtless muscle and blood and movement. I haven't felt this good in weeks, not since that night at Duke's, when I met Ethan, when—

Damn it, I don't want to think about him. I don't want to imagine him winging around in a private plane with his ex-girlfriend. An ex-girlfriend I'm responsible for shoving back into his life.

That door is shut, I remind myself. It never really opened.

I close my eyes, lift my arms into the air, trying to grab hold of that good feeling again, to pull the music back into me.

But I can't stop the images from coming. Ethan pushing Alison onto a bed, moving his lithe, athletic body over hers, brushing her blond hair aside to kiss her, to look at her the way he looked at me.

The thoughts and the mammoth drink catch up to me. I feel heat in my throat, and a wave of dizziness makes me stagger sideways a step. The crowd presses in on me, and my whole body feels super-charged with heat.

"I need to sit for a second," I shout at Beth.

She pulls her red bra strap back into her halter and nods. "Want me to come with?"

"No, I'm good."

Beth conveys my message to Skyler, but I turn away before her concerned look can reach me.

I aim myself for a narrow alcove at the far end of the club, where bodies writhe together on low sofas. Everything feels weird now, sexually intense and alien. I'm jealous of everyone. The people on the dance floor whose brains can shut down for more than ten minutes. The people on these couches, who can touch each other, be with each other, even if maybe they should do a little less of it within full view of dozens of other people.

I perch on the edge of a velvet-covered chaise, trying to ignore the noisy grinding inches away. I want another drink. Or ten. I want to do something with myself, but I can't decide what.

Someone on the couch next to me gives a little gasp, and a cascade of fragments come to me—bits of my night with Ethan. Just dizzying, random images. Not enough to make a full picture.

His dark hair, wet and clinging to his neck, that deep groove of his collarbone and my lips there, sliding down his chest. The two of us, tangled on his sofa, giggling under the Pendleton blanket, until his tongue parted my lips, and I buried my hands in his wet hair.

The music recedes, and the memories crash inside me. I decide that what I want to escape most is myself.

Beth's right: I'm not Sleeping Beauty. I go after what I want.

But I didn't, and now it's too late.

I fish out my cell phone, and its white glow goes off like a flare in this dark corner. For a long time, I stare at it. Then I scroll back through our texts, and feel myself smile.

It's too late. I know this. And I'm drunk. But maybe I can let it go if I tell him. I don't know what exactly, but I feel like I need to exorcise the regret in some way, need to let it all go, truly, so I can be free.

Mia: I wish I remembered more of that night.

That's true, but it's only part of it.

Mia: I'm pretty sure you rocked my world.

And I am. As sure as I am that he's still rocking it, though I keep trying to bring it back to some steady state.

Running my finger over the touch screen, I will him to text back, to reach out from wherever he is and tell me he feels the same. Just that. I'll be happy with just that.

I wait for a long time. My heart thumps a merciless rhythm in my chest. Bodies move around me while I sit there, as still as a stone in a river.

But a reply never comes.

So I get up, put my phone away, and head back to my friends.

Chapter 42

Ethan

Q: Champagne: special occasions only
or whenever the mood strikes?

The three-mile walk from old town Fort Collins to my house is a blur. I don't see the bars and coffee shops, the quaint streets that gradually give way to my neighborhood.

No. It's like a movie. I'm leaving Jimmy's, then I'm puking in a bush, then I'm stumbling into my kitchen, where I am now.

I throw on the faucet and take huge gulps from the tap until I feel like I might vomit again. Then I straighten, swipe my sleeve over my chin and stare at the darkness.

I can't see much besides the microwave clock and the shine of stainless steel, but I feel the steadiness of these walls. My lifetime—and Chris's—is recorded in the dented cabinets and scuffed floorboards around me.

I close my eyes, and the sour taste on my tongue sweetens until it's champagne, the taste of Mia, and I'm back in my apartment in LA that first night I met her. We had come back there after meeting at the bar at Duke's. For whatever reason, standing in my tiny kitchen with her, I got it in my head that we should celebrate.

"Celebrate?" Mia asks. She leans her hip against the counter and smiles. "What's the occasion?"

"You, Curls. You're the occasion."

I wonder if it sounds like a line to her, but I mean it. I've only known her a few hours, but she's eclipsed everything else in my world. This girl with her green eyes, her wild hair, and her gorgeous smile is amazing. Funny and smart and hot. Christ, she's hot. She is absolutely worth celebrating.

Mia's smile widens. "Curls, huh?"

I step toward her and reach up, twirling a strand of soft hair around my finger. "It suits you."

Mia leans into my touch, resting her cheek against my hand, and I flash back to the cab ride here. My fingers had been buried in her hair, and she'd been halfway on my lap. We're combustible together, every time I touch her I want more. I want her now, right now, but there's no need to rush. I lean in and kiss her lips quickly, then duck into the refrigerator for the bottle of champagne Jason stashed in there a few weeks ago.

"You just happen to have bottles of Cristal waiting around for moments like this?"

I grin and shake my head. "My roommate, who showed up at the bar?" I unwrap the foil top and toss it in the sink, then slowly twist the cork to let pressure out of the bottle. "He just started his second year of med school, so his parents sent this to him. It's something they do every—"

The cork slams into my palm, jerking my hand up. Champagne shoots from the bottle, arcing into the air, and dousing Mia. She lets out a squeak and lurches off the counter, curling her back like a startled cat.

"Whoops," I say, trying not to laugh.

Her blue dress has a dark splatter line from hip to shoulder where the material is soaked. She pushes a dripping curl away from her face and straightens her back. Then she runs her tongue over her lower lip. "Tastes pretty good, actually."

It's the sexiest damn thing I've ever seen, and I have to clear my throat to find my voice. "I can't say I'm sorry that happened."

"You don't seem sorry. . . . but you will be." She lifts the bottle from my hand. "Let's see how you like it." She gives the bottle a shake my way.

Champagne spills onto my shirt, a cool, liquid lash against my chest that I barely feel. It's like my body has one setting. Like it's suddenly programmed to only feel her.

"Wasn't that bad." I take the bottle back and step forward. "There's something I should probably tell you about me," I say.

She steps back, retreating, but I keep going until I have her cornered against the counter. "I'm highly competitive. And I always finish what I start."

"That's actually two thi—"

Mia gasps, swallowing the rest of her words as I tip the bottle over her—over us, since we're pressed together.

Her hands shoot up, bracing my chest as she sucks in a breath, but she doesn't stop me as I soak every inch of her.

When the bottle is empty, I set it on the counter. "There."

The only sound is the champagne dripping onto the floor and Mia's quick little breaths. I don't know where to look first. Her face is priceless, her green eyes bright. Almost glowing with shock. The curves of her body are perfectly outlined by her clinging dress, and I want to high-five myself because she's fucking beautiful this way, shivering and wet and holding onto me like she'll fly away if she lets go.

"Well, then," she says finally. "We're all wet."

I can't resist her anymore. I catch a glimpse of her eyes widening in surprise just before I kiss her. I want to take my time, but it's like holding back a tidal wave. I kiss her hard, my tongue sliding against hers, her taste cool and sweet from the champagne. She makes a small needy sound and tilts her head up, giving me a better angle, giving me exactly what I wanted, like we're connected in some primitive way, our bodies fluent in their own language.

Some part of me knows we're drunk, both of us, but that this is real. How could it not be?

Dipping my head, I take the soft part of her ear between my teeth, pressing a gentle bite there. "You're so sweet, Mia. So hot."

She reacts urgently to my words, framing my face with her hands and guiding my mouth back to hers. Her body presses against me and I'm instantly hard, fighting the urge to drive into her right now.

When have I ever wanted a girl this much? Have I ever?

"You taste incredible," I say, sucking the champagne off her warm skin. I work my way down to her collarbone, and then to her breasts. She's soft, the weight and shape of her so fucking perfect. I can't push her dress and bra aside enough, so I suck through the wet layers and feel her nipple tighten into a bud beneath my tongue.

"Ethan . . ." Mia grips my hair and arches her back. "That's amazing."

"It's going to get better." I glance up. Her eyes are unfocused and heavy with desire. Seeing her that way only makes me want her more. She's like liquid fire under my hands, so responsive. "But you know what's getting in our way, Curls?" I smooth my hand down her hip and over her thigh, finding the hem of the wet fabric. "Your dress."

Chapter 43

Mia

Q: When was your last truly memorable night?

I fall onto my bed, drunk and spinning, trying to fix on the bright double squares of my bedroom window, which Sky's opened so I can get some fresh air. I taste the night on my tongue—that metallic tang, like pennies, that comes right before rain. The breeze is cool and shivery and flutters along my sheet like fingers, so light, touching every bit of me.

Of course I think of Ethan, wishing for *his* fingers, *his* lips. Remembering.

"But you know what's getting in our way, Curls?" he says, and his hands travel along my body like he's taking the measure of me, like he's sculpting me to life there in his dimly lit galley kitchen. "Your dress."

He turns me around and nudges me toward the refrigerator.

"What are you doing?" I ask, but I don't care, not
really. I just know I want him, want to taste him again,
his tongue warm and darting in my mouth, his body
pressed against me again, firm and powerful and radiating with desire.

"Zipper," he says, bending close to my ear.

I put my hands against the cool surface, and it feels
so good. I should be chilled, drenched in champagne—I
remember now—but I'm feverish, floating, wanting his
hands on me to keep me rooted.

The zipper gently scrapes my flesh, and I feel his
closeness like a palpable force, keeping me there. The
soft fabric of my dress brushes against my legs, traveling over my upper thighs, my belly, my breasts, until I'm
free of it, and it disappears in the shadows like it never
existed.

His hands come around me and caress the sheer wet
fabric of my bra, closing over my breasts with just the
right firmness, everything exactly the way I like it.

And the way I realize it's never been before, never
perfect like this.

He thumbs my nipples, squeezes them, then pushes
my hair out of the way so his lips can touch my shoulder,
my neck, his teeth grazing me, tongue warm against my
skin.

"That's not fair," I protest.

"What's not?"

"You're still dressed."

He laughs. "For now." His mouth against my ear, he

says, *"You taste like champagne. Jesus, I want more of that."*

Not as much as I want you, I think and push back against him, needing the feel of his body again. It's more than just a perfect physical match, more than just him knowing how to touch me. It's this feeling of being perfectly free to express every part of me, especially my longing for him.

I move my hand off the refrigerator, needing to touch him, but he traps my hand and returns it to the cool stainless steel.

"I'm right here," he tells me, and presses against me, hard against the small of my back. *"Don't move. Stay just like that."*

His arm comes around me again, wrapping around my waist. He bends me forward just a little, pushes a leg between my legs so that I feel his rock-hard thigh, the rough texture of his jeans pushed up against me. I groan and rest my face against my arm, feeling the stickiness of the champagne, the cool vibration of the refrigerator.

Ethan spreads my legs apart, and his other hand slides beneath the lace waistband of my panties, slipping down to rest against me, against the pulsing warm center of my body.

And then I can't think. I can only feel. The brush of his fingers against me. Over and over. Perfect. So absolutely perfect. His lips on my back, my neck, his arm tight across my waist. I move against him, my body seeking his touch, my legs trembling from the impossibility of staying upright while his hand moves against me, while I move against his hand.

"Fuck," he groans, and the sound of his voice makes me weak, makes me wish that stainless steel weren't so goddamn slippery. "You feel good. So fucking good."

He holds me hard against his body, his fingers coaxing me, making my breath come faster, making my whole body tremble.

I can't stand how good it feels, like a miniature sun is burning inside me, radiating through my every cell. Like I'm about to go supernova.

And then I do.

He slips a finger inside me, and heat rushes through every part of me, the delicious intense pulse of it almost knocking me off my feet. It rolls through me in wave after wave, sharp and overpowering, almost painful but the opposite of pain. My body can't stop moving against his fingers. Every part of me craves more, and I'm drenched in this place of dizzying, gorgeous surrender.

"Holy shit." I want to kiss my own hand in gratitude for being part of my body, with blood and nerves and skin. I'm only upright because he's holding me upright, because I only exist where I connect with his powerful arm, his skilled, beautiful touch.

My breathing slows, and his hand slips out of my panties to join the other one resting against my stomach. "Thanks," he replies, and I can imagine his slow, satisfied smile, which may very well be my undoing.

I turn in his arms. His hands plunge into my hair, and I rise up on tiptoes to kiss him, to tongue all my pleasure and gratitude into his body, to give him a little bit of what he just gave me. We kiss and kiss for what feels like hours but like no time at all, like there will never be enough time to taste him, to know all there is to know about his lips against mine.

My fingers move down his neck, trailing across the sturdy "V" of his chest, slipping down the contours of his stomach to the button on his jeans.

"Now you," I say, so hungry with the need to touch him that my fingers are clumsy.

"Not yet, Curls," he tells me, and before I know it, he's lifted me off my feet, like I'm nothing. His hands settle beneath me, and my legs come around his waist. I wrap around him, and he kisses me again, then starts to carry me toward the living room, his lips still pressed against me so we're clumsy, bumping into the walls.

"What are we doing?"

I feel his smile against my own, and then he settles me on the couch. Vaguely, I think we should probably go to his bedroom, but most of me doesn't care. I just want more of this. Want to swim in it.

"First, I think we need to get you out of the rest of your wet clothes," he says, with mock concern. "And then I've got a few ideas."

Chapter 44

Ethan

Q: What's your favorite hangover cure?

*E*than?" Mom knocks on my bedroom door. "Time to wake up. It's six o'clock."

"Sleep. My head . . . needs more sleep."

I sound like Frankenstein. With strep throat.

"It's six *p.m.*, Ethan. Your head's slept all day."

"What time?" My face is mashed against my pillow, and I can't lift it. I think they may have become one. I peer at my window, seeing the fading daylight through the blinds.

"Are you decent?" my mom says, cracking the door open. "Guess not."

"Geez, Mom." I drag the sheet higher so it covers my ass. "How about some privacy?" I say, but I'm used to living in a family where nothing is sacred.

Mom looks from the clothes I wore last night piled on the floor, to the bottle of aspirin on my nightstand, with the same analytical blue eyes as Chris. "Looks like you accomplished your goal of making yourself sick."

She waits for a beat, and I know she wants me to talk to her. She wants to know what's going on, but I'm about ten years past the point of telling her. What I want to tell her is that I'm fine, but I can't do that, either. Lying to people you care about is fucked. I thought so even before Alison.

"I'm a goal-oriented kind of guy," I croak.

She laughs. "I just ordered pizzas and Matt's on his way."

I push myself onto my elbows, riding the swells of a monstrous headache as I try to figure out who Matt is. Then it clicks. "Coach Williams is coming?"

"He's not your coach anymore. You can call him Matt now. He'll be here in half an hour—and he's bringing his wife, Tricia."

I have no idea how my former coach found out that I was home, or why he's coming to the house, but it'll be good to see him. I feel myself crack a smile—which makes my mom smile—which gives my mood an honest boost.

"You called him?" I ask.

"Maybe I did, but he was the one who invited himself over. Now get your butt into the shower. I'll make you a vanilla milk shake and a grilled cheese."

Half an hour later, I feel halfway human as Matt and Tricia Williams step into the house with a bottle of wine for dad and a bunch of sunflowers for mom.

My parents hug Matt, and then I do, which feels more normal than weird. He's my peer now, but it's something I'm still getting used to.

Four and a half years ago, he came to this house to recruit me and stood exactly where he is now. His brown hair didn't have any silver in it, and he wore a UCLA soccer sweatshirt instead of the Air Force

Academy one he wears now, but other than that, he doesn't seem to have changed at all. His vibe is still pure calm and positivity—the kind that quietly seeps into the people around him. Two minutes into his visit, and I already feel it.

Tricia is very pregnant, and I hear a steady flow of excited questions from my mom, who disappears with her into the living room. Dad, Matt, and I settle in the family room, where an MLS soccer game is playing on the television.

Soccer's a small world. Matt coached or played with a couple of the guys who sprint across our flat screen, and I know a few of them, too, so for a little while, we talk about them and the game while Dad chills in his recliner, listening. Then Matt asks about LA, and I catch him up on Jason and the rest of the guys.

"I've got a youth team I'm coaching," I tell him. "They play Saturdays too, so I can't always make it to the pick-up games, but I see everyone almost every week."

"You're coaching a team?" my dad asks.

It's the first thing he's said since we sat down.

"Yeah. Boys. Under nines. It's basically a squad of puppies, but they're good kids. We're seven and one right now. And I just added a kid who's going to make us unbeatable as soon as I get him to buy in."

Matt leans forward and sets his beer down on the coffee table. "What's stopping him?" he asks, genuinely interested.

"He came in late, so getting him integrated with a team that'd already bonded pretty tight wasn't easy. The main thing, though, is a confidence issue, but I think I've got a handle on that."

Matt and my dad fire off tons of questions about Parker, so the whole damn story comes out, from Raylene to bowling night. For reasons unknown to me, my dad laughs his ass off when he hears I had to go on dates for work, but Matt only becomes more interested, asking me questions about the other kids on my team, and then about Parker and Raylene.

"So you got through to him?" he asks. "The team outing worked?"

"I haven't had a chance to work with him since bowling night, but I think so. I want to get him out a few times a week to work on his finishing skills."

"Can I make a suggestion?" Matt weaves his fingers together— a familiar cue, telling me he's about to say something he believes with conviction.

"Of course."

"Don't work with him privately. If you're going to work with him outside of practice, bring Tyler or one of the other boys out too. The last thing Parker needs, I'm guessing, is to feel like he's being singled out."

I sit back, absorbing the wisdom of his suggestion. "Thanks. I'll do that."

Matt smiles. "You've done the hard part already, Ethan. That's just a minor point." I shrug, trying not to grin like an idiot over his praise. "So, how're the law school plans coming?" he asks. "Last we spoke, you were getting ready to study for the LSAT?"

"Right . . . LSAT," I mutter. "I haven't had a chance to get to it yet, with work and coaching."

We're quiet for a few moments, watching the television, but I know both Matt and my dad are focused on me. Their attention makes the blood rush to my face. My sole preoccupation becomes not fidgeting. Just staying calm.

"Ethan, I was thinking about something on my way here." There's a serious note in Matt's voice that makes my heart beat faster. "I had my squad work with a specialist this year. Mike Mc-Carthy. He's a psychologist who focuses on high-level athletes. The guy was incredible. Every single one of my players made massive strides in their training and game performance after working with him. Unfortunately for me, he's leaving Colorado."

There's a pause, and I know I'm supposed to fill it. So I do.

"Yeah? Where's he going?"

"Out your way, actually. USC. He's starting a new graduate program there. Masters and doctoral degrees in sports psychology. I've told him about your interest in psychology and your playing history. Mike thinks you'd make an ideal candidate for the program. I'd be happy to put you in contact with him if it's something you think you might be interested in."

My lungs stop working for a few seconds. I stare at the television, trying to get my breathing to become unconscious again.

"I appreciate the offer, Matt. But—"

What can I say? My bank account is hovering at a hundred and thirty bucks right now? It wasn't the plan?

Think of a reason, Ethan. Think of one decent goddamn reason to turn down his offer that doesn't have to do with money or pride.

I hear the front door open and close. "Pizza!" Chris yells.

A stroke of luck. Matt picks up his beer and quietly leaves, but my dad stays back.

"Ethan." He stops me with a hand on my shoulder, then he waits until he knows I'm really listening. "Do me a favor, son. Think about what Matt said?"

It's the favor thing I can't say no to. Of course I'm going to do whatever he asks when he says it that way.

"I will, Dad," I promise. Then I make a break for the bathroom.

I need to get some cold water on my face before my head explodes.

As I turn the corner into the hallway, I run right into Chris.

"Sup, bro?" His smile is so big, it looks painful. "How's your day going?" He holds up my cell phone. "Because it's about to get *so much* better."

"You little shit." I lunge for him, but Chris dodges and slams into the wall, almost knocking down a framed picture of us skiing.

"Who's Mia and what did you do to her?" He's shouting and

laughing, and I have never had a clearer goal in my life. I catch his shirt and get him in a headlock, snatching the phone away. Then I pull up my texts and read Mia's message.

Holy Mother of God.

I read the two lines again, but Chris swipes the phone out of my hand. He tears into the dining room. I'm right behind him, but it's too late.

"Dear Ethan," he says, embellishing words that are perfect just the way they are. "I wish I remembered more of our magical night. I'm pretty sure you *rocked my world*. Love, Mia."

Laughter explodes from my mom and dad. Matt puts his arm around Tricia and grins. I can tell he's at least trying not to lose it.

"Thanks, Chris," I say. "Real cool of you to share that with everyone. With my coach."

"I'm not your coach anymore, Ethan. Anyway, by the sound of it, I'm the one who should be getting pointers from you."

Tricia rests her hands over her huge stomach. "I think you do just fine."

"I guess the apple doesn't fall far from the tree," my dad proclaims, like he's making a public service announcement. "You know what they say. Like father, like son."

And here comes the cliché part of the night.

I catch my brother's eye across the table. "You're going to die, Chris. As soon as I have the energy, your life is over." Then I drop into a chair and prepare myself to answer a million questions about Mia.

"Ethan, what are you doing?" my Mom says. "Don't be rude. Go text her back!"

Matt nods. "Prudent advice."

"Keep making me proud, son." Dad barely gets the words out before he's in stitches again.

Chris tosses my phone across the dinner table. I catch it, and I'm out the door, in my room, and texting Mia in less than two seconds.

Ethan: Hey, Curls. Just saw this.

Ethan: I spent most of my night remembering what we did. Remembering you. You rocked my world too.

I drop onto my bed, kick off my Nikes and stare laser beams at the phone. Thankfully, her response comes right away.

Mia: You remember?

Ethan: Most of it.

Ethan: Enough to know I want more of you.

No answer.

No answer, no answer, no answer.

Finally, it comes through.

Mia: What about work? What about Alison?

Ethan: Mia

Mia: Yes?

Ethan: I want YOU.

Another pause. Then,

Mia: You keep rendering me textless.

Mia: And I want you, too.

I stare at those words for a few seconds, my heart doing double gainers in my chest. It takes all my willpower not to call her, but it wouldn't be a quick conversation, and I don't want to say what I want to say on the phone, anyway. And, as understanding as my parents and Matt seem to be about the situation, it'd be rude to spend the rest of the night in my room on the phone with Mia instead of with them.

So I go to plan B.

> **Ethan:** Need to see you. ASAP.
> **Mia:** When are you back?
> **Ethan:** Tomorrow at 6. Feel like picking me up at the airport?
> **Mia:** YES.
> **Ethan:** All caps yes?
> **Mia:** !!!YES!!!
> **Ethan:** OK. One more thing.
> **Ethan:** Send me a picture of you.

I stare at the phone until the picture pops up.

Mia lies on her bed, and the light is all golden and soft, like it's coming from the lamp at her bedside. Her dark hair spills over the soft pink pillows around her, and what I can see of her shoulders is smooth, bare skin with only the thinnest black strap of a tank top or bra. Her green eyes shine with anticipation, and yet her smile is mellow and sultry—and inviting as hell.

She looks like she's at the point of smiling, and at the point of asking me to rock her world, and I know I'm past the point of going crazy for this girl.

Damn.

I know I'll be staring at this picture all night. Imagining a thousand different scenarios, all of them starting with this moment, and ending with her quivering and saying my name. There's no doubt about that. But right now, I need to get back downstairs. So I send her one last text.

> **Ethan:** You're beautiful, Mia. I'll thank you for this tomorrow.

Chapter 45

Mia

Q: Who taught you about true love?

In some alternate world, I'd be able to walk around like a normal person without bumping into furniture. Or I'd be able to focus on my poor Nana, who's having a good day for once but whose words wink in and out in my mind like fireflies.

Thirty minutes until I leave to pick up Ethan.

That is literally the only thought I seem able to hold on to today. Of course, I started with *twenty hours until I pick up Ethan*, which has rendered the day useless in pretty much every arena. Like I had to keep checking to make sure I put on pants before leaving the apartment today.

Twenty-nine minutes, and Ethan likes you in just panties.

Or out of them.

Shut up, brain.

I drift into my mom's studio, where she's stretched across her chaise, backlit by the sun and holding a photographer's loupe up to a contact print. I notice she's only polished one set of toenails—exactly the kind of thing I might do today.

"What're you working on?" I ask, though I know I won't remember a thing she tells me.

Twenty-seven more minutes. . .

"New series," she says, handing me the sheet and the loupe.

I sit on the edge of the chaise and bend toward the sunlight to get a better look. The images are raw: simple photos of people I don't recognize, along with close-ups on some of their features—a flat pink scar against glossy brown skin; a trace of feathered lipstick above a full upper lip. There's a starkness and an intimacy to them that's so different for my mom. Quiet compared to the bold, exaggerated work she usually does.

I tell her so, and she smiles. "I like change. That's why I keep telling you to play. The artist you are at twenty-one isn't the same as the one you'll be at forty. Or sixty. It's important to be curious and open. Not fret so damn much."

Today, that angst feels miles away. Ethan's coming home. We'll be together. And I definitely do plan to play.

I hand her back the sheet. "What drew you to this new idea?" I ask. "Or, like, to these particular people?" Part of me feels excited for her to make new discoveries and take new paths in her art. And part of me feels sad to think that part might not include me.

She smiles. "I just follow the light. All of these people had a kind of glow. From the inside. Do you know what I mean?"

"Yeah." Ethan has that, I think. Bright and intense, like the flare of a match in the dark.

"You've got it too, my darling," she says and cups my cheek.

Nana appears in the doorway, carrying a hinged brown leather box. Settling into a stiff-backed chair, she says, "She's right, you know."

"Thanks, Nan." I feel so grateful to be here on this day, when her own light is so bright.

I point to the box. "What have you got there?"

"Oh, I just wanted you to have a few things." She props open the lid and pulls out a handful of yellowing photographs. They're pictures of my grandmother and grandfather on the beach at Coney Island. I flip them over for the date: July 1964.

My grandfather's stretched out on his stomach in the sand, a pair of aviators resting on his curly dark hair and a sleepy grin on his face. My grandmother—who looks so young and so much like Audrey Hepburn here, it's crazy—lies with her head on his back, a thick hardcover book resting against her chest, smiling up at the camera. It's amazing how modern they look, though my grandmother's white two-piece bathing suit has a high waist and is cinched with a thick gold belt.

It occurs to me to get my camera, to capture more of my grandmother's life on a day when she's happy and lucid. I run into the kitchen, fish it from my bag, and run back into the studio. I switch it on and focus on her.

"Do you remember what you were reading?" She can remember so much more of her past than she can of the present. I want to keep her talking, keep her happy and sounding like her old self for as long as I can.

She takes back the photograph and studies it. "Oh, it had to be *The Group*," she tells me. "My girlfriends and I were all reading it. I'm surprised your grandfather looks so happy here. That book made me so mad at him. Well, at all men." Winking at my mother, she adds, "It's a miracle you were born the next year."

My mother laughs. "Judging by how often you two locked me out of your room, it's more of a miracle that I only have two brothers."

"What was it like back then?" I ask. "Dating, I mean. Or relationships. Did you have a lot of single friends?" I want to ask if it's always been like this—confusing. Exhilarating.

She shakes her head. "We all married young. Your age or younger. But maybe that was a little like dating."

"What do you mean?"

"It took me a long time to get to know your grandfather," she says. "We were practically strangers when we got married, but that's what you did. You wanted someone, and then you married him. If you were lucky, you fell in love."

"I don't know if that's everyone's experience," says my mother.

"Maybe not." She takes back the photographs, closes the box, and hands it to me. "There's a movie reel in there, too," she says. "It's from the march."

"Jesus, Nana." I practically start to drool. "You have film from the march on Selma in here?"

She nods. "I think it's the day I fell in love with your grandfather. I mean really in love."

"You were already pregnant with me!" my mother exclaims.

"What happened that day?" I think about Ethan because I can't stop thinking about Ethan, because I have to leave in—I check my phone—*seven minutes* to get him and because I suddenly see myself in the future, sitting with my own children. Will I be telling stories about *him*? Am I *in love* with him?

I don't know. I only know I want to see him, just to sit with him, breathe the same air. Okay, maybe attack him like an expensive buffet.

"So you were pregnant when you and Grandpa marched in Selma?"

"Yes. About six months along."

"What made you fall in love with Grandpa that day?"

She runs her hand along the edge of the box, her expression dreamy. "A policeman knocked me down by accident, and your grandfather went crazy and attacked him. Grabbed a baton right out of the officer's hand and beat the man with it."

"He did?" I can't put the sweet lazy smile in the photograph together with a man who'd attack a police officer.

"He did and got fifteen stitches for his trouble," she says. "But you know him. He can be hot-headed."

Anxiety flares at her use of the present tense, but I don't correct her. "I guess we all can."

"Stan was so mad at me that day, too. He wanted me to stay home because he knew it would be dangerous. But we'd been working side by side with all the other people in the law office to organize, to help do something about the terrible situation in the South. And I was naïve. Even though I saw the news reports myself, I didn't believe they'd do anything. I guess I didn't believe they'd hurt a cute Jewish girl from New York."

I imagine the crowds and the chaos, picture my grandfather as a young man so filled with protectiveness and rage that he'd go up against an officer in riot gear, with a shield and baton.

"He picked me up and carried me, six months pregnant and no feather in those days, away from the crowd." She touches her temple. "He had blood gushing from his face where they'd split it open. And he was like . . . like he'd mow down anyone in his path, police or no police. I think he could have walked through a wall if it meant getting me to safety."

"I can see why you fell in love with him." Again I think about Ethan, about him lifting me, no feather myself, and carrying me into his living room. And I think about how fair he is, and how loyal. He'd do what my grandfather did. I know that much.

Suddenly, I can't wait another minute to get to see him.

I switch off my camera. "I have to get to the airport," I tell Nana and my mom.

"Do you want to bring Ethan back for dinner?" my mom asks, but her smile quirks, and I can see she's teasing me, that she knows—like she always knows—what's on my mind.

"Um, maybe another night," I tell her and give her a kiss on the forehead. Then I kiss and hug Nana. "I'm glad you fell in love," I tell her.

Then I run for the door.

Chapter 46

Ethan

Q: How do you like to be kissed: hard, soft or any which way?

I spot Mia's Prius just as she swings the door open and bolts out of it. She jumps into my arms, and my duffel slips off my shoulder as I catch her. I kiss her and feel the world fade back.

We're officially the cheesy airport reunion couple, and I don't care.

I'm consumed by her. By feeling her body against me, smelling the clean floral scent of her hair, tasting her soft, hungry mouth under mine. Everything becomes *her*, and only a tsunami could bring me back to myself.

Or an LAX parking enforcement attendant.

"Take it somewhere else, you two! I am three seconds away from giving you a ticket *and* having that Prius towed!"

After talking with Alison this morning and telling her as gently as I could about Mia, I decided to fly back on my own. Now Alison's hurt, which defeats the purpose of us trying to move forward, but I can't put her first anymore. That place is taken.

"Hi," Mia says, smiling up at me. "Where to?"

I feel like I can finally look at her without trying to hide anything. I can finally look at her like she's *mine*. She looks incredible in tight faded blue jeans and a purple sweater. It's a change from the work clothes I'm used to seeing her in. Sexy in a way that makes me think of long afternoons in bed. Which is going to happen soon and often.

My life just got so fuckin' great.

"Mind if we stop at the office?" I toss my duffel into the backseat. "I need to grab something."

With Vegas only days away, my preparations for the trade show are almost finished. I need to pick up the check for Zeke—the final payment for the virtual boomerang game.

Mia's smile falters.

"What is it, Curls? Work's not what you had in mind?"

She shakes her head. "No, that sounds *awesome*."

I grab her hand, stopping her from slipping into the driver's seat. "Mind if I drive?"

"Sure. But . . . why?"

"Safety consideration. It's the only way I'll be able to keep my hands off you for the next half hour." I bend down and kiss her before she can reply, taking the keys out of her hand.

"How was home?" she asks, hopping in the passenger seat.

"Inebriated in part, but also enlightening." I pull away from the airport, and we fall into easy conversation. I tell her about my disastrous Friday night, and about how Chris has changed. Then I ask about her weekend and she tells me about Nana, and we go back and forth, catching up. When I tell her about Matt's visit, Mia drops her face into her hands.

"Oh, God. So your family *and* your former coach know you rocked my world?" she says, her voice muffled.

"Yes, but it was an accident, you see."

She looks up. "I don't think I've ever embarrassed myself to complete strangers on this scale before. Not even for art's sake."

"Well, they're not really complete strangers." I've told her plenty about my parents and Chris. Despite the bumps we've had over the past weeks, Mia knows more about what's going on in my life than Alison, or even Jason. "And they know a lot about you now. Dinner Saturday night was pretty much a press conference about Mia Galliano."

Mia smiles. She starts to say something, then seems to change her mind. "I'm glad you got to see your coach," she says instead, her voice soft with sincerity.

"Thanks." We're quiet for a few moments. The silence is comfortable, filled with only the quiet sounds of the road. Then I realize I want to tell her more.

"I never realized how much he influenced me until this weekend. Matt's always trying to bring out the best in others—it was really apparent to me—and it got me thinking that maybe I got that from him, you know? Maybe I picked that up from him, or maybe that was already part of me and he just sharpened it, as a coach. As someone I had to listen to."

"That's the enlightening part of your weekend," she says, more a statement than a question.

I nod.

Mia rests her head against the car seat and watches me for a few seconds. Then she smiles. "That's amazing, Ethan." Her gaze moves out the front window and she grows pensive.

"Nana's the same for me, I think," she says after a little while. "She kind of keeps our family history. But it's more than that. She was part of such a big movement, something so pivotal to where we are today. I think that's why I want to make this documentary so much. She inspires me, and I always want to be shaped by her. I don't want her influence on me to ever go away."

She gives her head a small shake, like she's said too much, but I could hear her talk this way all day long. She's smart and funny, and hotter than should be legal, but there's an old soul inside of her. I want to protect that part of her. I want to stand guard in front of it so it's always safe.

"You want to hear the *best* part of my weekend?" I ask.

She smiles. "What's the best part of your weekend?"

"There are actually a few: thinking about you. Getting your text messages. Getting picked up at the airport. Right now . . ." I smile at her. "See anything in common?"

Putting this kind of stuff out there so bluntly is a new thing for me but it feels natural with her. And it's more than worth the reward.

Mia takes up some slack in her seat belt and scoots up to her knees. She leans over the center console and kisses my cheek. Then she hovers by my ear, and when she speaks, I feel her warm breath.

"If you're that easy to please, then your weekend's going to get *much* better. We still have a few hours left."

I turn and kiss her, managing to steal a taste of her before I have to look back to the freeway.

"You were right," she says. I see a glint of desire and surprise in her eyes before she settles back into her seat. "We really are a road hazard."

"I had it covered, Curls." I reach over for her hand. It feels soft and so small compared to mine. "I'd never put you in harm's way."

"Still," she says. "Making out while we're going seventy miles an hour is a bad call."

"Disagree. Dangerous make-out sessions with you give my life meaning."

"Fair enough, but should we at least try not to?"

"Do or do not. There is no try."

"Is that one of Matt's sayings?" she asks, smiling.

I look at her like I'm shocked. "Curls, you *know* that's Yoda!" Which is true, she does. "And you call yourself a film student."

"I know. I'm a disgrace," she says. "So are we doing or not doing?"

"Are you kidding me?" I tip my head, motioning her my way. "Get back over here."

Mia laughs. Then she scoots back onto her knees, and we kiss again.

Half an hour later, we step into the Boomerang offices. On a Sunday night, with only half the recessed lights on and the expansive glass windows full of night, it's eerily quiet and dark.

"I asked Rhett to open up for me. He'll come back later to lock up," I explain to Mia as we make our way to his office. I don't bother to flip the lights on; there's enough light filtering through the glass walls, and we're only staying for a minute.

The check for Zeke rests on Rhett's keyboard, just like he promised.

"What's so urgent that it can't wait for tomorrow?" she asks, perching on the edge of the desk.

"It's not the urgency. We just couldn't risk cutting the check during regular hours. Rhett came in late Friday night to do it." I've told her about the situation with the virtual game and Cookie, so she knows why we had to do it this way. "Zeke and I are driving out to Temecula tomorrow to check out the game before it's shipped to Winning Displays. From there, it'll get trucked to Vegas with the rest of the booth." I hold up the check. "But I need to pay him."

"Ah," Mia says, "got it." But her expression clouds with worry, and I know why.

I drop the check back on the desk and step in front of her, taking her face into my hands.

"This thing with Boomerang," I say, staring into her eyes, "the competition for the job . . . we'll figure it out."

After this stunt I'm pulling with Cookie, I know I'm going to lose the job anyway, and I don't care. I know how much Mia wants to do the film of Nana, and I don't see anymore how her winning could feel like my loss.

"But, Ethan, I—"

"It's going to be all right, Curls. I promise." Leaning down, I brush my lips against hers. I meant it to be a light kiss, but Mia's mouth is firm, insistent. Her tongue slips between my lips. I pull her against me, and like the strike of a match, I'm hard for her.

"Ethan," she breathes, and presses her hips into me.

I pick her up, and her legs wrap around me, linking behind my back. My tongue plunges into her mouth and her arms tighten around me. I'm suddenly seeing images of her laid out on this desk, naked, her legs wrapped around me just like they are now. Me, buried inside of her.

"You can't tempt me like this, Mia."

"Why not?"

The office lights flip on, and the brightness is blinding. Raw instinct fires through me, and I get Mia behind me in a quick move.

Cookie stands at the door, tapping her foot.

"Actually," she says, "I can think of a few reasons."

Chapter 47

Mia

Q: Are you easily embarrassed?

The light in the office feels bright enough to sear the flesh from my bones but not half as intense as the look of total disgust Cookie directs my way. It takes forever for my mind to process the fact that we've been caught. By the worst possible person.

On earth.

She steps into the office and closes the door behind her. Immediately, it feels like she's sealed off all the oxygen in the place. My throat tightens, and every part of me goes clammy.

"Cookie," I start to say, but she's riveted on Ethan.

Smiling, she says, "Well, first of all, you're fired."

Oh, God. "No!" I exclaim. "That's not—"

"Oh, it is," she says, that satisfied smile glued to her face. "Fair, I mean. That's what you were going to say, right?"

"If you want to know what she has to say, then let her talk,"

Ethan says. He stands there, cool and upright. But I can feel the anger coiled in his body. And I know I'm the cause of it.

Cookie leans back against the door, folding her arms. Her expression challenges him to dig a bigger hole. I can't let him do it.

"Listen," I try again.

"I don't need any explanations, Mia," says Cookie, though her gaze barely flicks in my direction. For once, she's not barking her anger, but the chill in her words is much, much worse. "I just need the two of you to leave. And I need not to see Mr. Vance ever again. Seems simple enough."

"Why only Ethan? Why not—?"

"Fine," he interrupts. "But answer something for me first."

"You're not really in a position to make requests."

"How did you find out about Alison?"

My whole body heats, and my mouth goes Sahara dry. I reach out to touch his arm, but he moves it just as I make contact, thrusting his hands into the pocket of his jeans.

"You sound like a paranoid lunatic," Cookie says. "You know that, right?"

"Right. I'm the lunatic. I'm not the one who pried into someone else's life to try to sabotage his career."

Cookie snorts. "What career? You're an *intern*. You were never going to be anything else."

A flush creeps up his neck, and he steps forward. Cookie shrinks into herself, like she's scared he'll get physical with her.

This is awful. I need to put a stop to it. "Please, listen—"

"And you made sure of that, didn't you?" Ethan says. "You really get off on playing God, right? Once you got tired of threatening Paolo and Sadie, why not move on to me?"

"You have an exaggerated view of your own importance," Cookie says. "And you're lucky I'm just firing you. I should have you arrested."

"Arrested? For what?"

She stalks over to the desk and snatches up the envelope with Rhett's check inside. "How does embezzling seventeen thousand dollars sound to you?"

He laughs, and it's a raw, brutal sound. "Come on. That's weak, even for you."

"That's crazy," I protest. "He wasn't embezzling. He was trying to do a good job for Adam and the investors."

"The investors don't care what a couple of *interns* have to say about anything. Now get out."

She crosses back to the door and whips it open.

"Wait," I say. My pulse rushes in my ear, loud as the ocean's roar. "Fire me if you have to fire someone. It's not Ethan's fault. I'm the one who messed with the Boomerang setups."

"What?" he says. "Mia, you don't have to—"

"I know," I tell him, still unable to look at him but wanting to, desperately. "It's dumb. I should have said something sooner. I was going to, but—"

"But you couldn't know Alison was my ex. How—"

"I didn't know," I say. Finally, I look up at him, and his expression is as confused and deeply hurt as I feared. "I just got . . . jealous and stupid, and I tried to pick someone I thought you'd hate."

He raises an eyebrow, and a hardness comes into his gaze, piercing me. "Really? Of all the girls in the Boomerang system, you just *happened* to find Alison?"

"I know it sounds crazy, but yes."

"And then you let me make an ass of myself in front of Frosty here?" He jerks a thumb at her. "You didn't think it'd be a good idea to tell me this *before* I committed career suicide?"

I can't bear to have Cookie hear all of this, to see her angled up against the door again, an expression of amusement on her face. And Ethan and me as the source.

"Let's go talk about this somewhere else, okay?"

"You know what?" His tone is brittle as dry leaves. "I'm good."

"What does that mean?"

He strides up to Cookie and whips the check out of her hand. "I'm paying my vendor because he did the work. If you want to call the police, then call the goddamn police." Gripping the doorknob, he gives her a look that dares her to keep him from leaving.

"Ethan, wait."

"I'm going to walk home," he says. "We'll talk later."

My stomach hollows at his words. I've ruined this evening. Maybe I've ruined everything.

"Ethan, it's too far. Let me drive you."

But he's already out the door and doesn't hear me. Or he does, and he ignores me. I turn back to Cookie, and she meets me with a cool, impassive gaze.

"You're going to come to Vegas, and you're going to set up that booth," she tells me. "It had better be the best thing you've ever done."

"Or what?" I ask. Suddenly, this job feels like nothing to me. I just want to punch Cookie in the throat and go make things right with Ethan. "You can't fire us both."

"Of course I can," she says, but there's a flicker of hesitation in her eyes.

I don't care if it costs me the job. I have to find some way to redeem this night. Not for me. I don't give a damn at this point. But I can't be responsible for Ethan losing this opportunity. I just can't.

"Vegas is in five days," I remind her. "And like it or not, Adam entrusted two *interns* with the most critical job of the convention."

"A decision I've questioned from the start." She sniffs. "But I'm sure we can manage just fine without you."

"Fine. Let's test that theory." It literally feels like my insides are trembling. I'm terrified she'll call my bluff. "I'm sure you have time to make a totally new *custom* display, right? Or maybe you can just pull the old one out of storage. I'm sure Adam would love to see that again."

"Who do you think you are?"

But I ignore her. "And I'm sure Paolo, Sadie, and Pippa will be really happy to pitch in on the creative side, since you're always *so good* to them."

Her fists ball at her side, and she tries to eviscerate me with her eyes, but I don't care.

"Fine," she says. "I'll see you in Vegas."

That's not good enough. That's not the point of all this. "You'll see us *both*, you mean."

She stares at me, and I stare at her. I'm pretty sure another ice age unfolds while we stand there, eyes locked.

"Goodnight, Ms. Galliano," she says, and I know I've won.

Cookie turns and flicks out the light, leaving me with only the glow of the hallway's recessed lights. I watch her leave, her skin ghostly pale, posture erect as a rake.

In the parking lot, I run to the car and whip open the door. Getting behind the wheel makes me want to cry. What happened to this night?

I throw the car into gear and zoom out onto the main road. In no time, I spot Ethan, jogging along the shoulder.

Pulling up alongside him, I roll down the window. "Ethan, hold on," I call, trying not to crash or run him over. "Cookie's letting us both come to Vegas. I told her I wouldn't go if you didn't."

He thrusts his hands into his pockets but doesn't look my way. "Great."

"It is, right?" I swerve a little and correct. "Ethan, can you please get in the car? I'm going to kill you or myself, trying to talk this way."

Finally, he stops and turns to me, so I slam on the brakes, almost breaking my own nose on the steering wheel.

"Are you getting in?"

He hesitates for a moment but then opens the door and slips into the car.

Every part of me soars, just having him with me again. I put my hand on his shoulder, and he lets me keep it there, but his eyes stay fixed on the windshield in front of him.

"You're not fired," I try.

"Yeah, I heard."

"But . . . That's good, right?"

"Like I said, it's great."

This is all so screwed up and wrong that it's all I can do not to get out of the car and walk myself. It hurts to have him sit there, all warmth and connection obliterated. And it hurts worse to know that it's one hundred percent my fault. "I . . . I'm really so sorry, Ethan. I didn't mean for any of this to happen. I was just being . . ." What, Mia? Stupid? Selfish? Words feel too small to contain everything I want to say. "You have to believe I never wanted this."

"It's fine, Mia," he tells me, in a tone that suggests the very opposite. "Just take me home."

Chapter 48

Ethan

Q: What stays in Vegas for you?

Rhett and I check into the Mirage at 11 p.m., which is the equivalent of happy hour in Vegas time.

"Should we get some food first?" Rhett asks. "Then play some blackjack?"

This is our only night "off." The convention floor opens to exhibitors in the morning. We have the day to set up before the show starts on Monday morning.

"I'm not hungry," I say. "Let's just get a drink and gamble."

Rhett gives me a look.

I've been seeing it a lot this week.

We detour into a bar, and I order a Jack and Coke. Rhett gets a beer, but when our drinks arrive we don't leave for the casino. We don't even talk about it, we just stay in the bar.

It occurs to me that I did some gambling of my own recently. I took a risk. I trusted a girl again—and was sucker-punched again. I'm pissed at myself for making the same mistake. I hate even more that I understand Mia's reasons for doing what she did. Just remembering Robby DTF and the other dude, Brian, makes me want to punch somebody. I didn't want her going on those idiotic dates either.

I'm not angry that she brought Alison back into my life. It's working out all right. Forcing me to come to terms with the past. And I can't blame Mia for being the reason I won't get the job either. Regardless of how it started, I'm the one who went head-to-head with Cookie that morning, and then went behind her back with the video game.

I can't really tell *what* I'm pissed about. The goddamn no-dating office policy? Maybe none of this would've happened if I'd just gone after Mia like I wanted to in the first place.

"The virtual game's going to be awesome, Ethan," Rhett says, breaking our silence.

It's surprising to hear him call me by my full name, since he usually calls me "E" now. That bugged me a few weeks ago, but now I can't imagine why.

"Maybe you went rogue on it," he continues, "but Adam appreciates trailblazers. He'll be more impressed by your initiative than pissed that you went around Cookie."

He has no idea what happened between me, Mia, and Cookie at the office on Sunday night. As far as I can tell, no one except the three of us does.

"I don't care what he thinks," I say, but it's a lie. I'm here because I do care. I'm here because I finish what I start, and because I still want the job. I don't want Mia to lose, but losing isn't an option for me either. I don't know where that leaves me. Or us.

"You don't mean that," Rhett says, his intuition spot-on as usual.

But my pride won't let me concede the point, so I shrug and take a long sip of my drink. Then I square my shoulders and focus on being here. In this moment.

Sin City is firing on all cylinders tonight. The vibe around us is charged with the promise of money and sex.

Businessmen. Professional escorts. Bachelor parties. Girls' weekends. They're all here to let go of themselves, and it's close. I can feel it in the air. In two hours' time, their last thin layers of cool reserve will crack under the pressure of mountains of pent-up desire.

My gaze pulls to the dark-haired girl in a black dress entering the bar.

Mia.

I'm not surprised to see her walk in with Sadie and Paolo. We're all staying here; it was only a matter of time before she appeared.

I've done a spectacular job of avoiding her this week.

Monday I spent the day at the gaming vendor's warehouse.

Tuesday I was at Winning Displays to check on the booth design.

Wednesday she went there to do the same for her design.

Thursday I worked in the conference room.

And Friday I came into the office at 6 a.m., left at noon, and worked the rest of the day from my apartment.

Where I failed was every freaking night, when I pulled up her picture on my phone.

Rhett peels away from my side and joins Sadie and Paolo at a high bar table. The way they do this, so deliberately, makes me wonder if I've been wrong about no one knowing what happened. It's obvious now they all think Mia and I need to talk.

"Hi," Mia says, joining me.

I turn toward the bar and rest my elbows on it. "Hey."

"Haven't seen you much."

"Been busy getting ready for this and with practices." I stare at the spotlit liquor bottles against the back of the bar as I answer. I don't want to look into her green eyes. I don't want to see the sadness I know I'll find there.

"Right," she says. "Makes sense. How . . . um . . . how'd it go with Parker this week?" she asks after a moment.

My team practices were the only highlights of my week, and I want to tell her about it. I want to tell her how Parker's like a different kid out there; he and Tyler are this unstoppable duo now. And how Raylene comes to every practice and how she and Rhett have morphed into this cool, normal couple, mellowing each other out. Rhett sweats less now, I want to say. And Raylene isn't manic anymore. She's actually pretty nice.

But I don't tell her any of that.

"Good," I say. "He's coming around."

In my peripheral vision, I see Mia nod, but I get the feeling she senses how much I'm not saying. She pulls a chair over and sits. She orders a drink from the bartender when he comes around.

Then we sit there for long minutes, drinking our drinks, my heart pounding just from being near her.

"I wish you'd talk to me."

I face her. "That's what I think too, Mia. Why didn't you say something after that first date with Alison? Why did you let it go so long?"

"Because I was *afraid*," she says, but it comes out like she's angry. "For a while, it felt like all we had were reasons to *not* be together. The competition for this job . . . The rules. The way we started, with a one-night stand that neither of us could even remember. I didn't want to add one more thing. One more reason to drive us apart. Then you started seeing her again, and I—"

"I wasn't seeing her again."

"That's what it looked like. You went on dates with her. You went to *Colorado* with her. You and I . . . we haven't done *one thing* together that we actually chose."

I realize it's true. The first night, we happened to be at Duke's to-gether after meeting with Adam. The second time we kissed, in her mom's studio, my being there was a coincidence. Working together happened by chance. Even this moment, right now, is a coincidence.

A prickling sensation spreads over my skin, and I feel like I don't recognize myself. My internal compass is spinning. I've lost my north.

I've always gone after what I want, but I haven't done that with her. I don't think I've done that *for myself* either.

I'm fighting for this job and for my future. For money, so I can pay off my loans and go to law school, but something feels wrong, and I can't see what it is. It's like my life's gone blurry and unfo-cused.

"Sorry to interrupt your poignant silence," Paolo says, joining us, "but I just got a text from Mark. Adam's on fire over at the black-jack tables. I guess he's up twenty K already and he just sat down ten minutes ago. That's a must-see situation. At least it is in my book. What about your books?"

"Sure. I'm in." Mia looks at me, hope glowing in her eyes. We're not finished with our conversation, and it's not going to happen now, with Rhett, Sadie, and Pippa standing around us.

"I'm good," I say. "Maybe I'll catch up with you guys later."

"Okay," Mia says, her eyes dimming. She leaves with Paolo, Sadie, and Pippa. I don't watch her go, but I feel the rush of being with her fade.

Rhett takes the seat she just vacated. "You're Opposite Man to-night, E."

I smirk at him.

"It's true," he says, grinning. "You keep saying things that are the opposite of what you mean. 'Cause you didn't want to gamble, and you're not 'good' and I doubt you're meeting up with them later either."

"Opposite Man, huh?" I tip my drink back, sucking down the rest. "Well, in that case, I love the way you pry into my private life, Rhett. It doesn't make me want to punch you so you'll shut the hell up."

He laughs, and then we order another drink, and I make my purpose tonight finding a comfortable numbness. Maybe if I do that well enough, I won't pull up Mia's picture when I get back to my room.

Because I don't want to do that.

So says Opposite Man.

Chapter 49

Mia

Q: Bright lights, or quiet nights?

 O nly in Vegas does a hotel exhibit hall blaze with neon and feature carpeting patterned to look like someone fed a tiger into an industrial shredder. Soft techno ebbs and flows beneath a steady stream of conversation punctuated by bursts of shrieking laughter that make my entire body clench.

Of course, I'm on edge already, not just because I'm responsible for finally putting my part of the display together—with help from Paolo, thank God—but because I have to spend the entire day working side-by-side with Ethan, acting like I'm perfectly fine with the fact that we haven't spoken since I cornered him at the bar yesterday. Everything's still wrong. But I'm here now, and I'm determined to do the job Adam entrusted me to do.

All around us, people hustle elaborate displays into place, erecting massive vinyl banners, latching together platforms, hauling up shelves. And at every other booth, it seems, someone is having a full-on nervous breakdown.

Nearby, a man with a helmet of straw-gold hair and a shiny steel-gray suit paces back and forth with his cell phone glued to his ear and a face red enough to make me look around for EMTs. "I ordered the ten-foot chrome pyramids, and you sent me these fucking dinky shelves." He stands back and holds his phone out to capture a pair of triangular bookcases that stand about as tall as my shoulders. "Seriously," he says. "Are you seeing this shit?"

Just then, a massive ripping sound splits the air, and I look over to see two girls about my age, only tall, wearing dresses that look recently sprayed onto their bodies. Each holds half of a heart-covered banner, now torn neatly in two.

"Jesus Christ, Amy," one of the women, a redhead, shrieks and throws down her side of the banner. "What did you do?"

"What did I do? I told you to stop tugging at it!"

"This place is cray-cray," Paolo mumbles and unfolds a schematic of the cavernous space.

"What number's our booth again?" I ask for about the sixtieth time.

"We are"—he consults the diagram—"in the primo spot, right between the bar and the bathrooms. Number thirty-three."

Someone almost clips us with a giant wheeled backdrop of men in fatigues and a sign that says, "Love Is a Battlefield," which feels like an iffy approach to me but hey, I'm not *their* marketing intern.

Finally, I spot our display, and even from here I can see it's perfect. Shaped like two boomerangs back to back, it has an almost yin-yang effect, with Ethan's curved wall and floor a deep, glossy black and mine a gleaming white. LCD monitors line a narrow shelf running the length of his side, leading to a tall screen with a console in front of it that I know will run the boomerang game he commissioned. A message scrolls over and over again on every screen: *In the dating game, play to win.*

My side is softer, with café tables, comfy chairs, and a curved projection screen that runs almost the full length of my wall. I'll run a loop of the video I edited together with all the footage I got of the staff at the Boomerang office, my friends and neighbors, Paolo and Beth acting out "dates" in front of the green screen, which Brian helped me convert to dinner at a Parisian café, a picnic in Central Park, and—just for the hell of it—a Moroccan feast, with gossamer tent flaps rippling in the background and a starry moonlit sky beyond.

On each silk-covered table rests a pair of iPads, where clients can access the Boomerang site, create profiles, even enter a drawing for a year's free membership. Mostly, I want it to feel intimate and sexy here, with my film reminding them of what a big, lovely adventure dating can be.

As long as you're not me.

"Ethan, you stud!" exclaims Paolo, and jogs the last few yards to the display to give Ethan a vigorous bro hug, which consists of half handshake, half chest bump.

My own footsteps slow, and Ethan looks up at me. I smile, and he smiles, but I don't believe either of us.

Then he turns away and starts to confer with Rhett, who I now see is on his hands and knees on the floor, plugging cables into a chain of tidily arranged power strips.

Rhett sees me, gets to his feet, and dusts off his hands. "How's it going, Mia? You ready to rock Adam's world?"

My whole body goes cold, and I fire a look at Ethan. Did he tell Rhett about my text?

But Ethan gives me a subtle head shake, like he's reading my mind, and I feel a weird bubble of hysteria rising in me. Is everything—every casual comment—going to remind me of him? If I never see him again after this weekend, do I still have to carry him with me everywhere I go? And for how long?

"Mia?"

"Sorry, yeah." I say. "Just going to get the video connected and test run it a few times." Then I just have to wait for a banner delivery with my slogan: *Life is short. Make it an adventure.* Catering will come Monday morning.

"Sounds good. Let me know if you need help."

Apparently, Raylene agrees with Rhett. His face has fleshed out a bit in the last month or so. And he seems less coiled and intense. More teddy bear, less Skeletor.

It occurs to me how many couples have gotten together in the few months Ethan and I have been working together: Raylene and Rhett; Paolo and Mark, who used to work in accounting; Skyler and Brian. It's like we're some kind of a relationship version of Dorian Gray. Everyone around us hooks up, and we keep disintegrating.

Okay, Mia, focus.

I head around to the back of the display, where I'm going to connect my laptop to run the video.

"Hey, Paolo, do we have HDMI cables around here somewhere?"

Paolo comes around to my side of the booth, holding a set of cables in each hand.

"Is it the one with weird prongs that look like a smiley face?"

"Umm . . . No. I don't know *what* that is." I hold out my hand for both cables but don't recognize either. "Crap. Not what I need."

Music blares from Ethan's side of the display, followed by a sharp whooshing sound.

"Oh, that's *sick,* E," says Rhett, and I can't help myself. I have to see.

Over on Ethan's turf, I find Rhett wearing a vinyl glove with glinting metal plates on the knuckles. A screen in front of him displays a grid with heart-shaped signposts measuring distance in ten-foot increments.

"I'm going for thirty this time," Rhett says. He hefts an imaginary object in his gloved hand, then cocks his arm back and swings it at the screen. A red-and-blue boomerang, bearing the Boomerang logo, comes whipping in from the corner of the screen. It soars past the ten-foot marker, the twenty, and almost makes it to thirty before spinning in the air and coming back toward Rhett.

He bounces on his feet and lunges forward, hand closing on air. On the screen, an animated hand passes right through the boomerang, and it disappears from the screen. Red letters appear: "MISSED."

"You grabbed for it too quickly," says Ethan, and his tone carries the same amused patience it does when he coaches his kids. "Wait 'til it fills about a third of the screen and snap it up then."

"Got it." Rhett does it again, and after a couple of tries, he's flinging the virtual boomerang at least forty feet and nabbing it back on each try.

"There you go," says Ethan, and then he finally notices me standing there.

"It's looking really good," I tell him. "All of it."

And it's true. Everything looks polished and put together on this side. Appealing. Like him.

"Thanks." He brushes his bangs off his forehead, and I feel a full-body longing to do it for him. Just for an excuse to touch him.

"Hey, do you guys have an extra HDMI cable?"

"About six of them," Rhett says. "Help yourself."

I look to Ethan for confirmation that it's okay, but he's already bending over a tangle of cords to find me what I need. "Here you go," he says, and hands it over. "More here if you need anything."

We stand there for another awkward moment before I think to say thanks and retreat back to my side of things.

There I connect my laptop, power it on, and wait. Paolo drifts back over to Ethan's side, and I can hear the three of them taking turns on the game and talking about what time to bring in seating and food on Monday.

Once my desktop icons appear on the big projection screen, I go into the folder for my presentation. I click on it, and a box appears on the screen: "Error 2048—File type unsupported."

But I've run the file a dozen times already. I know it's supported. I try again. Same error.

A swell of panic laps at my brain, but I force it back. I stored an extra version of the file in the cloud, just in case.

But as I sign into the hotel's wireless and sign into my account, I feel the stirrings of nausea in my belly. I download and click on the file.

"Error 2048—File type unsupported."

Because of course I must have saved it *after* it became corrupted somehow. How else was this day going to go?

A taste of something metallic rises in my throat, and my body goes limp. I sink into a chair at one of the café tables.

I'm screwed. Ethan has the perfect, smart presentation going over there, and I've got nothing. A weird fake café with some iPads at the table. That's going to absolutely *dazzle* the investors.

But I don't really care about that. I just don't want to humiliate Adam—or myself. And I have no idea how to spare either of us.

"Mia?"

I look up, and of course, it's Adam, standing there in all of his elegant glory, in charcoal jeans and a tailored black oxford.

Then I notice that he's left a button in the middle of the shirt undone, and for the first time since we've met, his expression is grim.

"What's—"

"It's your mother," he says, holding his cell phone out to me. "She's been trying to reach you."

Chapter 50

Ethan

Q: Crises: wake you up or shut you down?

Zeke designed the advanced mode on the boomerang game so it's like skeet shooting: when you hit *Start*, a series of three targets— hearts, which I thought were going to be cheesy but actually look pretty badass—appear across the sky on screen. Only one of them is the "right" heart—distinguishable by the quick flash of red that illuminates it the instant before you have to throw. The goal is to hit that one while avoiding the others and still catch the boomerang when it comes back.

It's genius—and addicting.

The only problem, for me, is that the red is right in my color-blindness blind spot, which makes it almost impossible for me to see the cue.

Almost impossible.

I hit *Start*, wiggle my fingers in the glove, ready to try again. Most of my booth is set-up, and I can feel the other vendors' envy. Once Mia figures out her file problem, I'll have a little more competition, but right now, my display is the one to beat.

"Ethan," Rhett says, catching my arm just as I'm about to launch the boomerang. "You better get over here."

His tone of voice sends a shot of adrenaline through me, and I wonder if someone else is hurt. This exhibit floor is a hazard. One of the GetLucky.com people already fell off a stepladder and twisted an ankle. I follow Rhett, hoping none of our team is hurt—that Mia isn't—and that it's just the file problem she needs help with. But as I come around to her side of the booth, all bright white and stylish, I stop in my tracks.

Mia stands by one of the café tables, a cell phone pressed to her ear. Her shoulders are bunched, and she's still, like her entire body is bracing and distressed. Adam stands beside her. Adam, whose personal worth is about fifty million dollars over anyone else's in this convention hall, and who isn't supposed to show up until tomorrow, when the show starts.

As soon as he sees me, he waves me over. His hair is wet and uncombed like he had to rush from a shower, and he has a five o'clock shadow—which he's never had before.

"Her grandmother," he says quietly.

Jesus. My whole body goes numb. Nana.

Mia still hasn't said a word. She stares vacantly into space, listening to someone on the other end.

"What happened?" I ask.

"She's in the hospital," Adam says. "I don't know anything else. Mia's mother called me. She had my number from a piece I commissioned. I guess this hall is a dead zone for Mia's phone."

We stand there, me and Rhett and Adam, a small protective circle around Mia. Cookie wanders over, quiet and rigid. I give her a look, letting her know if she dares say a word—about anything—I will physically silence her, and she avoids my gaze, wisely choosing to stand down.

Across the booth, Paolo, Sadie, Pippa, and Mark watch—and even beyond, people have taken notice. Our booth was generating lots of buzz before. Now it's drawing the somber attention that only comes from tragedy.

"How critical, Mom?" Mia says finally, her voice thin and shaky. It's quiet again as she listens. Then, "but she's going to live, right? She'll be okay, right?"

Fuck the job. Fuck everything.

I put my arm around her shoulders, and her eyes are still far away, in Los Angeles, but her weight shifts slightly onto me.

"Okay," Mia says. "Okay. Don't worry about me. I'll be fine, okay? You just worry about Nana. I love you. Bye." She hands Adam his phone and says, "Thank you," and we're all standing there waiting for her to explain, but she doesn't. She's off the phone, but it's like she's still listening to her mother's voice.

"Mia," I say. "What happened to Nana?"

She looks up. When she speaks, it's only to me. "She was hit by a car. She's in bad shape. All broken. They don't even know how badly yet. And she has some internal bleeding, and she hit her head, and—" her voice breaks, and I tighten my arms around her.

"It's okay, Mia. What else?"

"The doctors don't know if she'll make it."

I draw her against me because she's so close to the edge now, so close to losing control. I can feel it like it's me, my own body. And I can't give her privacy but I can give her me. My arms will have to do right now.

"I'm going back with her," I say to Adam.

It should have been a question. He's my boss. But it wasn't.

Paolo's here. I only notice him when he speaks. "We just checked all the major airlines," he says. "Flights are booked out of Vegas until noon. You'd get there faster if you drove."

Adam looks from Paolo to me. He fishes his keys out of his pocket and holds them out. "It's faster than her Prius," he says, handing them to me.

I take them, tuck Mia under my arm, and we're gone.

Back to Los Angeles.

Chapter 51

Mia

Q: Who always has your back?

The drive back to Los Angeles goes by in a blur. Highway. Desert. Dust.

My dad calls at one point to fill me in, and I find out that my grandmother wandered down the canyon road in her nightgown. In the dead of night. The car that struck her had a seventeen-year-old girl at the wheel, the daughter of new neighbors my parents just had over for dinner.

I give Ethan the report. "Nana's in surgery to stop the bleeding and repair a punctured lung. She's got a broken hip, a broken nose, and one of her legs is completely shattered. They still don't know . . ." But I can't say the rest of it.

"It's going to be okay, Curls," Ethan says, his voice soft but so filled with certainty, he almost convinces me. He takes my hand and squeezes it. "Let's just get you there."

And he does. Faster than should be possible, we pull up to the entrance of Cedars-Sinai.

"I'll park and find you," he says. Then he lifts my hand to his lips, and immediately, the tears I've been working so hard not to shed spill out of me. "I'll be right there. Go."

Vision fogged, I race through the sliding glass doors and find my way through a maze of sterile hallways to the Surgical Intensive Care Unit, in a totally different building. There they have me call from the lobby before I'm allowed to head up to the surgical floor. By the time the elevator doors close, my body is drenched in sweat, and I can't stop the tears from coming. I feel like I'm in a nightmare where letters blur to nothing in front of my eyes and where every step feels like it takes an inhuman effort.

Finally, I find the waiting area. My mom sits on a vinyl-cushioned chair, staring up at a monitor that lists patient names and statuses. She sees me and gets to her feet. We collide in a clumsy hug, and my mom's tears wet my cheek. I tighten my arms around her, and we stand there for a bit, then she sinks into a chair and pulls me down beside her.

"Where's Dad?"

"He went for coffee," she replies. "And your grandmother's on her way out of her first surgery. They stopped the bleeding and repaired the damage to her lung. I guess they did what they could with her broken bones too. But . . ." It feels like my heart stops beating while I wait for her to finish. "We have to see if she wakes from surgery. Her brain's injured, and she just might not . . . regain consciousness."

I think about the photos she just showed me and of that bold, wry look on her face, the same expression I've seen a thousand times.

That girl who marched in Alabama, who was one of only nineteen women in all of New York State to receive a paralegal degree in 1963, still lives in my grandmother. I can't imagine this is the end of that person or the end of the life she's lived since.

Even though she's been slipping away for years, I'm not ready to let her go.

"She'll wake up," I say. "She's so strong."

"And stubborn."

I smile. "That too."

My dad arrives with a cardboard holder loaded with coffee cups. He sets them down on a scratched laminate table and gives me a fierce hug. Then he smooths the hair back from my face and kisses my forehead.

"Where's Ethan?" he asks.

"He'll be up soon."

"I'm glad he brought you," my mother says. "I couldn't stand to think of you traveling here alone."

I know what she means. I've had this feeling since we left Las Vegas of being more vulnerable, of having spent my life in some kind of protective bubble that burst with Nana's accident. I know it's crazy, that no such bubble exists, but I'm still drenched in that feeling of fragility.

"What happened? Why was she out there this time?"

My mom shoots a look at my dad, but neither of them speaks.

"What? What it is?"

My dad sits down next to me and puts a cup of coffee in my hands. "She got on a tear this afternoon. Going on and on about that girl again. The one she thinks keeps stealing things from her."

"Who *is* that girl? Is it one of the home health aides?" I don't believe she's stealing from Nana, but I can believe my Nana would get that idea in her head and not let go. "What was she missing this time?"

"Her photos," my mom says softly, and she gives me a strange, sad look. "And the film reel from Selma."

"She gave those to *me*." I start, and then the reality sweeps through me, and it's like a punch in the gut. "Wait. *I'm* the girl?" How can that be?

But I can't deny the sense of it. The way she constantly tried to give me things—her jewelry and old photos. That video. And the last home health aide I met was Grace, an older woman. I don't know why I didn't put it together sooner.

I sit with it for a while, a cold ache in my chest. It's devastating to imagine myself so thoroughly rewritten in my Nana's mind. It feels like such a betrayal. But I know that's wishful thinking in a way, like my protective bubble. Even though it's totally unfair, it's as real to my Nana as the rest of her unreliable thoughts.

A doctor comes out in scrubs, his surgical mask wadded beneath his chin. At the same moment, the elevator doors open, and Ethan steps out. Seeing the doctor, he hangs back, but my mom beckons him over.

"Well, she's a fighter," the doctor says. "She's coming around from the anesthesia."

I start to sob on the spot, I'm so happy.

My mom squeezes my hand. "Oh, thank God."

"But she's got a long uphill battle, and a tough one given your reports of dementia. Her leg's going to be held together with pins for months, and between that and damage to her spine, it's unlikely she'll ever walk again."

"But she's alive," my dad points out, and the doctor nods.

He goes on to detail her injuries, which were even more horrific and extensive than I'd imagined, and then takes us through her surgeries, which sound even more gruesome—though completely miraculous, too.

"When can we see her?" I ask.

"You can go in now, though she'll be asleep for a while still. They only let one person into SICU at a time and only for five minutes each hour. Your grandmother still requires a great deal of care, so we need to keep the room as clear as possible."

"Mia Moré," my dad says. "Why don't you go in first?"

"*Me*? Shouldn't that be Mom?"

But my mother shakes her head and says, "No, he's right. You go. Then we'll find you a flight back to Las Vegas."

"No, I don't need to—"

"Mia," my mother says. "Your grandmother's in excellent hands, *and* we're only allowed to see her for five minutes at a time. She'd be thoroughly livid to think she kept you from an opportunity. You can see her tomorrow morning and then head back."

"I can't leave her."

"We'll call you if anything happens, kiddo," my dad says. "And you'll be back in what? A day and a half? We'll be fine."

"And I know you don't want to let Adam down," my mom adds. "Okay?"

I look at the two of them and feel a surge of love so strong it practically lifts me off my feet.

"Fine," I tell them. "You win." To Ethan, I add. "I'll be out in five minutes, okay?"

He nods and takes a seat in one of the uncomfortable chairs. When he looks at me, his eyes are filled with warmth and concern. "I'll be right here," he says. "For as long as you need."

I follow the nurse down a long hall with glass-fronted recovery suites on either side. She pushes aside the drape in my grandmother's room and pats my shoulder as I pass.

"You come from strong stock, my dear," she says.

But at the moment, I feel anything but strong. I feel like my body's been pulled inside out, and all my nerves are on the outside, aching and exposed.

I tremble as I approach Nana's bed. Tears spill from my eyes; my nose runs; and I'm so afraid of what I'll see, but my feet move me across the linoleum floor to the shrunken figure lying half-buried between tubes and wires, encased in bandages.

This person looks nothing like Nana. Her face is bloated and has a strange, jaundiced sheen. Her eyelids are purple bruises, practically the only part of her visible atop an oxygen mask and a white sheet pulled up to her chin.

I hover there, taking a painful inventory of the metal cage encasing her leg, the bandages on her arms, across her chest, the blood seeping through gauze. I want to touch her, to give her a kiss, but I'm afraid I'll shatter her with even a breath.

Drawing a chair up to her bed, I see her arm dangling off the bed. I brush my fingers along a patch of soft skin on the inside of her wrist and then tuck her hand back beneath the sheet. I close my eyes and pray for her, sending all of my love and strength to her body.

"Mia," she said to me the other day. "It all goes so fast, but you never feel different inside." She'd put her hand on my heart and said, "We're the same age. In here."

I put my own hand against my heart, feeling her life beat inside me. Then I get up to go find Ethan.

Chapter 52

Ethan

Q: Finish this phrase: The feeling of skin on skin is____?

W here are we going?" Mia asks.

It's a testament to how deep in shock she still is that I'm almost pulling up to my apartment. She's been quiet since we left the hospital and it seemed more important to respect her mood than to get into logistics, so I didn't run my plan by her.

"My place." I edge Adam's Bugatti against the curb. This has to be the first time this car's ever been parallel-parked. "It's almost rush hour, so I thought we could make a pit stop for a few hours." I turn off the engine, and the deep thrum quiets. "You're exhausted, Mia. You need to rest. And you haven't eaten all day. I'd feel better if you had some food in you."

She looks at me for a long moment, and I can't tell whether she's worried about getting back to Vegas or Nana or what. But then she nods and says, "Okay. That sounds like a good idea."

My apartment is clean and empty. Mia stops just inside the door and looks around. "Your place looks so different," she says after a long moment.

It must. I've adjusted to the new furniture—the fresh flowers and colorful rugs and abstract prints on the walls—but I can only imagine how it's hitting Mia, considering what she saw the last time she was here.

"Isis," I say, dropping Adam's keys on a table. "She civilized us. They're out for the night, so we've got the place to ourselves." I realize that might sound like I'm looking for something to happen between us, so I add, "I figured you'd appreciate the quiet."

I lead her to the couch and make her sit down. Then I unzip her boots and set them aside. Mia watches me with tired eyes.

"What's all this about?" she asks.

My face goes a little warm, but I ignore my embarrassment. No more holding back. "Let me take care of you."

I need to. The need to ease her worry has been consuming me from the moment I saw her on the phone in Vegas.

She nods, and I pull a soft throw blanket from the back of the couch and tuck it around her. I bring her a glass of water, and put her cell phone on a pillow beside her. Then I turn off the lights, leaving only the small lamp on the side table lit.

"I'm going to throw something together," I say. "Give me ten minutes, and I'll be right beside you."

Isis is named after a goddess for a reason. Before she and Jason left tonight, she stocked the refrigerator. I see exactly what I was hoping for. Fresh bread. The right kinds of gourmet cheeses. In ten minutes, I have my mom's world-famous grilled cheese sandwich prepared. I wash a few strawberries and make some hot chocolate, and bring it all out to Mia.

She's lying down when I come back out to the living room. For a second, I think she's asleep, but she sits up and brushes her hair back and smiles.

"That smells so good."

"Wait until you taste it." I sit beside her and hand her the plate. "Good luck taking that apart," I add, remembering her habit of deconstructing sandwiches.

"Will you share it with me?"

"I'll eat what you don't finish."

We share the sandwich, hot chocolate, and strawberries—each and every taste sweeter, sharper in the almost dark. The moment feels familiar, like that afternoon after Winning Displays on the park bench, but better. I was fighting so hard to stop myself from liking her then. Nothing's standing between us now.

"Jason asked around," I say, setting the empty plate and mug on the coffee table. "He said your grandma's in the hands of the best specialists in the world. She's going to be all right, Curls. She's strong. She's a fighter, like you."

Mia pulls the blanket up and curls against me. It stops my breath how naturally she does it.

"I'm like her," she says, then adds, "Thank you, Ethan."

I tuck her close to my chest and her arm comes around my waist. We sit for a few moments, getting the feel of how we fit together in this new way. I take a lock of her hair and coil it around my finger. Right away, I know it's my new favorite thing to do.

Sounds drift up from the street. A car driving by, playing a thumping base. People walking past, their voices cheerful and laughing.

"Did I ruin the job for both of us?" Mia says.

I've been texting with Rhett throughout the day. They're making the booth work, he told me. But I don't want Mia to waste a single thought on Boomerang.

"I don't give a shit about the job."

"I don't believe that."

"I'm right where I should be, Mia."

Which I didn't feel for a second at that booth this morning.

The thought surprises me, and suddenly the feeling I had at the bar last night of my life's compass spinning around crazily is back. But this time it's calmer. It's settling toward north again, and I know Mia is part of that, part of me finding my way again. There's more though. I'm on the verge of making sense of something else. It's almost within my reach.

Mia looks up at me, and the feeling fades, making room for only her.

"I don't want to go back yet," she says.

"Then we won't. I'll stay here for the next month if it's what you want."

"But we'd run out of food."

"There's always pizza delivery."

"People might worry we'd joined a cult. A pizza-eating cult."

"Eff 'em. Pizza cults rock."

"What would we do with all that time?"

"Trust me, I've got you covered there, Curls." I can think of a hundred things I'd do with her if we had a month alone. I *have* thought of them. Over and over as I stared at her picture, or looked up at her across our workstations. But then I realize my ideas might not be exactly appropriate to point out right now. Seems rude to tell her I want her trembling beneath me, with everything else that's going on.

Mia's eyes drop to my mouth. "Ethan . . ." she says.

Damn. Looks like we're on the same page.

"Soon, Mia. I promise." I press a kiss to her forehead. "We have time."

I won't do this with her as a way to forget pain.

Instead of tucking back into my side, she leans up, bringing her lips to mine. I kiss her and gather her closer. She tastes like strawberries and chocolate, warm and sweet and perfect.

Mia's knee comes up over my leg, and she nestles against my

thigh. My self-control was already hanging by a thread, but now it buckles. I draw her leg over me, shifting her hips until she's straddling me. *Awesome job on not taking advantage of her, Ethan.* But I'm drowning in her. In seeing her how I've imagined her a million times. In her sweet scent and the soft coils of her black hair brushing against my cheeks.

Her hands find the top buttons of my shirt. "I want to feel your skin," she says.

I grin. "Okay."

She laughs, like I said something amusing.

It feels like it takes forever for her to undo the buttons, but my shirt finally comes off. Mia sits up, and studies me with her photographer's eye, but better. Like a picture could never be enough. Then her hands glide over me. Over my chest and my shoulders, and I let her until I can't be a passive participant anymore.

I lean up and take her mouth, and my hands slip under her shirt. I tug at her bra and the garment unclasps. Leaning down, I lift her shirt and explore her with my tongue, convinced I could do this— taste her, touch her, make her mine—forever. Mia lets out a whimper and arches her back. Her core pushes against me. She sucks in a breath, her eyes sparking with surprise as they meet mine and then drop lower.

Her looking at me—at us together—is unquestionably the hottest thing I've ever seen.

"That's what you do to me, Curls," I hear myself say.

"Good." She smiles and leans down, peppering soft kisses around my lips. She shifts her hips and grinds against me, and my mind empties of everything. I have one solitary need. One goal only. I might have rocked her world before, but I'm going to give her the universe this time.

My fingers find the top button of her pants. I pop it loose, and at that moment, there's a corresponding click in my brain. A downshift as a sliver of reason returns, and my hands freeze.

"Mia," I say.

Fuck, fuck, fuck.

Come on, Vance. Do the right thing.

"Curls . . . we shouldn't. Not yet. Not now."

The tension in her back relaxes, and she melts against me, burying her face into the crook of my neck. I wrap my arms around her and hold her close.

I know I don't have to say anything else. We got carried away. It happens every time we touch. But I want to make sure she understands.

"Mia," I say, smoothing back her hair, "you said something at the bar yesterday. You said I didn't choose you. That every time we've ended up together, it's been because of circumstance. Because we just happened to be at the same place at the same time. You were right. It has been that way, and you deserve better. I'm going to *give* you better. I want you to know that. When this happens between us, it won't be because we've been thrown together. It'll be because we both choose it. Okay?"

"Okay." Slowly, she slides to the side a little, still half on me, and says, "But you already did choose, Ethan. You came back with me. You're here with me."

I think about what she says for a long while as I hold her. How sometimes we're already doing the right things, and we don't know it. Long after she's fallen asleep and there are no more sounds drifting up from the street, I think about how sometimes, all we really need is the wisdom to see what's been there all along.

Chapter 53

Mia

Q: Best night of your life?

"First we need to get you out of these wet clothes," Ethan says. "And then I've got a few ideas."

He slides my panties down, and I lift my hips to help. Then I sit up and unhook my bra, flinging it to some corner of the room. A surge of giddiness washes over me. It's like I'm drunk in waves tonight, and I'm back at high tide.

Ethan rises from the couch, my underwear in his hands. The blanket slips off to the floor, but I don't mind.

"Wait . . ." I reach out for him, but he's already weaving off toward the kitchen. Guess I'm not the only one at high tide. "Where are you going?"

"We need to dry these off," he says. I hear him crash

into something and curse, but he's back in no time. He mumbles something that sounds like "toaster," but I'm too focused on his full lips, his perfectly masculine features, to really take in his words.

I sit up and pull him toward me, my whole body practically vibrating with need. I want more of his lips, more of his hands. I want to make him feel as good as he made me feel.

He kisses me, and his tongue teases my lips, slides slowly, playfully, into my mouth. I moan because I'm so ridiculously hungry for him. And I can't remember feeling this way before, like my body is a live wire, throwing sparks.

His lips still pressed to mine, he eases me back onto the sofa. Finally, I think, desperate for his weight, for the full, gorgeous length of him against me.

But he moves away to kiss my throat, his teeth grazing its hollow, tongue and hands darting everywhere. "Jesus, Curls," he says, as he brushes his lips over my nipple. "I've never seen anything as beautiful as you."

Again, I reach for him, dying for more. For everything.

And again, he eases my hand away. "Still your turn," he tells me, and his lips and tongue start a slow, maddening journey down my body.

"That's not fair," I protest, but his mouth grazes my navel, and he spreads my thighs apart with warm hands.

"Home team advantage," he says and dips his head lower.

I wake in Ethan's bed, and this time I know where my panties are: unfortunately, still on my body.

I can tell it's still nighttime, but I have no idea how long we've slept. Vaguely, I remember him leading me to his bedroom, helping me out of my clothes and giving me one of his t-shirts to wear. And I remember lying with my head against his chest as the final bits of our first night together filtered through my mind.

That night, he couldn't stop touching me, teasing me with his tongue, giving me pleasure over and over again until it felt impossible, like my body had been replaced by one meant to respond only to him.

Now he's stretched out next to me, a shaft of moonlight catching his strong jaw and angling down to his muscled shoulder and arm. His chest rises and falls, and his warmth surrounds me, along with that delicious fire and salt scent of his.

We need to get back to Vegas. But I can't move from this moment. Or I won't. Instead, I slide closer, brushing my lips against his throat, rising up against his body.

"Wake up," I whisper and run my tongue over his ear. I need him to be awake, to be fully with me the way I want to be with him.

"Mia?" He opens his eyes and smiles at me. I can't remember ever seeing something as beautiful as that. "What are you doing?"

"I'm choosing," I say, and kiss him. He tastes sweet, still, like the strawberries he fed me.

My body, my mind, every bit of me wants this. No more Sleeping Beauty. "I can't wait any more. Can you?"

He laughs and pulls me closer. "Hell, no."

We kiss and kiss until I feel drunk again, like that first night, like every molecule in my body wants to crash into every molecule in his.

I slip my hand under the sheet, brushing my fingers over the soft material of his boxers. My touch grows insistent, and he groans. The sound undoes me. It's possible I'll lose my mind if I can't have him. Not just in this moment but always.

I slip on top of him, straddling him, my thighs pressed against his hips. My eyes locked on his, I pull off the t-shirt he put on me last night. Then I smooth my body against his, brushing my breasts against his chest, skin against skin. I run my tongue over the delicious groove of his collarbone, up his throat, to his lips. I get lost there, in the taste of him, the feel of him beneath me. I slide my hips down, fitting myself against his hardness.

He gives a sharp inhale. "Wait, Mia," he says. "I need to tell you something first."

I graze his nipple with my teeth. "What is it?"

He tilts my chin up so that I'm looking at him. "I . . . I choose you."

"I know," I say. "You've probably told me a hundred times already, only I was too dumb to pay attention."

"But I need to say it in real words. And I need you to know it has nothing to do with . . ." His hands brush over me, and I shiver. "This."

"Really?" I press against him. "Nothing?"

He grips my hips and pulls me down harder, sending a shock of pleasure through my entire body. "Okay. Not nothing. But it's more than that. It's you, Curls. The whole package. The way you look when you've got your camera in your hands, like you can see through people, right down to their cores. And your crazy giant hair. Your laugh. How goddamn smart you are. All of it. I choose all of it."

I want to say it all back to him, tell him how much I love his focus, his generosity. His eyelashes. His perfect, straight nose. His intelligence and loyalty. The way I know I can trust him with every part of me.

I want to, and I will. I'll try to tell him that every day. And I hope those days stretch to the rest of my life. But for now, I just say, "Thank you," and I kiss him, hoping he knows what's contained in those words.

"You're welcome," he says, his hand slipping down to my panties. "Now let's get rid of these."

Laughing, we finish undressing each other. He finds and puts on a condom then pulls me back on top of him. We kiss for a long, long time, clinging to each other in a stream of bright moonlight. I suck on his tongue, and we both groan and then we laugh at ourselves.

But then he looks at me, and his deep blue eyes glimmer with intensity. "I want you so goddamn much, Mia," he says. "I can't wait anymore."

I feel molten inside, like liquid fire. I want to pour myself over him, envelop us both.

"Then don't," I say.

By some magic, our bodies find each other perfectly, and he presses himself slowly into me, pulling me down by the hips, filling every bit of me.

"Okay, we definitely haven't done *this* before," I gasp. But then we begin to move together, and I lose my words. Now it's only this stunning juncture of his body and mine, this perfect wavelike rhythm, ebbs and flows, like we're elemental. Meant to be.

His hands move over me, and I catch one and pull his long fingers into my mouth. Because I want even more of him. Because I'm not sure there's enough of him to satisfy this hunger he's created.

He rolls me over and pins me against the mattress. I want to cry at how good he feels on top of me, how solid and lovely and ridiculously hot. He slips a hand down between our bodies, all of him moving, his tongue in my mouth, his hips against mine, his fingers urgent and circling.

"But it's supposed to be your turn," I try to say. Only my body's selfish. It rises against him, urges him for more.

"Mia," Ethan groans. "You definitely . . . don't . . . have to worry about that."

I wrap my arms around him, drawing him closer. We burn against each other, chafing and igniting, and again, I feel that sun inside me, that radiating, cutting warmth. It builds and builds, and my whole body trembles, filled with how good this is. How good he is.

Then it tips over and explodes, catching me in this sharp electric current, hollowing me until I lose myself to it, burn and tremble and fracture into a million scintillating bits.

Ethan moans, and his movements grow intense, focused. A sheen of sweat glistens on his shoulder, and I taste the salt of his skin. His rhythm builds, and he buries his face in my neck, saying my name. The feel of him driving toward his own pleasure is more than I can take, and my body climbs to meet his.

My trembling makes him tremble.

His groans make me groan.

Finally, he grows rigid, and his arms pen my body, containing me. He gives a deep, long shudder, and it feels like my own body quivering.

Slowly, we stop moving, our breathing quiets. My heartbeat starts to feel like it's within normal human range.

"Wow, Curls," he murmurs.

I laugh, and hold him against me. "Yeah," I tell him. "Go, team."

Chapter 54

Ethan

Q: Do you chase dreams, or do you actually catch them?

*W*hy don't you hop in the shower?" I say. "I'll meet you in there."

Mia sits up, naked and gorgeous, and gives me a wry smile. "Shower? Why do I need to shower?"

I have to laugh because her hair is *gigantic*. "I thought maybe, uh . . ." I make a motion encompassing the black mountain of curls around her head. "I'm not quite sure how to describe what's going on here. I don't think Diana Ross or Bride of Frankenstein even come close, to be honest."

Mia play-punches me. "It's your doing." Then she pats her hair, feeling the dimensions of the awesomeness that surrounds her head. "Wow. This *is* impressive. I think I'm going to call this style *The Hat Trick*."

"You know what a hat trick means?"

"Sure do," she says, scooting off the bed. She stops at the door and looks back, grinning. "More importantly, I know how it *feels*."

Well, that settles that. I can die a happy man.

My work here is done.

Except it isn't.

I grab my cell phone from the nightstand and type two quick text messages—one to Beth and one to Matt—then I send a message to Rhett.

> **Ethan:** Hey man. Booth status?

It's 7 a.m. but he replies right away.

> **Rhett:** Questionable. We're trying.

That doesn't sound good. My side of the display is working, but a knot settles in my stomach. Mia's side obviously still isn't.

> **Ethan:** Keep trying.
> **Rhett:** Will do. Mia status?

I'm tempted to type *very satisfied*, but I know that's not what he means.

> **Ethan:** Holding up.

I let him know we'll be back by eleven, then I head to the bathroom, catch a glimpse of Mia in the shower, and realize I should've told Rhett noon.

But what the hell. They can wait.

In the shower, I wrap my arms around her and hold her. She's relaxed and tired, and I can tell yesterday drained her. I kiss her, playing with her soft lips, my hands exploring her body. I want to make her feel good again, but she shakes her head.

"Maybe a little later?" she says. "Sore."

"Sorry. Not sorry," I say. She laughs, and I trap the sound with another kiss and tell her, "I have some healing techniques . . . Tonight, Curls. Or sooner, if we don't get out of this shower."

Her smile grows wider. "Okay, tonight. Counting on it."

She's so sleek and beautiful this way. I can't resist her. I take her face in my hands and look into her green eyes. "Mia . . . we did this thing all wrong, at work and on dates that weren't even ours, but it doesn't change anything. It doesn't change where we are. You're mine now."

It sounds possessive and psychotic, but that's not how it feels. How it feels is like I want to become a human force field around her. Like I want to give her anything I can—*everything,* to keep her happy and safe. The truth isn't so much that she's mine as it is that I'm hers.

Mia shakes her head and smiles. "I already was yours, Ethan. The minute you put my panties in the toaster oven, I knew you were the one."

"Yeah? I'll admit that was an inspired move."

The shower starts to run cold, so I shut off the water and wrap a towel around her. Mia looks up at the sound of a cabinet slamming in the kitchen.

"Someone's here." She stares at the door, and then gasps as a loud laugh explodes from the other side. "Is that . . . *Beth?*"

"Sounds like Sky to me, but you would know."

Mia darts away from me, opens the door and bolts into the living room.

I grab another towel, wrap it around my waist, and follow her.

The chatter in the apartment stops. For a second, we all just stand there. Me and Mia, half-naked. Skyler, at the kitchen table. Isis, about to crack an egg against a mixing bowl on the counter. Beth, by the couch—which is covered in dresses and pants and shoes. Jason in the middle of everything like a startled animal that doesn't know where to flee.

"What is this?" Mia tugs her towel higher. "What are you guys doing here?"

Skyler lifts a coffee carrier from the kitchen table. "I brought lattes."

Beth spreads her hands like she's presenting the couch. "The usual for me. A fabulous assortment of clothes for you."

"I'm making pancakes," Isis chirps from the kitchen.

Jason shrugs, the corner of his mouth lifting in an embarrassed smile. "I just live here."

Mia looks at me, a question in her eyes.

"Seemed like the right time to call in the troops," I say. And I'm rewarded with a perfect smile before she's shuttled into my bedroom amid a barrage of condolences and questions.

"Damn," Jason says, when it's just him and me. "They're like a category five hurricane."

But at the moment, I'm too grateful that he's here—that they all are—to joke. "Thanks, J."

"Not necessary. It's not every Monday I get to drive a Bugatti to Malibu."

Jason's running Adam's car home for me this afternoon.

"I meant for letting us have the place last night, and for looking out for her grandma."

"Like I said, no thanks necessary."

"Okay." I turn around and stop, realizing I have no access to my room, and therefore my clothing.

"That sucks." Jason says behind me. But it doesn't. I love that Mia's in there, surrounded by her friends—old and new.

Jason sits at the table. "Pull up a chair, buddy. Here. Have a Skinny-Mocha-Chai-whatever-the fuck-this-is."

I sit and take the coffee.

"So," he says. "It appears you violated the code of conduct established by your employer."

Idiotic fucking office policies. They almost cost me Mia.

"Might have done that last night," I answer. "Might have done that this morning, too."

"Uh-huh," Jason says, with zero surprise. "And this professional"—he waves his hand in the air, searching for the right word—"*transgression . . .*"

"There was nothing wrong about it. Nothing."

"I hear you, brother. I do. It's about freaking time you two did the deed, but my question is this: you've got another week or so on the job—sorry, internship. Are you going to hide what's going on between you from Blackwood?"

"Too late for that," I say, remembering how I wrapped Mia in my arms in front of Adam yesterday. He's no idiot. He knows what's going on.

Jason takes a sip of coffee. "You don't seem too worried about it."

"I am for her."

"What are you for you?"

"Good. Real good," I say. Then I tell him about my conversation with Matt in Colorado. About the sports psychology graduate program. And about how I'm going to apply.

I only just decided to go for it this morning. Or maybe it was at some point in the night, holding Mia, but as I talk to Jason, I hear someone who's sure. Someone who has an unshakable confidence about the path he's chosen to walk. Grad school always felt right. I just had to find the angle that fits me.

"I just texted Matt," I say, finishing. "I'm going to get in touch with his contact. Get that ball rolling as soon as possible."

Jason sits back and studies me. There's a smile in his eyes. This feels right to him too, but he shakes his head. "Psychology, huh?"

I smile. "Yup."

"You know what?" he says, crossing his arms. "I'm going to be *pissed* if you become a doctor before I do."

An hour later, after Mia checks in with her parents and learns that Nana's condition is stable, we leave for Vegas. Sky and Beth drop us at the airport in time to catch the 10 a.m. flight, which gets us back to the hotel just before noon. As we walk through the casino to the exhibit floor, I feel Mia's dread mounting with every step.

During the flight, we brainstormed ways to work around the corrupted file containing the footage she's been shooting for the past weeks. We even made a list of people who might be able to help. Zeke, my gaming contact. Gayle, our IT expert, who was supposedly flying in this morning. And, in an act of supreme selflessness, I even suggested Brian.

"The point, Curls, is that it's not over yet," I told her.

She forced a smile but the reality was unavoidable: we didn't have much time.

And now, as we flash our badges at the security guards by the door, we have even less time. In only six hours, thousands of people will flood into this hall—along with Adam Blackwood and his cadre of top-tier investors.

"Oh, God," Mia says as our booth comes into view.

My side is lit up, the bright green playing field beneath a blue sky. I can't see who's using the game, but the boomerang whizzes across the sky and smashes into a heart, which explodes in a shower of probably red sparks.

It looks badass even from a distance, but I can't appreciate it. The walls on Mia's side are plain white—and they shouldn't be.

When we get to the booth, Mia is swarmed by Paolo, Sadie, and

Pippa. They all talk at once, and it's like the chaos at my apartment this morning, except frantic and stressed.

"We were up all night," Pippa says. "We kept going over everything and coming up with nothing."

Sadie holds up a USB drive. "We got new files with your images, but they aren't compatible with this system."

"Is your grandma okay?" Paolo says.

I want to tell everyone to shut the hell up, but this is Mia's gig.

Her silence eventually gets through to them, and they stand down, looking guilty for having bombarded her.

"Thanks," she says. "Thanks for . . . doing all of this."

All of this looks like nothing to my eyes, though I'm sure they spent the past twenty-four hours trying.

Mia looks up at me. I notice she's gone a little pale, but her voice is calm when she says, "We'll use your side, Ethan. We'll just send everyone that way. The game is great, and—"

"No," I say. "No way."

"It's too late."

"No, it's not. You worked too hard for this." I won't let her fail. Physically, I *can't* let that happen. I step closer and brush a curl away from her eyes. "We'll fix it, Mia. Together."

I can tell she wants to believe me, but she says, "In six hours?"

"Hell, yeah." I pop a kiss on her forehead, then I pull my suit jacket off and toss it on a café table. "Enough of this competition bullshit. Let's do this."

Chapter 55

Mia

Q: Happy behind the scenes, or strictly limelight?

Fifteen minutes before the doors to the convention officially open, I'm hunched over a toilet bowl, trying to keep down the chicken quesadilla I split with Sadie and not ruin the dress or expensive Gucci belt provided by my team of stylists back in LA. As it is, they'd be mortified by the condition of my hair. We're at Defcon Five, and the needle's tipping toward red.

But flop sweat will do that to a person, as will hauling equipment around on a humid convention floor, made even sultrier by the hyperventilations of hundreds of anxious vendors. Luckily, we have a small forest of neon-draped palms to suck up all the extra CO_2.

I take a few deep breaths, get up, and stagger over to the sink. Next to me stands a girl in a felt rocket ship costume, festooned with hearts and the words "Love Launcher" scrolling by on an LCD belt cinching her waist.

"What do you think?" she asks, smirking at me in the mirror as she dabs on bronze gloss. "Too subtle?"

"Oh, I think our audience is sophisticated enough to appreciate it."

I blot the sweat from my upper lip and run my hands through my hair, which makes things roughly a trillion times worse. One side is half curled, half straightened. The other side is mashed flat on top but curls out on the bottom. I've got Jekyll and Hyde hair, but I smile, thinking back on my night and morning with Ethan.

"Which is yours?" the girl asks me, and it takes me a second to realize she's asking about the booth.

"Boomerang."

"Oh, I've heard that's the one to beat," she says.

"If that's true, it's a miracle." We've spent six hours—Ethan, Paolo, Sadie, Pippa, and me—hatching a plan and then putting it into effect. We split apart the booths, reorienting them to push their walls to the outside, making a kind of heart out of the two boomerangs. Then we pushed my café tables together and slid Ethan's sleek black benches up to them. It looks fantastic, and Pippa's suggestion that people might prefer sitting in groups rather than at tables for two made a ton of sense.

But will it work, really? Does it only look good to us because our time is up and we're out of options? I don't know. I just know how grateful I am to everyone for working so hard. And I know I'll be buying us all very large drinks at the end of this night.

My belly still roiling, I tell Rocket Girl "good luck."

"Wait a sec," she says, and hands me a heart-patterned scrunchie from around her wrist. "For your hair."

It must be bad for perfect strangers to surrender hair accessories to me.

"Thanks." I exit the bathroom, tucking my ridiculous mane into the scrunchie with only the vaguest hope that it will help and hurry toward the Boomerang display. From a distance, it looks awesome. The glossy black and dreamy whites play off each other, creating a space that feels harmonious but sexy and inviting.

I take a second to text my mom for a status report. Apparently, Nana woke up a few times and even managed to have some broth.

Better than she has any right to be, her text says.

And I smile, feeling exactly the same.

"Cutting it close, Mia."

My blood freezes in my veins, and I turn to find Cookie stalking toward me. I'm shocked, though, because her hair's down and she's replaced her usual sharp, almost military, suit with a soft pink cashmere sweater and gray pants.

"Wow, Cookie," I say. "You look—" *Don't say, "almost human,"* my brain begs me, and for once I listen. "Nice."

"And you look"—she scrutinizes me—"rumpled. Now, shall we see what you've done? I need to know how big a cluster this is going to be."

"I think you'll be pleasantly surprised."

"If it's pleasant, I *will* be surprised." She gives an impatient wave. "Lead on."

Great. As if my anxiety levels needed further charging.

I lead Cookie past a few other booths and start to feel a bit better. Ours is centrally placed and really eye-catching. Though I couldn't recover my whole film, I was able to dig back into my raw clips and turn the best of them into simple animated GIFS. They play over and over again on the screens around the space, now miraculously integrated into Ethan's game.

I even transferred a few seconds of my grandparents, sepia-toned and lovely. It was so hard to leave Nana back in LA. I needed her here with me today. And there's something about the way she

and my grandfather look at each other, sitting side-by-side at a
picnic table somewhere in the Catskills, the regard and attraction
that projects through decades, that feels right, somehow.

I love the way it all looks—romantic yet modern. It feels like me.

My body starts to relax. We're good. This all looks good. Now
we just have to get the crowd to come interact with the space, and
we'll be money.

And then the GIFS wink off one by one, leaving us with a dozen
blank screens.

Oh, no. No. No. No.

I hurry over, and Ethan steps out from behind the wall on his
side, looking as queasy as I feel.

"What happened?"

"It's been like this for the past few minutes. Some kind of connection issue, but we can't figure it out."

Without the images, the space looks totally different. Unfin-
ished. Lacking.

"Two minutes 'til doors open, kids," says Paolo. Nervously, he
picks imaginary lint off his lapel.

"Let me see." I tear around behind the display and want to cry
at the tangle of cords littering the space. I dig through them, finding
where they connect, looking for loose couplings. It occurs to me
that Loose Couplings would make a great dating website name, and
I giggle.

I'm pretty sure I'm on the verge of hysteria.

I find a few cables, which all converge on some central power
supply, and follow the power supply's cord to a floor socket with a
loose plate. I push the plug in more firmly and lift the fat cord out of
the way to untangle it from some others.

"Yes!" Ethan calls. "We've got it."

"Awesome." I drop the cord back on the ground and start to
stand, but Paolo says, "Nope. Lost it again."

Merda. I pick up the cord.

"Okay, it's working," says Ethan.

I sit there, the cord in my hand suspended about eight inches from the floor. I'm afraid I know where this is going, but I start to lower it again.

"Damn it!" Ethan groans.

I look around, wondering if I can bring a box over, a chair, a small child—something to help prop this thing. I'll be damned if all our hard work is ruined by a cheap power supply.

The soft techno music swells, and I hear a surge of laughter and excited voices. A wave of exhilaration and raw anxiety sweeps over me.

Sadie peeks around the wall, her red hair swinging toward me like a pendulum. "Doors are open!"

"Is everything still working?"

"Yeah. It looks amazing!"

I want so much to see it. I want to be there while the crowds come and explore the space. I want to see their faces, watch Ethan show off what we've done. But I guess I'm going to sit here and hold a goddamn cord for the next few hours.

Cookie steps around behind the display and stands there, hands on her hips, beaming her usual nuanced blend of utter hatred and complete loathing at me.

Then she shocks the hell out of me by kneeling on the floor by my side. Reaching for the cord, she barks, "Give it to me, and get out there."

"But—"

"This is your show, Mia," she says, and something flashes in her expression—so fast I'm pretty sure I'm imagining it. Something that looks like compassion. "Go."

I get to my feet. "I'll find some way to prop it up. Or maybe we can plug into a new supply if I can find one."

"Yes, I'd appreciate not spending my entire night breaking my back down here. Now, go."

I rush to find Ethan. He, Paolo, and Sadie race around the space, making small adjustments, tidying up the tables and putting the last touches on the rows and rows of premiums: shot glasses with the Boomerang logo and real foam boomerangs, which I suspect may become a menace in the jam-packed hall.

A massive crowd heads toward us, a tide of beautiful, likely inebriated, people. They surge through the space like water rushing through tributaries.

I pan over the throng, and right away, I spot Adam, tall and elegant in an aubergine suit. A posse of suited dudes stride along beside him, their expressions skeptical and blasé. We have our work cut out for us, it seems, and I wouldn't have it any other way.

"Ready, Curls?" asks Ethan, as he slips an arm around my waist.

I lean against him for just a second, buoying myself with his strength.

"Bring it," I say.

Chapter 56

Ethan

Q: Is winning important, or how you play the game?

*A*dam betrays nothing as he introduces Mia and me to the five men who could potentially make him a billionaire. Nor does he show any surprise at the radical transformation the Boomerang booth has made since he saw it yesterday. The guy's poker face should be legendary.

Mia and I took a huge risk. It was my idea to load her images into my video game. Gone is the boring green field and flat blue sky. Now the boomerang hearts fly over images of people on dates, laughing, having fun—and falling in love, in Nana's case. Occasionally, someone hits a bull's-eye and the heart explodes, and it looks like fireworks rain down over a couple.

It's fucking perfect. Like we planned it. We couldn't have designed it any better.

As good as my idea was, Mia's idea—to invert the booth walls so the images are everywhere—has taken our booth to a whole other level. With that little stroke of genius, she made Boomerang exclusive, as tough to get into as any premier club in Vegas, and it becomes more obvious by the second that the conference attendees love that. The show's only been going for ten minutes, and already Rhett and Paolo have had to stand by the entrance to regulate the flow of traffic.

We're practically standing room only, the whole place thrumming with awesome music, thanks to DJ Rasputin, and with the laughter and fun that tells me something incredible is happening here.

But Blackwood, of course, looks like he must have at the blackjack tables the other night: cool and controlled, and like he could give a shit that his company is making trade-show history.

"Ms. Galliano filmed these images herself," he says, to a flushed, brick house of a man.

"They're very good," Brick House responds in a thick southern accent. "Talent runs in the family, I see."

I'm not sure what surprises me more: the fact that Adam's given these men a pregame briefing on Mia, or that Brick House is cultured enough to know Pearl's work.

"Thank you," Mia says. "The project's been tremendously rewarding for both Ethan and me."

I smile. "That's true," I say, nodding. "There are times I don't even feel right calling what we do work."

Adam's gaze finds me and I think it cools with warning, but I don't really care.

"The boomerang game," says Mr. Inoue, an investor from Japan. "It was furnished by which game-maker?"

"Zeke Lee," I answer. "He's a developer at Naughty Dog, but he did this on the side for us." The guy's not even looking at me as I

speak, he's so locked into the boomerang zipping across the screens.
"You want to try it?"

"Oh, yes," he replies.

"Great. Follow me." I take him to the playing pad and pull rank,
cutting in front of the long line of people waiting for their turn. I help
Mr. Inoue into the glove and give him a few pointers, then he's off,
flinging boomerangs like he was born in the outback. Inoue's feel for
the game is immediate, so I drop back and watch him laugh as he
literally breaks hearts left and right.

Adam stands beside me, his arms crossed, that same neutral expression on his face.

"I don't remember signing off on this," he says.

"You didn't," I say, and feel Mia nudge closer to my side.

I wait for him to say something else, but he doesn't. He just
stands there, but apparently that's enough to unnerve me a little.

I don't care what he says to me, but if he tries to drag Mia down,
I will bury my fist in his pretty rich-boy face.

When Inoue steps off the playing pad, grinning like a kid, he
comes over and asks me for Zeke's number, and then congratulates
Adam on a tremendous show.

Adam shakes his hand and smiles, charming and accommodat-
ing, but when Inoue leaves, he turns to me and Mia, his mood unreadable again.

"I'm calling a meeting in my suite tonight for all employees—
and interns. I'll see you both there."

Then he's gone, the crowd parting before him as he moves
through the booth.

"Jesus," I say. The guy's truly in his own category.

"A bit more like Moses at the moment," Mia says. Then her hand
slips into mine and squeezes. "We did it."

I look at her and smile, squeezing back. "Go team."

Chapter 57

Mia

Q: Real life, or fairy tale ending?

*W*e're about to step out of the elevator to Adam's penthouse suite when Ethan wraps his arms around me from behind, holding me there.

"Hang on a second," he says, pulling me against him and lifting my hair to kiss the back of my neck.

The door slides shut, and now it's just the two of us, reflected over and over in the mirrored wall panels.

"I guess if we never go into that hotel room, we can never be fired." I turn and lace my arms around his neck, drawing him down for a long, teasing kiss. "Is that the game plan, Coach?"

"Something like that."

I smooth down his collar and straighten his tie, remembering how badly I wanted to do it on our first day together, to give in to my need to touch him.

"We did good work today, Ethan," I tell him. "No matter what, we made that booth a success. Adam got *five thousand* hits to the site. In one night. That's crazy. Four hundred people signed up for accounts."

He smiles and kisses me again. "God, you're sexy when you spout statistics."

"And you're sexy when you *breathe*."

He laughs, but then his expression grows earnest. "Really, I just wanted to say that it's all going to be fine. I've got your back."

For a long moment, I look into his light-filled blue eyes and see a fathomless well of goodness and loyalty there. I snuggle in close and kiss his jaw, brushing my lips over the five o'clock shadow. "And I've got yours." I reach around and pat his butt. "Now, let's go get canned."

By the time we enter, the whole gang has gathered in the penthouse, except for Adam—and it's like being greeted by a hanging jury. Paolo slouches on the arm of a chocolate-brown sectional and rotates his cocktail nervously, making the ice clink. It's the loudest noise in the room.

"Awesome job tonight, kids," he says, and gives Cookie a challenging look before she even has an opportunity to form a facial expression.

Pippa, Sadie, and Rhett all murmur their agreement. Cookie looks down at her drink like she wants to strangle it to death.

"Thanks," I say. "Really, thank you all for everything. You saved our asses."

At least for tonight, if not for good.

"Well, Jesus Christ," Cookie blurts. "Sit down."

Ethan strides over to the mahogany dining table, pre-set with linen napkins, cut-crystal goblets, and gold-embossed plates, in the event of a spontaneous soiree. Behind the table, floor-to-fifteen-foot-ceiling windows reveal an amazing view of the strip, with the light atop the Luxor slicing through a starless black sky.

He brings over two chairs, and I sit, but he remains standing behind his. I know without him saying a word that the anxiety he's giving off has everything to do with me and nothing to do with himself. I'm gripped with the irrational fear that he might just tackle Adam to the deep-pile carpet the minute he steps through the door.

But then Adam comes from one of the bedrooms, looking relaxed and affable in jeans and a burgundy dress shirt. The man really loves his jewel tones.

"Thanks for coming," he says, as though our attendance wasn't fully mandatory. "I see you've helped yourself to the bar, Paolo. Anyone else?"

He plays bartender for a bit, but Ethan and I decline. My stomach's churning, and I feel flushed and shaky. I know some of it is just exhaustion and the residual effects of rushing home for Nana, worrying about her, worrying about this day. Now that I've left the safe haven of Ethan's bed, it's all crashing in on me.

I shift in my seat and remind myself that whatever happens here, I'll be fine. I've gotten something so much better than a job. It feels almost greedy to want anything more. But I do want it. Or I want Ethan to have it. I just don't want it to go to anyone else.

It takes Adam an excruciatingly long time to fix a few cocktails, and it's all I can do not to lose my mind when he starts to muddle mint for a mojito. He caps the club soda and comes back to the group. Handing the drink to Cookie, he settles in next to her and crosses his legs.

He folds his arms across his chest. "Well, I have to say you two surprised me." And that's all he says. It goes so quiet in the room, I can literally hear a clock ticking, and I don't actually *see* a clock on any of the walls.

Finally, Ethan asks, "Is that good or bad?"

Adam considers for a moment. "Well, let's see. You ordered a video game that cost almost twenty grand. You interfered with the field research I asked you to do. And you totally disregarded my no-dating policy."

My face grows warm. I know it's a lousy time to nitpick, but I say, "Ethan didn't interfere with my date except to get some creepy guy away from me. So that's all on me."

"Well, the video game's all on me," Ethan says, finally taking a seat beside me. "And I'll claim responsibility for breaking the no-dating rule. It's a dumb rule."

I laugh and take his hand, which is strong and warm. "I think we need to split that one fifty-fifty."

"Okay," he says, facing Adam with a soft half-smile on his lips. "We're going fifty-fifty on that last one, so I think that makes us about even. What else have you got?"

"I've got a position that needs filling," Adam says. "And I want you both."

"What?" Cookie sputters.

"What?" Ethan and I say in unison.

"Do you know what you did out there?" Adam asks. "You blew away the competition. Thoroughly. You impressed a bunch of old guys who are professional cynics. *And* you did all of that in the face of a relative's health crisis and with the distraction of what I'm guessing has been a long-simmering attraction. You also came up with a perfect slogan, not to mention getting me a cut rate on the works of my favorite photographer. So I want you both to come work for me. What do you say?"

I feel such a rush of euphoria, shock, and gratitude that I can barely speak. It's like I'm dreaming.

But then Ethan says, "I appreciate that. I really do. But I'm afraid I have to pass."

"Wait." I turn to look at him. "Why?"

He grins and massages his neck, suddenly sheepish. "I want you to have it. It's meant to be yours, Curls."

"What are you saying? You wanted the job every bit as much as I did."

Ethan shrugs. "I wanted the money. But you wanted the *job*."

"Lord, I'm confused," says Paolo. He drains his drink and gets up to refill at the bar.

"Me too." I take both of Ethan's hands and search his face for answers. "So, what will you do?"

"Well, I was waiting for the right time to tell you this."

"Now works," Sadie says.

"Yeah," Rhett agrees. "Works for me too."

Ethan looks around. "All right," he says. "Now it is." His eyes sparkle as they turn back to me. "While I was in Colorado, Matt told me about a graduate program at USC in sports psychology. He hooked me up with the guy who's starting it and . . ." He shrugs. "I'm going to do it."

"But what about the loans? What about—"

"I'm handling it. I'll look at becoming a trainer there—which would get me a free ride. And I'll take out more loans if I need to. But it's where I want to be." He looks at Adam. "I'm sure you understand?"

Adam nods. "It's a loss for me, but Rhett tells me you're very good with your team—and you've certainly helped bring the best out of my group. So, yes. I understand." He aims his thoughtful gaze in my direction. "What about you, Mia? You still aboard?"

"God, yes," I say. "Absolutely."

"Thank God," Paolo says. "Would have been hella dull there without you *both*."

"Yes," sniffs Cookie. "Thank God." But there's that hint of something that's unlike her again—just a flash. I can't be sure, but I think it's a smile.

Pippa gets to her feet and says, "I propose a . . . a . . . speech-type thing!"

"A toast?" laughs Sadie.

"Yeah, a toast."

Adam gets to his feet and then everyone does. "Excellent idea, Pippa. Let's get this party going."

We clamor around the bar, and Adam mixes more drinks. Rhett tells me to come in on Monday to fill out more forms, and Paolo says he'll find me a desk near his. I've been sprung from Intern Gulag.

We drink, and then we put on music.

Ethan and I dance and dance, and I'm not surprised to find he has excellent moves. The music slows, and I move into his arms, warm and exhilarated and amazed at the possibilities taking shape all around me.

"That night at Duke's," he says. "I watched you at the bar. And I couldn't stop looking. I kept finding my way back to you."

I smile. "Like a boomerang?"

Paolo bumps into us on his way back to the bar. "Oops." He weaves a little. "Hey, either of you want a refill?"

"No thanks," I say and pull Ethan down for a long, seriously unprofessional kiss. "I've got everything I need right here."

Acknowledgments

First, thanks to ALL of those in my amazing and far-reaching writing family, whose individual members will be impossible to name here. If you think you should appear on this page, believe me, I think so too. I'm so fortunate that so many of you have started as clients, students, and colleagues and have become lifelong friends.

To Don Maass, Erin Anderson, the awesome BONI faculty, and all the students who've attended over the years, thanks so much for your hard work and for providing constant inspiration. I'm grateful beyond the telling.

For students and faculty of WRW, thanks for wonderful evenings on the back porch at Marydale. In honor of Gary Provost and Robin Hardy, and with much appreciation to Gail Provost, Elizabeth Lyon, Carol Dougherty, and Jason Sitzes and his late-night texts.

To my literary agents, Josh and Tracey Adams; my editorial compatriot, Emma Dryden; and my fearless (and underemployed, by me) assistant, Kelsey Tressler—thanks for bringing the awesome, all the time.

To Roman (Chewy) White for impromptu toy instrument jam sessions and years of laughs; Katie Lu Krimitsos for sushi and butt-kicking; Kim Frost for her companionship on so many late-night drives; my local writing amigos, Tom, Chris, Liz, Larry, Usman (and Gemma and Geodie in spirit), for lots of great talks and a little bit of critiquing; to Jackie P. for modeling determination; and Kim L. for conversations about viscera.

Thanks, of course, to Tessa Woodward and everyone at Harper-Collins. And to my lovely coauthor, Veronica Rossi, for a ridiculous number of laughs and virtual high-fives along the way. It's an honor, Minty.

Lastly, to my crazy, hilarious, awesome family: Lisa, Mustafa, Alex(panda), Andrew, Dina, Samantha, and Abby. And to Brenda, Jose, Liz, Anna, and Kyle. We're weirdos, and I wouldn't have it any other way.

—LO

My deepest gratitude goes to the following people: Lorin Oberweger, for your friendship and general brilliance. Josh and Tracey Adams, for black-belt agenting. Tessa Woodward, for the support and editorial guidance—thank you. The rest of the William Morrow gang, Molly Birckhead and Megan Schumann especially, for all your efforts to spread the word about the Boomerang world. To my family and friends, thank you for being the reason why. Finally, to the bloggers and readers out there, thanks for taking another ride with me.

—VR

Don't Miss NEW BOOKS from your
FAVORITE NEW ADULT AUTHORS

Cora Carmack

LOSING IT A Novel
Available in Paperback and eBook

FAKING IT A Novel
Available in Paperback and eBook

KEEPING HER An Original eNovella
eBook on Sale August 2013

FINDING IT A Novel
Available in Paperback and eBook Fall 2013

Jay Crownover

RULE A Novel
Available in eBook
Available in Paperback Fall 2013

JET A Novel
Available in eBook
Available in Paperback Fall 2013

ROME A Novel
Available in Paperback and eBook Winter 2014

Lisa Desrochers

A LITTLE TOO FAR A Novel
Available in eBook Fall 2013

A LITTLE TOO MUCH A Novel
Available in eBook Fall 2013

A LITTLE TOO HOT A Novel
Available in eBook Winter 2014

Abigail Gibbs

THE DARK HEROINE A Novel
Available in Paperback and eBook

AUTUMN ROSE A Novel
Available in Paperback and eBook Winter 2014